THE SHAPE OF THINGS TO COME

"Body mass, two hundred kilos. Oxygen down below eight percent, and ammonia way up. Will John live?"

Ling went over to the tank and looked carefully at each of the read-outs. "I believe he will," he said at last. "The rates of change are down, and everything is very stable. I don't know if we will be able to return him to his former shape."

Ling looked at Wolf and caught the reflection of his own excitement.

"Look on the positive side," he said. "We've dreamed for centuries about our first meeting with an alien race." He nodded toward the great tank. "The first representative will be in there, ready to meet with us, a day or two from now."

SIGHT OF PROTEUS

Charles Sheffield

A Del Rey Book

BALLANTINE BOOKS • NEW YORK

A Del Rey Book
Published by Ballantine Books

ISBN 0-345-34433-2

Manufactured in the United States of America

First Ballantine Books Edition: April 1988

For Emma

BOOK I

"Have sight of Proteus rising from the sea,
Or hear old Triton blow his wreathed horn."

CHAPTER 1

The new fall catalog had arrived that morning. Behrooz Wolf, like millions of others, had settled in for an evening of browsing and price comparison. As usual, there were many variations on most of the old forms, plus an intriguing set of new ones that BEC was releasing for the first time. Bey keyed out the catalog displays, studying the images and the prices and occasionally marking a form for future reference.

After about an hour his interest began to fade and his attention wandered. He yawned, put down the catalog, and went to his desk in the corner of the room. He picked up and looked through a couple of texts on form-change theory, then, restless as ever, leafed through his casebook. Finally, he picked up the BEC catalog again. When the phone buzzed, he gave an instinctive mutter of annoyance, but the interruption was a welcome one. He pressed the wrist remote.

"Bey? Put me up on visual, would you," said a voice from the wall screen.

Wolf touched his wrist again, and the cheerful, ruddy face of John Larsen appeared on the wall holo. Larsen looked at the catalog that Bey was holding and smiled.

"I didn't know that was out yet, Bey. Tomorrow's the official release date. I haven't had the chance to see if mine has arrived. Sorry to call you at this hour, but I'm still over here at the office."

"No problem. I couldn't get too interested in this, anyway. It's the same old irritation. The forms that appeal the most need a thousand hours of work with the machines, or else they have a lousy life ratio."

"—or they require a whole mass of computer storage, if they're anything like last spring's releases. How are the prices?"

"Up again, and you're quite right, they need more storage, too. Look at this one, John." He held up the open catalog. "I already have a billion words of primary storage, and I still couldn't begin to handle it. Four billion words, or you shouldn't think of ordering it."

Larsen whistled softly. "That's certainly a new one, though. It's the closest thing I've ever seen to an avian form. What's the life ratio on it? Bad, I'll bet."

Wolf consulted the tables in the catalog and nodded agreement.

"Less than 0.2. You'd be lucky to last ten years with it. You might be all right in low-g, but not otherwise. In fact, there's a footnote that says it can achieve flight in a lunar gravity or less. I suppose they're hoping for USF sales."

He closed the catalog.

"So, what's happening, John? I thought you had a date —why the midnight oil?"

Larsen shrugged. "We've got a mystery on our hands. I'm baffled, and it's the sort of problem you thrive on. Do you feel up to a trip back to the office tonight? You're the boss, but I'd really like to get your opinion."

Wolf hesitated. "I wasn't planning to go out again. Can't we handle it over the holo?"

"I don't think so. But maybe I can show you enough to persuade you to come over here." Larsen held out a sheet so that it could be seen on the holoscreen. "Bey, what do you make of this ID code?"

Wolf studied it carefully, then looked back at Larsen questioningly. "It seems normal enough. Is it somebody I'm supposed to know? Let me just check it through my percomp."

Larsen watched in silence as Wolf entered the digits of the chromosome ID code that had replaced fingerprint, voiceprint, and retinal patterns as the absolute identification method. The link from his personal computer to the central data banks was automatic and almost instantaneous. When the response came, Wolf frowned at it for a moment, then looked in annoyance at John Larsen.

"What's the game, John? There's no such ID in the central files. Is it one that you made up?"

"I wish it were, but it's nothing so simple."

Larsen reached behind him and picked up a printed report.

"I told you, Bey, this is a strange one. I had a call about three hours ago from a medical student. This afternoon, he was over in the transplant ward of Central Hospital when a liver transplant case came in. He's been taking a course in chromosome analysis, and he'd missed one of the lab sessions where they were supposed to try the technique out on a real case. So he had the idea of doing an ID check on a sample from the donor liver—just to see if he had the technique correct."

"That's illegal, John. He can't have the licenses to use that equipment."

"He doesn't. He did it anyway. When he got home, he fed the ID code into central files and asked for donor identification and matching. The files couldn't produce a match."

Bey Wolf looked sceptical—but intrigued. "He must have made a measurement error, John."

"That was my first reaction. But he's an unusual young man. For one thing, he was willing to call us, even though he knew he might get in trouble for doing the ID analysis without proper permission. I told him he must have done something wrong, but he said he'd done it three times, twice the usual way and once with a shortcut method that he wanted to try out. It came out the same each time. He's sure that he handled the technique correctly and didn't make any mistakes."

"But there's no way to fake a chromosome ID, and every human being is listed in the central files. Your student is telling us that he tested a liver that came from a person who never existed."

John Larsen looked pleased. "That's what I wanted to hear you say. It was my conclusion exactly. Well, Bey? See you over here in an hour or so?"

The evening shower was over, and the streets were once again a wild, colorful chaos. Bey left his apartment and worked his way over to the fastest slideway, threading through the mass of people with practiced ease. With the population over fourteen billion, crowding was normal, night or day, even in the most affluent parts of the city. Wolf, preoccupied with Larsen's problem, scarcely noticed the throng that surrounded him.

How could anyone have escaped the chromosome typing? It was performed at three months, right after the humanity tests—and it had been that way for a century. Could the donor be old, a dying ancient? That was ridiculous. Even if the donor wanted it that way, no one would use a century-old liver for a transplant operation. Bey's thin face was puzzled. Could it be that the donor was an off-worlder? No, that wouldn't explain it either. The IDs for people from the United Space Federation were all separately filed, but they were still in the records at the central data banks. The computer response would have been delayed a little, but that was all.

He was beginning to feel the old mixture, a tingle of excitement modulated by a fear of disappointment. His job in the Office of Form Control was a good one—he didn't know of a better. But although he had been highly successful in it, somehow it was not completely satisfying. Always, he felt that he was waiting for the big challenge, the problem that would stretch his abilities to their limits. Maybe this could be the one. At thirty-four, he should know what he wanted to do with the rest of his life—it was ridiculous still to be full of the heart searching of adolescence.

In an attempt to suppress his illogical sense of anticipation and to prepare his mind for the problem ahead, Bey keyed his communication implant and tuned to the newscast. The familiar beaked nose and sloping brow of Laszlo Dolmetsch appeared, directly stimulated on his optic nerves. The people and the slideways were still faintly visible as a ghostly superimposed image—the laws forbade total exclusion of the direct sensory feeds. The early slideway deaths had taught that lesson.

Dolmetsch, as always, was holding forth on the latest social indicators and making his usual pessimistic prophecies. If the concentration of industry around the Link access points were not lessened, there would be trouble. . . . Bey had heard it all before, and custom had staled the message. Sure, there were instabilities in the social indicators—but that had been the case ever since the

indicators were first developed. Bey looked again at Dolmetsch's profile and wondered about the popular rumor.
Instead of using form-change to diminish that great beak,
the story went, Dolmetsch had increased it—to become an
unmistakable figure anywhere on Earth. That he certainly
was. Bey could not remember a time when Dolmetsch had
not been a prominent prophet of doom. How old was the
man now? Eighty, or ninety?

Bey mentally shrugged and switched channels. He had
to return to the real world for a moment, to move quickly
out of the way of two red-coated medical emergency staff
hurtling at top speed along the fastest slideway, then he
skipped through the other news channels. Not much there.
A mining accident on Horus, so far from most Solar System activities that it would take months for relief to reach
it; a promising discovery of kernels out in the Halo, which
meant fortune for some lucky prospector and more free
energy for the USF; and the perennial rumor of a form-
change that would give immortality to the wearer. That one
cropped up every couple of years, regular as the seasons. It
was a tribute to the continued power of wishful thinking.
No one ever had any details—just the vaguest of hearsay.
Bey listened scornfully and wondered again how people
could pay attention to such a flimsy prospect. He switched
back to Dolmetsch—at least the old man's worries were
comprehensible and had a solid basis of fact. There was no
doubt that the shortages and the violence were barely under
control, and the population, despite all efforts, was still
creeping upward. Could it ever hit fifteen billion? Bey re-
membered when fourteen had seemed intolerable.

The crowds surging along the slideways didn't seem to
share Wolf's worries. They looked happy, handsome,
young, and healthy. To people living two hundred years
earlier they would have seemed models of perfection. Of
course, this was the west side, closer to the Link entry

point, and that helped. There was plenty of poverty and ugliness elsewhere. But forget for the moment the high prices and the mass of computer storage that was needed. BEC—the Biological Equipment Corporation—could fairly claim to have transformed the world, that part of the world, at least, that could afford to pay. Here on the west side, affluence was the norm and use of the BEC systems a sine qua non.

Only the general coordinators shared Laszlo Dolmetsch's view of the problems in keeping the economic balance of the world. Earth was poised on a knife edge of diminishing resources. Constant subtle adjustments, calculated by application of Dolmetsch's theories, were needed to hold it there. Every week there were corrections for the effects of drought, crop failures, forest fires, epidemics, energy shortages, and mineral supplies. Every week the general coordinators watched the indices for violence, disease, and famine and waited grimly for the time when the corrections would fail and the system would run amok into worldwide slump and economic collapse. In a united world, failure of one system means failure of all. Only the off-Earthers, the three million citizens of the United Space Federation, could cling to their shaky independence—and the USF watched the economic indicators at least as closely and nervously as any Earth-based coordinator.

As he neared his goal, Bey Wolf kept an automatic eye open for illegal forms. Makeup and plastflesh could hide a great deal, but with the Office of Form Control he had been specially trained to see past the outward form, through to the shape of the underlying body structure.

Here, on the public slideways, the chances of running into an outlawed form were small—but Bey still had occasional nightmares about the feline form he had spotted less than a mile from here two years earlier. That had cost him two months out of action, in the accelerated change and recovery room of the Form Control Hospital unit.

As he made the transitions back to the slowest slideway, he noticed again the large number of rounded Elizabethan foreheads on the people he was passing. That had been a minor special of the spring catalog but had turned out to be a big hit. He wondered what the fall attraction would be— dimples? saber scars? an Egyptian nose?—as he printed into Form Control and went up to Larsen's office on the third floor.

As Bey Wolf was climbing the stairs, a few miles east of him a solitary white-coated figure dialed a vault combination and stepped through into the underground experiment room, four floors below City level. The face and figure would be familiar to any scientist. It was Albert Einstein —Einstein at forty, at the very height of his powers.

The man made his way slowly down the long room, checking the station monitors at each of the great tanks. Most received only a few seconds of attention and the occasional adjustment of a control setting, but at the eleventh station he halted. He examined the outputs closely, grunted, and shook his head. Several minutes passed while he stood motionless, deep in thought. At last he continued his patrol and went on into the general control area at the far end of the room.

Seated at the console, he called out the detailed records for the eleventh station and displayed them on the screen. Then he was again silent for many minutes, twisting around his forefinger a lock of his long, graying hair as he bent over the displays of feed rates, nutrient mixes, and other vital indicators. The program-swapping records occupied him for more long minutes, but finally he was finished. He emerged from his concentration, cleared the screen, and switched to voice recording mode.

"November second. Continued deterioration in tank

eleven. Response intensity is down by a further two percent, and there is a renewed instability in the biofeedback loops. Change parameters were recalibrated tonight."

He paused, reluctant to take the next step. At last he went on.

"Prognosis: poor. Unless there is improvement in the next two days, it will be necessary to terminate the experiment."

He sat for a moment longer, visibly shaken. At last he stood up. Moving quickly now through the dimly lit room he reset the monitors at each station and switched on the telltales. He took a final look around the room, locked the vault, and entered the elevator that would take him back to ground level. More than ever now, the face was that of Einstein. Over the warmth, intellect, and humanity was etched the pain and torment of a man who worried and suffered for the whole world.

CHAPTER 2

John Larsen, still fresh-faced and cheerful despite the late hour, looked at Bey closely when he came in.

"Late nights don't seem to agree with you," he said. "You look tired. Been neglecting your conditioning program again?"

Wolf shrugged and involuntarily blinked his eyes several times.

"It shows, does it? I was born a bit myopic, you know. If I don't work out regularly, I get eyestrain. I'll have a full session on the bios—first thing tomorrow."

Larsen raised a sceptical eyebrow. Bey was famous for his "tomorrow" statements. He claimed he had inherited subtlety and shrewdness from his Persian mother, along with tenacity and attention to detail from his German father. But from his Persian side had also apparently come a gift for extreme procrastination. Bey swore that there was no word just like *mañana* in the Persian language—there were a dozen related words, but none of them had that degree of urgency. His tendency to delay didn't seem to extend to his work. He was highly effective there. Dark-haired, dark-complexioned, of medium height and build, he had an uncanny ability to efface himself totally and disappear into any crowd—a useful talent for an investigating agent in the Office of Form Control.

Larsen picked up a typed sheet from his desk and offered it to Wolf.

"There it is. The signed, sworn statement of Luis Rad-Kato—that's the medical student. It has the whole story. Gives the time, tells just what he did, quotes the liver ID, and shows where he filed his results in the data banks."

Wolf took the paper and glanced over it. "I suppose you already pulled the records on this out of Central Data to make sure he filed it the way he said he did?"

"Sure. I did that as soon as I received his report. It was still held in the scratch file. I'll read it out again for you."

He dialed the entry code, and the two men waited as the data search was performed. The wait lengthened. After a minute or so Larsen frowned in perplexity.

"There shouldn't be this much delay. The response last time I checked was almost instantaneous. Maybe I goofed on the access code."

He hit the priority interrupt key and reentered the code. This time the message light blinked on, and the display screen filled: ENTRY CODE DOES NOT CORRESPOND TO ANY RECORD IN FILES. CHECK REFERENCE AND REENTER.

"Damnation. That can't be right, Bey. I used that same code less than an hour ago."

"Let me have a go. I know the supervisor entry codes for that area of central storage."

Wolf, much more at home with computers than Larsen, took over the console. He entered the control language statements that allowed him access to the operating system and began to screen the storage files. After a few minutes work he froze the display.

"This is the area, John. Look at it—talk about bad luck! The data dump shows a hardware malfunction in the medical records section, less than an hour ago. A whole group of records has been lost—including the area where the file we want was stored. They were all erased when the system went down."

Larsen looked miserable. He shook his head in disgust.

"It was a lousy time for it to happen, Bey. Now the whole thing will be a pain to follow up. We'll have to call Central Hospital and ask for a new check on the liver transplant ID. They won't like that, but if we reach Dr. Morris in the Transplant Department, he'll probably arrange to do it for us."

"Tonight?"

"No." Larsen looked apologetic. "It can't be done. It's almost eleven now, and Morris works the day shift. We won't get any action until tomorrow. The best I can do is call and leave a stored request for the morning."

He sat down at the video link and prepared to call the hospital, then paused. "Unless you want to go over in the morning and check it in person? We'd actually get faster action that way."

Wolf shrugged. "Might as well. Tonight's shot anyway. Let's leave it all until tomorrow."

Larsen was still apologetic. "It must have been a million to one chance, losing the record we wanted like that."

"More than that, John. The scratch record is copied into a master file, soon after entry, so that there's always a backup copy. The accident must have happened before they could get the copy for permanent storage. I've never even heard of such a thing before—it must be a one in a billion rarity, maybe one in a trillion."

He wore a thoughtful and dissatisfied expression as they went together into the still-crowded streets.

"I've had no dinner, and I broke a date to follow through on this thing," said Larsen. "Do you know, I haven't been outside the office for a minute since I arrived this morning. What's new on the slideways?"

Wolf looked amused. "If you mean women, as you usually do, I wasn't looking too much on the way over. I saw a couple of new ones this afternoon, though—styles straight from old Persia. Fantastic eyes. It would be nice if they caught on and came into fashion."

They merged into the slidewalkers. Like most members of Form Control, Wolf and Larsen were wearing simple forms, close to those given by nature. Years of form-change training, reinforced by the chilling exposure to the outlawed forms, made form-change for pleasure or entertainment a doubtful attraction to them. It took an intriguing form indeed to tempt them to experiment. The biofeedback machines in the Office of Form Control were used for work and for health, almost never for cosmetics. Before Bey went to bed he took a short program on his own equipment for his myopia, and resolved to take a more complete physical overhaul—tomorrow.

CHAPTER 3

The meeting was running well over its scheduled one hour. That happened often. Every year the list of petitioners grew longer, and every year the committee had to weigh more factors in deciding the new legal forms.

Robert Capman, committee chairman, looked at his watch and called the meeting again to order.

"We're late, ladies and gentlemen. This must be our final decision for today. Turn, if you please, to the description of the twentieth petition. Perhaps I can summarize it for you in the interests of speed.

"The basic form is mammalian aquatic. You will see that fourteen variations are also being applied for in simultaneous petition. The developer of the forms points out that one of these variations has a life ratio a little better than 1—about 1.02, to be more precise. This could translate to an extension of a couple of years on a user's life span. BEC has already stated that they would be willing to handle this form and all its variations as Type 1 Programs, fully certified and supported by BEC warranties. Could I now have your comments, please."

Capman paused. He had a gift—part instinct, part experience—that allowed him to control the pace of the meeting completely. There was a stir at the far end of the long table.

"Yes, Professor Richter. You have a comment?"

Richter cleared his throat. He was a lean, fastidious man with a neat black beard. "A question, really. I notice that the basic form can supposedly be reached with less than two hundred hours of machine interaction. I know that the main external change, apart from the skin and eyes, is just the addition of gills to the human form, but that interaction time seems to me to be too little. I question its accuracy."

Capman smiled and nodded. "An excellent point, Jacob. I had the same thought myself when I reread this petition."

Richter warmed to the praise in Capman's voice.

"However," continued Capman, "I now believe that the statement is accurate. This petitioner seems to have achieved a real breakthrough. As you know, a form is usually reached with less effort when it corresponds to one somewhere in our own genetic history."

Richter nodded vigorously. "Indeed, yes. I have always thought that to be the reason why the avian forms have proved so difficult to realize. Are you suggesting that the petitioner has developed a form that relates to our own descent?"

"I believe so. More than that, in his application he points out a new use of form-change. Since the number of hours of machine interaction seems to correlate directly with a form's closeness to human genetic heritage, our own remote history can actually be explored through systematic form-perturbation. Whenever we suspect that a new form lies close to the line of our own species development, we should look for the perturbations that decrease machine interaction time. Those changes will generally take us closer to our evolutionary path. Thus this petitioner has not only contributed to the present science of metamorphosis, he has also given us a new tool to examine our own evolutionary heritage."

There was a stir of excitement around the table. Capman rarely offered personal comment on a petition. He left it to the committee to make their own evaluation and recommendation. His praise carried weight. The approval for the use of the new form was swiftly given, and the ecstatic petitioner received the formal congratulations of the committee.

He left in a blissful daze—with good reason. Adoption of his forms by BEC as Type I Programs made him an instant millionaire, in either Earth riyals or in USF new dollars.

As soon as he had gone, Capman called the meeting once more to order.

"That concludes the consideration of petitions for today. There is, however, still one extraordinary item of business that I want to bring to your attention before we leave. We cannot resolve it now, but I urge you to think about it in the weeks until our next meeting."

He motioned to one of the minutes secretaries, who handed him a pile of thin folders, which he distributed to the committee members.

"These contain some details of an unusual petition request that we received last week. It has not been through the conventional screening process, because after a quick look at it I judged that we should consider it directly in this committee. It has a life ratio close to 1.3."

There was a sudden hush. Committee members who had

been straightening their papers before leaving stopped and gave Capman their full attention.

"The petitioner does not emphasize this," went on Capman, "but the extensive use of this form could increase the average life expectancy to almost one and a half centuries. The appearance of the form is outwardly normal. The changes are mainly in the medulla oblongata and the endocrine glands."

At the far end of the table, Richter had again raised his hand.

"Mr. Chairman, I urge great caution in discussing this form anywhere outside this committee. We all can guess the public reaction if people see a chance to increase their life spans by thirty percent. It would be chaos."

Capman nodded. "That was going to be my next point. There is still another reason why this form must be handled with special care. As many of you may know, I also serve as consultant and technical adviser to the general coordinators. It is in that role that I am most worried by this petition. The widespread use of any form with a life ratio this high could eventually push the population of Earth up above twenty billion. We could not support such a level. If Dolmetsch is correct, we are already crowding close to the absolute limit of population stability."

He closed his notebook.

"On the other hand, I'm not sure that we have the right to suppress any petition for such arguments. The petitioner presumably knows his legal rights. I would like to get your opinion on this next month, after you have all had time to think about it.

"The meeting is now adjourned."

He smiled his thanks at the participants, gathered his papers, and hurried from the room. After the other committee members had also left, the minutes secretaries remained to clear up and compare notes. The junior of the two skipped through his recording, then compared it with the written transcript.

"I show one clean acceptance," he said, "two conditional acceptances subject to further tests, two more to be continued with sponsored research grants. If my count is right, that leaves us fifteen outright rejections."

"Check. Funny, isn't it, how the percentages seem to run about the same each time, no matter what the petitions are?" The blond girl tried an experimental flutter of her eyelashes and a pout of the lips. Getting the form of the Marilyn variations was fairly easy as far as the outward shape was concerned, but the mannerisms took lots of practice. "There, how was that?"

"Not too bad. You're improving, but you're not there yet. I'll let you know when you have it perfect. Look, do you think we should make any special notes on the rejected forms? There's at least one that might be worth a comment."

"I know. The petitioner who tried to develop the wheeled form? I don't know what we could put in the transcripts. 'Widespread and ill-concealed laughter from the committee members'? They had a hard time controlling themselves, the way he was hopping and rolling all over the room. It's probably better to say nothing. I wonder why somebody would go to all that trouble to make a complete fool of himself."

"Come on, Gina, we both know why."

"Oh, I guess you're right. Money will always do it."

Of course.

. . . *would you like to be rich, really rich? Then why not develop a new form to catch the public fancy? You will get a royalty from every user. . . .*

It sounded easy, but it was not. All the simple forms had been explored long before. The change specialists were driven all the time to more exotic and difficult variations.

Any proposal had to pass the stringent requirements of the petition board, and only one in a million hit the jackpot.

. . . BEC will sell you a low-cost experimental package. It includes everything that you need to create your very own form-change program. . . .

Few of the enthusiasts signing up for form-change experiments worried about the fine print at the end of the contract: *. . . BEC takes no responsibility for reduced life expectancy, physical damage, or unstable physical-mental feedback resulting from form-change experiments made with BEC equipment. . . .*

For the one in a million lucky or clever enough to hit on a really successful form, there was still a hidden catch: the form would have to be marketed through BEC. The royalty was factored into BEC's prices, and they made more than the developer.

The statistics were seldom publicized. Licensed form-change experimenters: 1.5 million. Living millionaires from new form inventions: 146. Deaths per year directly attributed to form-change experiments: 78,000.

Form-change experiment was a risky business.

The minutes secretaries didn't realize it, but in the final petition board they saw only the cream of the crop—the ones that could still walk and talk. Less than one in fifty made it to the board. Many of the failures finished in the organ banks.

"We should include a summary on the humanity-test proposal, Gina."

"I guess so. I sketched out a short statement while they were still debating it. How about this? 'The proposal that the humanity test could be conducted at two months instead of three months was tabled pending further test results.'"

"I think it needs a bit more detail than that. Dr. Capman pointed out what an argument the present humanity test caused among the religious groups when it was first introduced. BEC had to show success in a hundred thousand test cases before the council would approve it."

He skimmed rapidly through the record. "Here, why don't we simply use this quote, verbatim, from Capman's remarks? 'The humanity tests remain controversial. Unless an equally large sample is analyzed now, showing that the two- and three-month test results are identical, the proposal cannot be forwarded for consideration.'"

They were both much too young to remember the great humanity debates. What is a human? The answer had evolved slowly and taken many years to articulate clearly, but it was simple enough: an entity is human if and only if it can accomplish purposive form-change using the bio-feedback systems. The definition had prevailed over the anguished weeping of millions—billions—of protesting parents.

The age of testing had been slowly pushed back to one year, to six months, to three months. If BEC could prove its case, the age would soon be two months. Failure in the test carried a high penalty—euthanasia—but resistance had slowly faded before remorseless population pressure. Resources to feed babies who could never live a normal human life were simply not available. The banks never lacked for infant organs.

Gina had locked her recorder. She pushed back her blond hair with a rounded forearm and threw a smoldering look at her companion.

"Still not quite right," he said critically. "You should droop your eyelids a bit more and get a better pout on that lower lip."

"Damn. It's *hard*. How will I know when I'm getting it right?"

He picked up his recorder. "Don't worry. I told you before, you'll know from my reaction."

"You know, I ought to try it on Dr. Capman—he'd be the ultimate test, don't you think?"

"Impossible, I would have said. You know he only lives for his work. I don't think he has more than two minutes a day left over from that. But look"—only half joking—"if the hormones are running too high in that form, I might be able to help you out."

Gina's response was not included in the conventional Marilyn data base.

The telltales on the experiment stations glowed softly. The only sounds were the steady hum of air and nutrient circulators and the click of the pressure valves inside the tanks. Seated at the control console, the lonely figure looked again at the records of experiment status.

It had been necessary to abort the failure on the eleventh station—again the pain, the loss of an old friend. How many more? Fortunately, the replacement was going very well. Perhaps he was getting closer, perhaps the dream of half a century could be achieved.

He had not chosen his outward form lightly. It was fitting that the greatest scientist of the twenty-second century should pay homage to the giant of the twentieth. But how had his idol borne the guilt of Hiroshima, of Nagasaki? For that secret, he would have given a great deal.

CHAPTER 4

The unexpected loss of the data set containing the unknown liver ID had nagged all night like a subliminad. By the time Bey Wolf reached the Form Control offices his perplexity was showing visibly on his face. As they set off together for Central Hospital, Larsen mistook Wolf's facial expression for irritation at being called out on a wasted mission the previous night.

"Just another hour or two, Bey," he said, "then we'll have direct evidence."

Wolf was thoughtful for a moment, chewing at his lip.

"Maybe, John," he said at last. "But don't count on it. I don't know why it is, but it seems that whenever I get involved in a really interesting case, something comes along and knocks it away. You remember how it was on the Pleasure Dome case."

Larsen nodded without comment. That had been a tough

one, and both men had come close to resigning over it. Illegal form-changes were being carried out in Antarctica as titillation for the jaded sexual appetites of top political figures. Starting from a segment of ophidian skin picked up in Madrid, Wolf and Larsen had followed the trail little by little and had been close to the final revelation when they had suddenly been called off the case by the central office. The whole thing had been hushed up, and left to cool. There must have been some very important players in that particular game.

While the slideways transported them toward the hospital, both men gradually became more subdued. It was a natural response to their surroundings. As the blue glaze of the newer city's shielded walls became less common, the buildings seemed drab and shabby. The inhabitants moved more furtively, and the dirt and the refuse became noticeable. Central Hospital stood at the very edge of Old City, where wealth and success handed over to poverty and failure. Much of the world could not afford the BEC programs and equipment. In the depths of Old City, the old forms of humanity lived side by side with the worst surviving failures of the form-change experiments.

The bulk of the hospital loomed at last before them. Very old, built of gray stone, it stood like a massive fortress protecting the new city from Old City. Inside it, the first BEC developments had been given their practical tests—long ago, before the fall of India—but the importance of the hospital's work lived on, deep in human memory. All moves to tear it down and replace it with a modern structure had failed. Now it seemed almost a monument to the progress of form-change.

Inside the main lobby, the two men paused and looked about them. The hospital ran with the frantic pace and total organization of an ants' nest. The status displays in front of the receptionist flickered all the colors of the rainbow, constantly, like the consoles of a spaceport control center.

The young man seated at the controls seemed able to ignore it completely. He was deep in a thick blue-bound book, his consoles set for audio interrupt should attention be needed. He looked up only when Wolf and Larsen were standing directly in front of him.

"You need assistance?" he asked.

Wolf nodded, then looked at him closely. The face, now that it was no longer turned down to the pages of the book, looked suddenly familiar—oddly familiar, but in an impersonal way. Bey felt as though he had seen him on a holograph without ever seeing the man in person.

"We should have an appointment with Dr. Morris of the Transplant Department," said Larsen. "I called him first thing this morning to arrange some ID tests. He told us to come at ten, but we are a little early."

While Larsen was speaking, Wolf had managed to get a closer look at the book sitting on the desk in front of them. It had been a while since he had seen anyone working from an actual bound volume. He looked at the open pages; very old, from the overall appearance, and probably made of processed wood pulp. Bey read the title word by word, with some difficulty since the page was upside down: *The Tragical History of Doctor Faustus* by Christopher Marlowe. Suddenly, he was able to complete the connection. He looked again at the man behind the desk, who had picked up a location director, keyed it on, and handed it to Larsen.

"Follow the directions on this as they come up. It will take you to Dr. Morris's office. Return it to me when you leave, please. To get back here, all you have to do is press RETURN and it will guide you to the main lobby."

As Larsen took the director, Wolf leaned over the desk and asked, "William Shakespeare?"

The receptionist stared at him in astonishment. "Why,

that's quite right. Not one visitor in ten thousand recognizes me, though. How did you know? Are you a poet or a playwright yourself?"

Wolf shook his head. "I'm afraid not. Just a student of history, and very interested in faces and shapes. I assume that you get a positive feedback from that form or you wouldn't be using it. Has it helped a lot?"

The receptionist wrinkled his high forehead in thought, then shrugged. "It's too soon to tell. I'd like to think it's working. I thought it was worth a try, even though I know that the form-change theorists are sceptical. After all, athletes use the body forms of earlier stars for their models, so why shouldn't the same method work just as well for an artist? It was a hassle changing to it, but I've decided to give it at least a year. If I don't see real progress in my work by then, I expect I'll change back to my old form."

Larsen looked puzzled. "Why not stay as you are? The form you have now is a good one. It's—"

He stopped abruptly in response to a quick kick from Bey, below desk level. He stared at Wolf for a second, then looked back at the receptionist.

"I'm sorry," he said. "I seem to be a bit dense this morning."

The receptionist looked back at him with a mixture of amusement and embarrassment. "Don't apologize," he said. "I'm just surprised that either of you could tell. Is it all that obvious?" He looked down ruefully at his body.

Bey waved his hand. "Not at all obvious," he said reassuringly. "Don't forget we're from the Office of Form Control. It's our job; we're supposed to notice forms more than other people do. The only thing that tipped me off was your manner. You still haven't adjusted that totally, and you were behaving toward us more like a woman than a man."

"I guess I'm still not completely used to the male form.

It's more difficult than you might think. You can get used to the extra bits and the missing bits in a few weeks, but it's the human relationships that really foul you up. Some day when you have a few hours to spare, I could tell you things about the adjustment in my sex life that other people find hilarious. Even I laugh at it now—mind you, I never saw the humor at the time."

Wolf's own interests extended to anything and everything and quite overshadowed his tact. He found that he couldn't resist a question. "People who've tried both usually say they prefer the female form. Do you agree?"

"So far, I do. I'm still learning to handle the male form properly, but if it doesn't pay off in my writing, I'll be very pleased to change back."

He paused and looked at the panel in front of him, where a cluster of yellow and violet lights had suddenly started a mad blinking.

"I'd like to talk to you about your job sometime, but right now I have to get back to the board. There's a stuck conveyor on the eighth level, and no mechanics there. I'll have to try and borrow a couple of machines from Parthenogenetics two floors down." He began to key in to his controller. "Just go where the location director tells you," he said vaguely, already preoccupied completely with his problem.

"We're on our way. Good luck with the writing," said Wolf.

They went over to the elevators. As they continued up to the fifth floor, Larsen could see a trace of a smile on Wolf's thin face.

"All right, Bey, what is it? You only get that expression when there's a secret joke."

"Oh, it's nothing much," said Wolf, though he continued to look very pleased with himself. "At least, for the sake of our friend back there I hope that it's nothing much.

I wonder if he knows that for quite a while there have been
theories—strong ones—that although the face he is wearing may have belonged to Shakespeare, all the plays were
written by somebody else. Maybe he'd be better off trying
to form-change to look like Bacon."

Bey Wolf was a pleasant enough fellow, but to appeal to
him a joke had to have a definite twist to it. He was still
looking pleased with himself when they reached the office
of the director of transplants. One thing he hadn't mentioned to John Larsen was the fact that a number of the
theories he had referred to claimed that Shakespeare's
works had been written by a woman.

"The liver came from a twenty-year-old female hydro-
ponics worker who had her skull crushed in an industrial
accident."

Dr. Morris, lean, intense, and disheveled, removed the
reply slip that he had just read from the machine and
handed it to John Larsen, who stared at it in disbelief.

"But that's impossible! Only yesterday, the ID tests
gave a completely different result for that liver. You must
have made a mistake, Doctor."

Morris shook his head firmly. "You saw the whole process yourself. You were there when we did the microbiopsy
on the transplanted liver. You saw me prepare the specimen
and enter the sample for chromosome analysis. You saw
the computer matching I just gave you. Mr. Larsen, there
are no other steps or possible sources of error. I think you
are right, there has been a mistake all right—but it was
made by the medical student who gave you the report."

"But he told me that he did it three separate times."

"Then he probably did it wrong three times. It is no new
thing to repeat a mistake. I trust that you are not about
do that yourself."

Larsen was flushed with anger and embarrassment, and

Morris, pale and overworked, was clearly resentful at what he thought was a careless waste of his precious time. Wolf stepped in to try to create a less heated atmosphere.

"One thing puzzles me a bit," he said. "Why did you use a transplant, Dr. Morris? Wouldn't it have been easier to redevelop a healthy liver, using the biofeedback machines and a suitable program?"

Morris cooled a little. He did not appear to find it strange that a specialist in form-change work should ask such a naive question.

"Normally you would be quite right, Mr. Wolf. We use transplants for two reasons. Sometimes the original organ has been so suddenly and severely damaged that we do not have time to use the regrowth programs. More often, it is a question of speed and convenience."

"You mean in convalescence time?"

"Certainly. If I were to give you a new liver from a transplant, you would spend maybe a hundred hours, maximum, working with the biofeedback machines. You would need to adjust immune responses and body chemistry balance, and that would be all. With luck, you might be able to get away with as little as fifty hours in interaction. If you wanted to regrow a whole liver, though, and you weren't willing to wait for natural regeneration—which would happen eventually, in the case of the liver—well, you'd probably be faced with at least a thousand hours of work with the machines."

Wolf nodded. "That all makes sense. But didn't you check the ID of this particular liver before you even began the operation?"

"That's not the way the system works." Morris went over to a wall screen and called out a display of the hospital operational flow. "You can see it easiest if you follow it here. When the organs are first taken from their donors, they are logged in at this point by a human. Then, as you can see, the computer takes over. It sets up the tests to determine the ID, checks the main physical features of the donor and the organ, fixes the place where it will be stored, and so on. All that information goes to the permanent data banks. Then, when we need a donor organ, such as a liver, the computer matches the information about the physical type and condition of the patient with the data on all the available livers in the organ bank. It picks out the most suitable one for the operation. Everything after the original logging in is automatic, so the question of checking the ID never arises."

He came back from the wall displays and looked questioningly at Wolf, whose face was still thoughtful.

"So what you're telling us, Doctor," said Bey, "is that you never have any organs in the banks which didn't have an ID check made when they first entered it?"

"Not for adults. Of course, there are many infant organs that don't have their IDs filed. Anything that fails the humanity tests is never given an ID—the computer creates a separate file in the data bank for the information about those organs."

"So it *is* possible for a liver to be in the organ banks and yet have no ID."

"An infant's liver, from a humanity-test failure. Look, Mr. Wolf, I see where you're heading, and I can assure you that it won't work." Morris came to the long table and sat down facing Wolf and Larsen. He ran his hand over his long jaw, then looked at his watch. "I have things that I must do, very soon, but let me point out the realities of this case. The patient who received the liver, as you saw for yourself, was a young adult. The liver we used on her was fully grown, or close to it. I saw it myself at the time of the operation. It certainly didn't come from any infant, and we would never use infant organs except for children's operations."

Wolf shrugged his shoulders resignedly. "That's it, then. We won't take up any more of your time. I'm sorry that we've been a nuisance on this, but we have to do our job."

They rose from the table and turned to leave. Before they reached the doorway, a gray-haired man entered and waved casually to Morris.

"Hi, Ernst," he said. "Don't let me interrupt you. I noticed from the visitors log that you have people in from Form Control, so I thought I'd stop by and see what's happening."

"They were just about to leave," said Morris. "Mr. Wolf and Mr. Larsen, I'd like to introduce you to Robert Capman, the director of Central Hospital. This is an unexpected visit. According to the hospital daily scheduler, you have a meeting this morning with the Building and Construction Committee."

"I do. I'm on my way there now." Capman gave Wolf and Larsen a rapid and penetrating look. "I hope that you gentlemen were able to get the information that you wanted."

Wolf smiled and shrugged. "Not quite what we hoped we'd get. I'm afraid that we ran into a dead end."

"I'm sorry to hear that." Capman smiled also. "If it's any consolation to you, that happens to us all the time in our work here."

Again, he gave Wolf and Larsen that cool and curiously purposeful look. Bey felt a sudden heightening of his own level of attention. He returned Capman's measured scrutiny for several seconds, until the latter abruptly nodded at the wall display and waved his hand in farewell.

"I'll have to go. I'm supposed to be making a statement to the committee in four minutes time."

"Problems?" asked Morris.

"Same old issue. A new proposal to raze Central Hospital and put us all out in the green belt, away from the tough part of the city. They'll be broadcasting the hearings on closed circuit, if you're interested, Channel Twenty-three."

He turned and hurried out. Wolf raised his eyebrows. "Is he always in that much of a hurry?"

Morris nodded. "Always. He's amazing, the work load he tackles. The best combination of theorist and experimenter that I've ever met." He seemed to have calmed down completely from his earlier irritation. "Not only that, but you should see him handle a difficult committee."

"I'd like to." Wolf chose to take him literally. "Provided that you don't mind us staying here to watch the display. One more thing about the liver." His tone was carefully casual. "What about the children who pass the humanity tests but have some sort of physical deformity? You did mention that you use infant organs in children's operations. Are they taken from the ones who fail the tests?"

"Usually. But what of it?"

"Well, don't you sometimes grow the organs you need, in an artificial environment, until they're the size you want for the child?"

"We try to complete any repair work before the children can walk or speak; in fact, we begin work right after the humanity tests are over. But you are quite correct; we do sometimes grow an organ that we need from infant to older size, and we do that from humanity-test reject stock. However, it's all done over in Children's Hospital, out on the west side. They have special child-size feedback machines there. We also prefer to do it there for control reasons. As you very well know, there are heavy penalties for allowing anyone to use a biofeedback machine if they are between two and eighteen years old—except for medical repair work, of course, and that is done under very close scrutiny. We like to get the children away from here completely, to prevent any accidental access here to form-change equipment."

Morris turned to the display screen and lifted the channel selector. "I suppose that I should admire your persistence, Mr. Wolf, but I assure you that it doesn't lead anywhere. Why, may I ask, do you lay all this emphasis on children?"

"There was one other thing in the report from Luis Rad-Kato—the medical student. He says that he not only did an ID check on the liver, he did an age test, too. The age he determined was twelve years."

"Then that proves he doesn't know what he's doing. There are no organs used here from child donors. That work would be done over at Children's Hospital. Your comment to Capman was a good one—you are trying to pursue this whole thing through a dead end. Spend your time on something else, that's my advice."

While he was speaking, the display screen from Channel twenty three came alive. The three men turned to it and fell silent.

"From choice, I wear the form of early middle age."

Capman, in the few minutes since he had left the Transplant Department, had found the time to remove his hospital uniform and don a business suit. The committee members who listened to him were wearing the same colorful apparel and appeared to be composed largely of businessmen.

"However," went on Capman, "I am in fact quite old—older than any of you here. Fortunately, I am of long-lived stock, and I hope that I have at least twenty more productive years ahead of me. I am also fortunate enough to be blessed with a retentive memory, which has made my experiences still vivid. It is the benefit of that experience that I wish to offer to you today."

"On his high horse," said Morris quietly. "He never

goes in for that sort of pomposity when he's working in the hospital. He knows his audience."

"My exact age is perhaps irrelevant," continued Capman, "but I can remember the days before 'Lucy's in the Water' was one of the children's nursery songs."

He paused for the predictable stir of surprise from the committee. Larsen turned to Wolf.

"How long ago was that, Bey?"

Wolf's expression mirrored his surprise. "If my memory is correct, it is very close to a century. I know it was well over ninety years ago."

Wolf looked with increased interest at the man on the screen. Capman was *old*. "Lucy's in the Water," like "Ring-a-Ring-a-Rosy" long before it, told of a real event. Not the Black Death, as in the older children's song, but the Lucy massacre, when the Hallucinogenic Freedom League—the Lucies—had dumped drugs into the water supply lines of major cities. Nearly a billion people had died in the chaos that followed as starvation, exposure, epidemic, and mindless combat walked the cities and exacted their tribute. It was the only occasion in four hundred years when the population had, however briefly, ceased its upward surge.

"I remember the time," went on Capman, "when cosmetic form-change was unknown and medical form-change was still difficult, dangerous, and expensive; when it would take months of hard work to achieve a change that we can manage now in weeks or days; when fingerprint and voiceprint patterns were still in use as a legal form of identification, because the law had yet to accept the elementary fact that a man who can grow a new arm can easily change his larynx or his fingertips."

Wolf frowned. The audience that Capman was addressing seemed to be lapping it up, but he was almost certain that the speaker was indulging in a little artistic licence. The first developments Capman was referring to had begun even further in the past than the Lucies. In a sense, they had begun way back in the nineteenth century, with the first experiments on limb regeneration of amphibians. Many lower animals could regrow a lost limb. A man could not. Why?

No one could answer that question until two fields, both mature and well explored in themselves, had come together in a surprising way in the 1990s: biological feedback and real-time computer control.

It was already known in the 1960s that a human could use display feedback devices to influence his own involuntary nervous system, even to the point where the basic electrical wave rhythms of the brain could be modified. At the same time, computer-controlled instrumentation had been developing, permitting electronic feedback of computed signals continuously and in real time. Ergan Melford had taken those two basic tools and put them to work together.

Success in minor things had come first, with the replacement of lost hair and teeth. From those primitive beginnings, advances had come slowly but steadily. Replacement of lost fingertips was soon followed by programs for the correction of congenital malfunctions, for the treatment of disease, and for the control of the degenerative aspects of aging. That might have been enough for most people, but Ergan Melford had seen far beyond that. At the time that he had founded the Biological Equipment Corporation, he already had his long-term goal defined.

The dam broke on the day Melford released his first general catalog. Programs were listed for sale that would allow a user to apply the biological feedback equipment to modify his appearance—and all the world, as Melford well knew, wanted to be taller, shorter, more beautiful, better proportioned. Suddenly, form-change programs could be purchased to allow men and women to be what they chose to be—and BEC, seventy-five percent owned by Ergan Melford, had a monopoly on the main equipment and programs and held all the patents.

On the screen, Capman continued to build his case. "I remember, even though most of you do not, the strange results of the early days of form-change experiments. That was before the illegal forms had been defined, still less understood. We saw sexual monsters, physical freaks, all the repressions of a generation, released in one great flood.

"You do not remember what it was like before we had an Office of Form Control. I remember it well. It was chaos."

Larsen noticed that Morris was looking across at him. "It's not far from chaos now in the office we're in. We still see the wildest forms you can imagine. I suppose the policy now is to get the chaos off the streets and into the Office of Form Control."

Wolf waved him to silence before he could go into details with office anecdotes. Capman, still on screen, was again building his edifice of logic and persuasion. He had tremendous presence and conviction. Bey was beginning to understand the basis for the respect and reverence that showed through when Morris and others at the hospital spoke about their director.

"All these things I remember, *personally*—not by secondhand reporting. Perhaps you, as members of this committee, wonder what all this has to do with the proposal to tear down Central Hospital and build a new facility outside the city. It has a great deal to do with it. In *every one* of the events that I have referred to, this hospital—Central Hospital, this unique structure—has played a key and crucial role. To most people, this building is a tangible monument to the past of form-change development. Much of that past

has been disturbing and frightening, but we must remember it. If we forget history, we may be obliged to repeat it. What better reminder of our difficult past could
there be than the continued presence of this building as an
active, working center? What better assurance can we have
that form-change is under control and is being handled with
real care?"

Capman paused for a long moment and looked around
the committee, meeting each man or woman eye to eye as
though willing their support.

"I should finish by saying one more thing to you," he
said. "To me, the idea of removing such a monument to
human progress is unthinkable. I do not relish the idea of
working, myself, in any other facility. Thank you."

Capman had swept up his papers, nodded to the committee, and was already on his way out of the room before
the applause could begin.

"That was the clincher," said Morris. He looked ready
to applaud, himself. "I wondered if he'd say that last point.
The committee is terrified of the idea that he might resign
if they go too far. They'd get so much grief from everybody else, they won't press the point."

He had clearly lost all signs of his earlier irritation with
Wolf and Larsen. As they prepared to leave the hospital, he
even assured Wolf of his continued cooperation, should
anything new be discovered. They said polite farewells inside the hospital, but once outside they felt free to let their
own feelings show.

"*Tokhmir*! Where do we go from here, John? That got
us absolutely nowhere."

"I know. I guess we'll have to give it up. Rad-Kato
made a mistake, and we've chased it into the ground. Isn't
that the way it seems to you?"

"Almost. The one thing I still can't swallow is the loss
of those data records last night. The timing on that was just

too bad to be true. I'll admit that coincidences are inevitable, but I want to look at each one good and hard before I'll accept that there's only chance at work. Let's give it one more try. Let's call Rad-Kato again when we get back to the office."

CHAPTER 5

"**I** am quite sure, Mr. Larsen." The medical student was young and obviously a little uncomfortable, but his holo-image showed a firm jaw and a positive look in his eyes. "Despite what you heard from Dr. Morris, and I think I can guess his views, I assure you that I did *not* make a mistake. The ID that I gave to you yesterday was correctly determined. More than that, I can prove it."

Larsen pursed his lips and looked across at Wolf, standing beside him. "I'm sorry, Luis, but we went through all that already, in detail. The liver for the patient who received the transplant was given a microbiopsy for us today. We were there, and we watched every stage of the process. We found a different ID, one that's in the central data bank files."

Rad-Kato was clearly surprised, but he looked stubborn.

"Then perhaps they got the wrong patient, or perhaps they made a mistake in their testing."

"Impossible, Luis." Larsen shook his head. "I tell you, we watched the whole thing."

"Even so, I can prove my point. You see, I didn't mention this last night, because I didn't think it was relevant, but I wanted to run a full enzyme analysis on the sample that I took as well as doing the chromosome ID. I didn't have time to do all the work last night. So I stored a part of the sample in the deep freeze over at the hospital. I was going to do the rest of the work tonight."

Wolf clapped his hands together exultantly. "That's it, John! It's time we had a break. We've had nothing but bad luck so far on this. Look"—to Rad Kato—"can you stay right where you are until we get over there? We need part of that sample."

"Sure. I'm in Fertility. I'll ask the receptionist to send you to this department when you arrive."

"*No*—that's just what you *don't* do. Don't tell *anybody*, not even your own mother, that you have that sample. Don't do anything to suggest that Form Control is interested in it. We'll have someone over in twenty minutes."

Wolf cut the connection and turned to Larsen. "John, can you get over there at once and pick up the tissue sample? Bring Rad-Kato with you and do the test with him in our own ID matching facilities. I would go with you, but I'm beginning to get ideas on what may be going on in this business. I need to get to a terminal and work with the computers. If I'm right, we've seen some very fast footwork in the past twenty-four hours. I want to find out who's doing it."

Before Larsen had even left the room, Wolf had turned to the terminal and begun to call out data files. It was going to be a long, tedious business, even if he was right—especially if he was right. He was still feeling his way through the intricacies of the software that protected files from outside interference when Larsen returned with the results of their own test of the liver sample. Rad-Kato had been right. He had made no mistake in his previous analysis; the liver ID corresponded to nothing in the central data bank files. Wolf nodded his satisfaction at the results, waved Larsen away, and carried on with his slow, painstaking search.

In the eighteen hours that followed Wolf moved only once from his chair, to find the bathroom drug cabinet and swallow enough cortamine to keep him awake and alert through the long night. It wasn't going to be too bad. The old tingle of excitement and anticipation was back. That would help more than drugs.

In the hidden underground lab three miles from Wolf's office, two red telltales in the central control section began to blink and a soft, intermittent buzzer was sounding. When the solitary man at the console called out the monitor messages, the inference was easy. Certain strings of inter-rogators were being used to question the central medical data files. His software that looked for such queries was more than five years old and had never before been called upon. He thanked his foresight.

One more tactic was available, but it would probably be only a delayer, and not much of that. The white-coated figure sighed and canceled the monitor messages. It was the time he had planned for, the point where the phaseout had to begin and the next phase be initiated. He needed to place a call to Tycho City and accelerate the transition. Fortunately, the man he wanted was back on the Moon.

"Sit down, John. When you hear this you'll need some support."

Wolf was unshaven, fidgety, and black under the eyes. His shoes were off, and he was surrounded by untidy heaps of output listings. Larsen squeezed himself into one of the few clear spots next to the terminal.

"You look as though you need some support yourself. My God, Bey, what have you been doing here? You look as though you haven't had any sleep for a week. Did you work right through?"

"Not quite that bad. A day." Wolf leaned back, exhausted but satisfied. "John, what did you think when you found out that Rad-Kato was right?"

"I was off on another case all yesterday and this morning, so I haven't been worrying too much about it. I thought for a while that Morris must have done something like palming the sample and substituting another one for it. The more I thought about that, the more ridiculous it seemed."

Wolf nodded. "Don't be too hard on yourself. That was the sort of thing that was going through my head, too. We were both watching him, so it was difficult to see how he could have done it—or why he would want to. That's when I began trying to think of some other way that it could have happened. I began worrying again about the computer failure and the loss of the records that we wanted the first night on the case. Two days ago, was it?"

Wolf leaned back again in his chair. "It feels more like two weeks. Anyway, I used the terminal here to ask for the statistics on the loss of medical records due to hardware failure, similar to the one that happened to us. That was my first surprise. There were *eighty* examples. It meant that the loss of medical data was averaging *ten times* higher than other data types."

"You mean that the medical data bank hardware is less reliable than average, Bey? That doesn't sound plausible."

"I agree, but that's what the statistics seemed to be telling me. I couldn't believe it, either. So I asked for the medical statistics, year by year, working backward. There was high data loss every year in the medical records, until I got back to a time twenty-seven years ago. Then, suddenly, the rate of data loss for medical information dropped to about the same level as everything else."

Wolf had risen from his chair and begun to pace the cluttered office.

"So where did that leave me? It looked as though some medical records were being destroyed *intentionally.* I went back to the terminal to ask for a listing of the specific data areas that had been lost in the medical records, year by year. The problem was, by definition, that the information about the missing areas had to be incomplete. Anyway, I got all I could, then I tried to deduce what it was that the lost data files must have contained."

Larsen was shaking his head doubtfully. "Bey, it doesn't sound like a method that we can place much reliance on. There's no way that you could check what you deduce. That would need a copy of the missing files, and they are gone forever."

"I know. Take my advice, John, and don't ever try it. It's like trying to tell what a man is thinking from the shape of his hat. It's damned near hopeless, and I could only get generalities. I squeezed out four key references with twenty-two hours of effort."

He stopped and took a deep breath. "Well, here's something for you to chew on, John. Did you ever hear—or can you suggest any possible meaning—of research projects with these names: Proteus, Lungfish, Janus, and Timeset?"

Larsen grimaced and shook his head. "I don't know about the possible meanings, but I can tell you right now that I've never heard of any of them."

"Well, that's no surprise, I'm in the same position. I got those names by going to the index files that define the contents of data areas, then querying for the missing files. Apart from the names I came up with, I found out only one other thing. All the four have one common feature—the same key medical investigator."

"Morris?"

"I wouldn't have been surprised if it had been that, John. But it goes higher: Capman. I think that Robert Capman has been purging the data files of certain records and faking it to make it look as though the loss is the result of a hardware failure. I told you you'd need a seat."

Larsen was shaking his head firmly. "No way, Bey. No way. You're out of your mind. Look, Capman's the director of the hospital—you'd *expect* his name to show up all over the medical references."

"Sure I would. But he isn't just the overall administrator of those projects, John, he's the single, key investigator."

"Even so, Bey, I can't buy it. Capman's supposed to be one of the best minds of the century—of any century. Right? He's a consultant to the general coordinators. He's a technical adviser to the USF. You'll have to offer a motive. Why would he *want* to destroy data, even if he could? Can you give me one reason?"

Wolf sighed. "That's the real hell of it. I can't give you a single unarguable reason. All I can do is give you a whole series of things that seem to tie in to Capman. If you believe in the idea of convergence of evidence, it makes a pretty persuasive picture.

"One." He began to check off the points on his fingers. "Capman is a computer expert—most medical people are not. He knows the hardware and the software that's used in Central Hospital better than anyone else. I asked you how we could get the wrong liver ID when Morris did the test. I can think of only one way. Morris put the sample in correctly—we saw him do it—but the data search procedures that handle the ID matching had been tampered with. Somebody put in a software patch that reported back to us with the wrong ID. Morris had nothing to do with it. Now,

I'll admit that doesn't really do one thing to link us to Capman—it's wild conjecture.

"Two. Capman has been at the hospital, in a high position, for a long time. Whatever is going on there began at least twenty-seven years ago."

"Bey," broke in Larsen impatiently, "you can't accuse a man just because he's been in a job for a long time. I'm telling you, if you tried to present this to anyone else, they'd laugh you out of their offices. You don't have one scrap of *evidence*."

"Not that I could offer in a court of law, John. But let me keep going for a while. It builds up."

Wolf had on his face a look that John Larsen had learned to respect, an inward conviction that only followed a long period of hard, analytical thought.

"Three. Capman has full access to the transplant organ banks. He would have no trouble in placing organs into them, or in getting them out if he wanted to. He could have disposed of unwanted organs there, and the chance that he would be found out would be very small. It would need a freakish accident—such as the test that Luis Rad-Kato did the other night, by sheer chance.

"A couple more points, then I'll let you have your say. According to the records, Robert Capman personally does the final review of the humanity-test results that are carried out at Central Hospital. If those results were being tampered with, Capman is the one person who could get away with it safely—anybody else would run the risk of discovery by Capman himself. Last point: Look at the hospital organization chart. All the activities I've mentioned lead to Capman."

Wolf flashed a chart onto the display screen, with added red lines to show the links to Capman. Larsen looked at it with stony scepticism.

"So what, Bey? Of course they all lead to him. Damn it,

he's the director, they *have* to lead to him. He's ultimately responsible for everything that's done there."

Wolf shook his head wearily. "We're going around in circles. Those lines I added end with Capman, sure—but not in his capacity as director. They end far below that, at a project level. It looks as though he chose to take a direct and personal interest in those selected activities. Why just those?

"There are a couple more things that I haven't had the time to explore yet. One of them would need a trip back to the hospital. Capman apparently has a private lab on the first floor of the place, next to his living quarters. No one knows what he does there, and the lab is unattended except for the robo-cleaners. Capman's an insomniac who gets by on two or three hours sleep a night, so he usually works in the lab, alone, to three or four in the morning. What does he do there?"

Wolf looked at his notes. "That's about it, except for a couple of points that are less tangible."

"*Less* tangible!" Larsen snorted in disgust, but Wolf was not about to stop.

"Didn't you find it peculiar, John, the way that Capman 'dropped in' on our meeting with Morris? He had no reason to—unless he wanted to get his own feel for what we were doing on the investigation. I don't know how aware of it you were, but he looked at the two of us as though he had us under a microscope. I've never had such a feeling before of being weighed and measured by someone.

"One final point, then I'm done. Capman has had absolute control of that hospital for forty years. Everybody there knows he's a genius, and they do whatever he wants without questioning it much. If I know anything at all about human psychology, he probably thinks by this time that he's above the ordinary laws."

Larsen was looking at him quizzically. "That's all very

nice, Bey. Now give me some real evidence. You have a lot of circumstantial points. With one piece of solid fact about the case, I'd even be convinced. But everything you've said is still guesswork and intuition. I'll be the first to admit that you're rarely wrong on this sort of hunch, but—"

He was interrupted by the soft buzz of the intercom. Wolf keyed his wrist remote and fell silent for a few seconds, listening to the private line accessing his phone implant. Then he cut the connection and turned to Larsen.

"Real evidence, John? Here's your solid fact, as hard a one as you could ask for. That was Steuben himself on the phone, and he was relaying a message from two levels higher up yet. There is a request for our services—the two of us, specifically, by name—to help investigate a form-change problem for the USF on Tycho Base."

"When?"

"At once. We have orders to drop any other cases that we're working on—Steuben didn't say what they were, and I doubt if he even knows—and leave tomorrow for the Moon. Apparently the request came direct from the office of the general coordinators. When does coincidence get to be past believing?"

"I don't know anybody at all in the general coordinators' office, Bey, and I'm pretty sure they don't know me. Do you know people there?"

"Not a soul. But somebody there—or one of their special consultants, such as you know who—seems to want us off the case we're on now. So somebody knows us and what we're doing. Like to take a bet?"

Larsen's face had begun to flush red. He looked again at the display of the Central Hospital organization, with its glowing lines leading to Capman, and swore softly.

"Bey, I won't take that twice. The business with Pleasure Dome was the last time I'll let them call me off. But they've got us trapped on this. We can't refuse a valid assignment—and for all we know the Tycho Base job is a real one. If only we had more time here. What can we do in one day?"

Wolf looked pale, but he was ready for a fight. He rose to his feet. "We can do at least one thing, John, before they can stop us. We can take a look at Capman's private lab."

"But we'd need a search warrant from head office before we can do that."

"Leave that to me. It reveals exactly what we're doing, but that can't be helped. We have to get over there this afternoon, while Morris is still on duty. I don't know how far we'll get, but we may need some assistance."

"What are you expecting to find, Bey?"

"If I could tell you that, we wouldn't need to go. I feel the same as you do—I'm not willing to be pulled off a case so easily this time, no matter where the order comes from. I want to know how those projects in the missing files— Proteus and the rest of them—tie in to that unidentifiable liver in the Transplant Department. We don't have much time. Let's plan to get out of here half an hour from now."

CHAPTER 6

On the way to the hospital, Larsen became silent and uncommunicative. Wolf noticed that he was listening intently to his phone implant and guessed at the reason.

"Any change in the situation at home, John?" he asked when Larsen finally cut the connection. He thought he could guess the answer.

Larsen looked somber. "Only the change you might expect. My grandfather's still with her. She's going down fast, and she knows it. It won't be more than another day or two. Damn it, Bey, she's a hundred and six years old—what can you expect? She's still using the machines, but it's not doing any good."

He drew a deep breath. "We love Grandmother, but what can we say to her? How do you tell someone you love that the right thing now is to go gracefully?"

Wolf could not give him an answer. It was a problem

that every family dreaded. Just as BEC's work had provided an answer to the old question of defining humanity, it also provided a definition of old age. Life expectancy was still about a century for most people; fertile, healthy years spent in peak physical condition. Then one day the brain lost its power to follow the profile of the biofeedback regimes. Rapid physical and mental decline followed, each reinforcing the other. Most people chose to visit the Euth Club as soon as they realized what was happening. An unfortunate few, afraid of the unknowns of death, rode the roller coaster all the way down.

Larsen finally broke the silence. "You know, Bey, I've never seen old age before. Can you imagine what it must have been like when half the world was old? Losing hair and teeth and eyesight and hearing." He shuddered. "A couple of hundred years ago, I suppose it was all like that. How could they stand it? Why didn't they become insane?"

Wolf looked at him closely. With a difficult time coming at Central Hospital, he had to be sure that Larsen was up to it.

"They had a different attitude in those days, John," he said. "Aging used to be considered as normal, not as a degenerative disease. In fact, some of the signs used to be thought of as assets—proof of experience. Imagine living a couple of hundred years before *that*, if you really want to scare yourself. Life expectancy in the thirties—and no anesthetics, no decent painkillers, and no decent surgery."

"Sure, but somehow you *can't* really think of it. You only really know it when you see it for yourself. It's like being told that in the old days people lived their whole lives blind, or with a congenital heart defect, or missing a limb. You don't question it, but you can't imagine what it must have been like."

They moved on, and finally Wolf spoke again.

"Not just physical problems, either. If your body and

appearance were fixed at birth, think how many emotional and sexual problems you might have."

The outline of Central Hospital was looming again before them. They left the slideways and stood together in front of the massive granite columns bordering the main entrance. Each time they entered, it seemed that old fears were stirred. Both men had taken the humanity tests here, although of course they had been too young to have any memory of it. This time it was Larsen who finally took Wolf by the arm and moved them forward.

"Come on, Bey," he said, "They won't test us again. But I'm not sure you'd pass if they did. A lot of people in Form Control say part of you isn't human. Where did you get the knack of sniffing out the forbidden forms the way you do? They all ask me, and I never have a good answer."

Wolf looked hard at Larsen before he at last relaxed and laughed. "They could do it as well as I can if they used the same methods and worked at it as hard. I look for peculiarities—in the way people look or the way they sound and dress and move and smell—anything that doesn't fit. After a few years it gets to be subconscious evaluation. I sometimes couldn't tell you what the giveaway was on a forbidden form. I'd have to give it a lot of thought, after the fact."

They were through the great studded doors. The same receptionist was on duty. He greeted them cheerfully.

"You two seem to have caught Dr. Capman's fancy. He gave me this code for you. You can use it anywhere in the hospital—he said you would need it when you got here."

He smiled and handed an eight-digit dial code to Wolf, who looked at Larsen in surprise.

"John, did you call and say we were coming?"

"No. Did you?"

"Of course not. So how the devil did he—"

Wolf broke off and walked quickly to a wall query

point. He entered the code, and a brief message at once flashed onto the viewing screen. MR. WOLF AND MR. LARSEN ARE TO BE GIVEN ACCESS TO ALL UNITS OF THE HOSPITAL. ALL STAFF ARE REQUESTED TO COOPERATE FULLY WITH OFFICE OF FORM CONTROL INVESTIGATIONS. BY ORDER OF THE DIRECTOR, ROBERT CAPMAN.

Larsen frowned in bewilderment. "He can't have known we'd be here. We only decided it half an hour ago."

Wolf was already walking toward the elevator. "Believe it or not, John, he knew. We'll find out how some other time. Come on."

As they were about to enter the elevator, they were met by Dr. Morris, who burst at once into excited speech. "What's going on here? Capman canceled all his appointments for today, just half an hour ago. He told me to wait here for you. It's completely unprecedented."

Wolf's eyes were restless and troubled. "We don't have time to explain now, but we need help. Where is Capman's private lab? It's somewhere on this floor, right?"

"It is, along this corridor. But Mr. Wolf, you can't go in there. The director has strict orders that he is not to be disturbed. It is a standard—"

He broke off when Wolf slid open the door, to reveal an empty study. The other two followed him as he went in and looked around. Wolf turned again to Morris.

"Where's the private lab?"

"Through here." He led the way into an adjoining room that was equipped as a small but sophisticated laboratory. It too was empty. They quickly examined both rooms, until Larsen discovered an elevator in a corner closet of the lab.

"Doctor, where does this lead?" asked Wolf.

"Why—I don't know. I didn't even know it was there. It must have been left over from the time before the new lift tubes were installed. But that's over thirty years ago."

The elevator had only one working button. Larsen

pressed it, and the three men descended in silence. Morris was counting to himself. When they stopped, he thought for a moment and nodded.

"We're four floors underground now, if I counted them correctly. I don't know of any hospital facilities this deep under the building. It has to be very old—before my time here."

The room they stepped out into, however, showed no signs of age. It was dust-free and newly painted. At its far end stood a large vault door with a combination lock built into the face. Wolf looked at it for a few seconds, then turned to Larsen.

"We don't have too many options. Good thing it's not a new model. Think you can handle it, John?"

Larsen walked up to the vault door and studied it quietly for a few minutes, then nodded. He began to move the jeweled key settings delicately, pausing at each one. After twenty minutes of intense work, with frequent checks on his percomp, he drew a deep breath and carefully keyed in a full combination. He pulled, and following a moment's hesitation the great door swung open. They walked forward into a long, dimly lit room.

Morris pointed at once to the line of great sealed tanks that ran along both walls of the room.

"Those shouldn't be here! They're special form-change tanks. They are like the ones we use for infants with birth defects, but these are ten times the size. There shouldn't be units like this anywhere in this hospital."

He moved swiftly along the room, inspecting each tank and examining its monitors. Then he came back to Wolf and Larsen, eyes wide.

"Twenty units, and fourteen of them occupied." His voice was shaking. "I don't know who is inside them, but I am quite certain that this whole unit is not part of the hospital facilities. It's a completely unauthorized form-change lab."

Wolf looked at Larsen with grim satisfaction. He turned again to Morris.

"Can you tell us just what change work is going on in here?"

Morris thought for a moment, then replied. "If this is the usual layout, there has to be a control room somewhere. All the work records on the changes should be there—computer software, experimental designs, everything. It's not at this end."

They hurried together along the length of the room. Morris muttered to himself in satisfaction when he saw the control room there. He went to the console and at once began to call out records for each of the experiment stations in turn. As he worked, his face grew paler and his brow was beaded with sweat. At last he spoke, slowly and in hushed tones.

"There are missing records, but I can already tell you something terrible—and highly illegal—has been going on here. There are humans in fourteen of those tanks. They are being programmed to adapt to prespecified forms, built into the control software. And I can tell you one other thing. The subjects in the tanks are definitely of an illegal age for form-change work—my rough estimate puts them between two years old and sixteen years old, all of them."

It took a few seconds for that to sink in. Then Larsen said quietly: "You are telling us that there are human *children* in those tanks. That's monstrous. How can a child assess the risks that go with form-change?"

"They can't. In this case, the question of knowing the risk does not arise. The arrangement is a very special one, never used legally. We've known how to apply it, in principle, for many years. The stimulus to achieve a programmed form-change is being applied directly to the pleasure centers of their brains. In effect, they have no choice at all. These children are being forced to strive for the programmed changes by the strongest possible stimulus."

He leaned back in the control console chair and put both hands to his perspiring forehead. When he finally spoke again, his voice was slurred and weary.

"I can't believe it. I simply can't believe it, even though I see it. In Central Hospital, and with Capman involved. He's been my idol ever since I left medical school. He seemed more concerned for individuals, and for humanity as a whole, than anyone I ever met. Never cared for money or possessions. Now he's mixed up in this. It makes no sense. . . ."

His voice cracked, and he sat hunched and motionless in his chair. After a few seconds, Wolf intruded on his troubled reverie.

"Doctor, is there any way that you can tell us what form-changes were being used here?"

Morris roused himself a little and shook his head. "Not without the missing records. Capman must have kept those separately somewhere. I can get the computer listings through the display here, but it would be a terrible job to deduce the program purpose from the object listings. Even short subroutines can take hours to understand. There's a piece of code here, for example, that occurs over and over in two of the experiments. But its use is obscure."

"What do you think it is, Doctor?" asked Bey. "I know you can't tell us exactly, but can you get even a rough idea?"

Morris looked dubious. "I'll be reading it out of context, of course. It looks like a straightforward delay loop. The effect is to make each program instruction execute for a preset number of times before moving on to the next one.

So everything would be slowed down by that same factor, set by the user."

"But what would it do?"

"Heaven knows. These programs are all real-time and interactive, so it would be nonsensical to slow them all down." He paused for a second, then added, "But remember, these programs were presumably designed by Robert Capman. He's a genius of the first rank, and I'm not. The fact that I can't understand what is being done here means nothing. We need Capman's own notes and experimental design before we can really tell what he was doing."

Wolf was pacing the control room, eyes unfocused and manner intent.

"That's not going to be easy. Capman has left the hospital, I'll bet my brains on it. Why else would he have given us free run of the place? I don't understand why he did that, even if he knew we were on to him. Somehow he must have tracked what we were doing and decided he couldn't stop us. But unless we do trace him, we may never know what he was doing here."

He turned to Larsen in sudden decision, "John, go and get a trace sensor. It's my bet that Capman has been here, in this room, in the past hour. We have to try and go after him, even if it's only for his own protection. Can you imagine the public reaction if people found out he had been stealing human babies for form-change experiments? They'd tear him apart. He must have taken the children by faking the results of the humanity tests. That's why their IDs aren't on file."

Larsen hurried out of the vault. As he left, Morris suddenly looked hopeful.

"Wait a minute," he said. "Suppose that Capman was working with subjects that had *failed* the humanity tests. That wouldn't be as bad as using human babies."

Wolf shook his head. "I had that thought, too. But it can't work. Remember, the whole point of the humanity test is that nonhumans *can't* perform purposive form-change. So they must be humans he's using, by definition. Not only that, remember that the liver we found came from a twelve-year-old. Capman didn't just have experiments, he had *failed* experiments, too. The organ banks were a convenient way of disposing of those, with small risk of discovery."

He continued to pace the room impatiently, while Morris sat slumped in silent shock and despair.

"God, I wish John would hurry up," said Wolf at last. "We need the tracer. Unless we can get a quick idea where Capman went, we're stuck."

He continued his pacing, looking at the fittings of the control room. The communicator set next to the control console looked like a special purpose unit, one of the old models. All the response codes for setting up messages had changed since they were used—which meant any dial code might key different responses. Bey thought for a moment, then entered the eight-digit dial code that had been left for him by Capman at the main lobby. This time, instead of the earlier message requesting cooperation with Form Control, a much longer message scrolled steadily into the viewer. Bey read it with steadily increasing amazement.

DEAR MR. WOLF. SINCE YOU ARE READING THIS, YOU ARE IN THE PRIVATE VAULT AND HAVE, AS I FEARED AFTER OUR FIRST MEETING, DEDUCED THE NATURE OF MY WORK HERE. I HAVE KNOWN FOR MANY YEARS THAT THIS DAY MUST COME EVENTUALLY, AND I HAVE RESIGNED MYSELF TO THE FACT THAT THIS WORK WILL PROBABLY NOT BE COMPLETED UNDER MY DIRECTION. MR. WOLF, YOU MAY NOT KNOW IT YET, BUT YOU AND I ARE TWO SPECIMENS OF A VERY RARE BREED. IT WAS APPARENT TO ME VERY QUICKLY THAT THIS

WORK WOULD PROBABLY END WITH YOUR INVESTIGATION. I
REGRET IT, BUT ACCEPT IT.

LONG AGO, I DECIDED THAT I WOULD PREFER TO LIVE
OUT MY LIFE IN QUIET ANONYMITY, SHOULD THIS WORK BE
DISCOVERED, RATHER THAN ENDURE THE EXTENSIVE AND
WELL-MEANING REHABILITATION PROGRAM THAT WOULD
BE INFLICTED ON ME AS PUNISHMENT FOR MY CRIMINAL
ACTS. TO MOST, THESE DEEDS MUST APPEAR UNSPEAKABLE.
TO YOU, LET ME SAY THAT MY WORK HAS ALWAYS HAD AS
ITS OBJECTIVE THE BENEFIT OF HUMANITY. TO THAT END, A
SMALL NUMBER OF HUMAN LIVES HAVE UNFORTUNATELY
BEEN SACRIFICED. I FULLY BELIEVE THAT IN THIS CASE THE
END JUSTIFIES THE MEANS.

IN ORDER TO ACHIEVE THE ANONYMITY I DESIRE, IT WILL
BE NECESSARY FOR ROBERT CAPMAN TO VANISH FROM THE
EARTH. IT IS UNLIKELY THAT WE WILL MEET AGAIN. THE
RISK FOR ME WOULD BE TOO GREAT, SINCE I SUSPECT THAT
YOU AND I WOULD ALWAYS RECOGNIZE EACH OTHER. AS
HOMER REMARKS, SUCH KNOW EACH OTHER ALWAYS. MR.
WOLF, LEARN MORE FORM-CHANGE THEORY. YOUR GIFT FOR
THE PRACTICAL IS ASTONISHING, BUT ITS TRUE POTENTIAL
WILL BE WASTED UNTIL YOU MASTER THE THEORETICAL
ALSO. DO THAT, AND NOTHING WILL BE BEYOND YOU.

THIS MORNING I COMPLETED ALL THE NECESSARY PLANS
FOR MY DEPARTURE, AND NOW I MUST LEAVE. BELIEVE ME,
THERE IS A POINT WHERE FAME IS A BURDEN, AND A QUIET
LIFE AMONG MY RECORDINGS AND HOLOTAPES IS DE-
VOUTLY TO BE WISHED. I HAVE REACHED THAT POINT. SIN-
CERELY, ROBERT CAPMAN.

That was the end. Wolf and Morris watched the screen
intently, but nothing further appeared.

"I'm beginning to understand why you people in the
hospital regard him as omniscient," said Wolf at last. "But
I'm sure you realize that I can't let him get away. If I can

track him down, I have to do it. As soon as John Larsen gets here, we'll try and follow him—no matter where he's gone."

Morris did not reply. He seemed to have had more shocks than he could take in one day. He remained at the seat of the control console, slack-jawed and limp, until Larsen appeared at last through the great vault door.

"Sorry that took so long, Bey," he said. "I thought I'd better go by Capman's apartment and train the sensor on a couple of his clothing samples. It should be pretty well tuned now to his body chemistry. We can go any time, as soon as we get a faint scent. The sensor kept pointing this way, so somehow he must have been able to exit from here. See any signs of a concealed way out?"

The two men began to search the wall areas carefully, while Morris looked on listlessly and uncomprehendingly. Finally, John Larsen found the loose wall panel behind an air-conditioning unit. Working together, they lifted it aside and found that beyond it lay a long, narrow corridor, faintly lit with green fluorescence. Larsen held the trace sensor in the opening, and the monitor light glowed a bright red. The trace arrow swung slowly to point along the corridor.

"That's the way he went, Bey," said Larsen. He turned to Morris. "Where will this lead?"

Morris pulled himself together and looked around him. "I'll have to think. The elevator was in the west corner of the study. So that would mean you are facing just about due east."

Bey Wolf pinched thoughtfully at his lower lip. "Just about what I expected," he said. "Where else?" He turned to Larsen. "That's the way we'll have to go, John, if we want to catch Capman. See where we'll be heading?—straight into the heart of Old City."

CHAPTER 7

Take the toughest and seediest of the twentieth-century urban ghettos. Age it for two hundred years and season it with a random hodgepodge of over- and underground structures. Populate it with the poorest of the poor and throw in for good measure the worst failures of the form-change experiments. You have Old City, where the law walked cautiously by day and seldom by night. Bey Wolf and John Larsen, armed with cold lights, stun guns, and trace sensor, emerged from the long underground corridor just as first dusk was falling. They looked around them cautiously, then began to follow the steady arrow of the tracer, deeper into Old City.

The evidence of poverty was all around, in the cracked, garbage-strewn pavements, the neglected buildings, and the complete absence of slideways. Travel was on foot, or in ancient wheeled vehicles without automatic controls or safety mechanisms.

"Let's agree on one thing, John," said Wolf, peering about him with great interest. "While we're hunting Capman, we'll not be worrying too much about the usual forbidden forms. For one thing, I expect we'll see more of them here than we've ever seen before. Look there, for example."

He pointed down the side alley they were passing. Larsen saw a hulking ursine form standing next to a tiny, rounded man no more than two feet tall. They had a reel of monofilament thread, which they were carefully unwinding and attaching to a frame of metal bars. Wolf kept walking.

"Run into that," he said, "and it would shear you in two before you knew you'd been cut. They're obviously setting a trap. It's not for us, but we'd better watch how we go in here."

Larsen needed no reminding of that fact. His eyes tried to move in all directions at once, and he kept his hand close to his stun gun.

"They don't look much like failed attempts at the usual commercial forms, Bey," he said. "I suppose that's what happens when some poor devil who's really twisted in the head gets hold of a form-change machine."

Wolf nodded. "They probably try and fight against taking those forms with their conscious minds, but something underneath dictates their shapes. Maybe in another hundred years we'll understand what makes them do it."

As he spoke, Wolf was coolly assessing all that he saw and storing it away for future reference. Old City was off-limits for all but real emergencies, and he was making the most of a rare opportunity. They hurried on through the darkening streets, becoming aware for the first time of the absence of streetlights. Soon, it was necessary to use the cold lights to show their path. The tracer arrow held its steady direction. As night fell, the inhabitants of Old City who shunned the day began to appear. Larsen held tighter to the handle of his gun as the sights and sounds around them became more alien.

They finally reached a long, inclined ramp, leading them again below ground level. Larsen checked the tracer, and they continued slowly downward. Their lights lit up the tunnel for ten yards or so, and beyond that was total blackness. A gray reptilian form with a musty odor slid away from them down a side passage, and ahead of them they heard a chitinous scratching and scuttling as something hurried away into the deeper shadows. Wolf stopped, startled.

"That's one to tell them about back at the office. Unless I'm going mad, we've just seen someone who has developed an exoskeleton. I wonder if he has kept a vertebrate structure with it?"

Larsen did not reply. He lacked Wolf's clinical attitude, and he was becoming increasingly uncomfortable with their quest. They moved on, and the surroundings became damp and glistening as the ramp narrowed to an earth-walled tunnel with a dirt floor. Ahead of them, a slender figure mewled faintly and slithered away with a serpentine motion down another side passage.

Wolf suddenly stopped and fingered the metal shaft of the tracer he was holding. "Damn it, John, is it my imagination or is this thing getting hot?"

"Could be. I think the same thing is happening to the gun and the flashlight. I noticed it a few yards back."

"We must have run into an induction field. If it gets any stronger, we won't be able to carry metal with us. Let's keep going for a few more meters."

They moved on slowly, but it was soon apparent that the field was strengthening. They backed up again for a council of war.

"The tracer signal is really strong now, John," said

Wolf. "Capman can't be far ahead of us. Let's leave all the metal objects here and scout ahead for another fifty meters. If we don't spot him after that, we'll have to give up."

Both men were feeling the strain. In good light, Wolf would have seen the reaction that his suggestion had produced in Larsen. As it was, he heard a very faint assent, and leaving guns, lights, and trace sensor behind, they went on into the darkness, meter by cautious meter.

Suddenly, Larsen stopped. "Bey." His voice was a faint whisper. "Can you hear something up ahead?"

Wolf strained his ears. He could hear nothing.

"It sounded like a groan, Bey. There, again. Now do you hear it?"

"I think so. Quietly now, and carefully. It's only a few yards in front of us."

They crept on through the musty darkness. They heard another low groan, then heavy and painful breathing. Suddenly, a weak voice reached them through the gloom.

"Who's there? Stay where you are and for God's sake don't come any closer."

"Capman? This is Wolf and Larsen. Where are you?"

"Down here, in the pit. Be careful where you tread. Wait a second. I'll show you where it's safe to go."

A thin beam of light appeared, coming from the floor in front of them. They moved hesitantly forward and found themselves standing at the edge of a twelve-foot drop. At the base of it they could see Capman lying helpless, limbs contorted. He was holding a small flashlight and shining it toward them.

"This pit wasn't here a couple of days ago," he said faintly. "It must have been dug by one of the modified forms that live in these tunnels. A big one, I think. It came this way a few minutes ago, then went away again. That way."

He shone the flashlight along the bottom of the pit.

They could see a large tunnel running away from the base of it. Capman seemed weak and obviously in pain, but he was still perfectly rational and composed.

"If it survives down here, it's probably carnivorous," he said. "I wonder what the basic form is."

Wolf was astonished to hear a note of genuine intellectual curiosity in Capman's tone. He advanced closer to the edge and tried to see farther along the tunnel in the pit.

"I don't know what you can do to help me," went on Capman calmly. "If you can't get me out, it's vital that I give my records to you. I should have left them at the hospital. They are a crucial part of the description of the work I've been doing. Make sure they get into the right hands."

He broke off suddenly and swung the light back along the wall of the pit. "I think it's coming back. Here, I'm going to try to throw this spool up to you. Step nearer to the edge. I'm not sure how well I can throw from this position."

Capman shone the flashlight on the wall of the pit to give a diffuse light above and threw a small spool awkwardly upward. Reaching far out, almost to the point of overbalancing, Larsen managed to make a snatching one-handed catch. Capman sighed with relief and pain and sank back to the dirt floor. They could hear a deep grunting, and a scrambling noise was approaching along the pit tunnel. While they watched in horror, Capman remained astonishingly cool.

"Whatever happens here," he said, "remember that your first duty is to get those records back to the hospital. Don't waste any time."

He turned the flashlight again into the pit. In the uncertain light, Wolf and Larsen had an impression of an enormous simian shape moving toward Capman. Before they could gain a clear view of it, the light fell to the floor and was suddenly extinguished. There was a grinding noise and a bubbling cough from the pit, then silence.

Wolf and Larsen were seized suddenly with an understanding of their own defenseless position. Without another word or a wasted moment, both men turned and sped back through the tunnel. They picked up guns, lights, and tracer and continued at full speed through the dark ways of Old City. Not until they were once more in the elevator, rising through Central Hospital to Capman's laboratory, did Larsen finally break the silence.

"I don't know what Capman did in that vault, but whatever it was he paid for it tonight."

Wolf, unusually subdued, could do no more than nod agreement and add, "Requiescat in pace."

They went at once to the Transplant Department, where Morris received the precious spool of microfilm. At Wolf's urging, he agreed to have a team assigned to an immediate analysis of it, while they told him of the strange circumstance of its passage to them.

CHAPTER 8

An hour before sunrise, Wolf and Larsen were break-
fasting in the visitors' section on the highest floor of Central Hospital. At Morris's insistence they had taken three
hours of deep sleep and spent another hour in programmed
stress release. Both men were feeling rested and fit and had
accepted a substantial meal from the robo-servers. Before
they had finished, Morris came bustling in again. It was
clear from his appearance that he had not slept, but his
eyes were bright with excitement. He waved a handful of
listings and sat down opposite them.

"Fantastic," he said. "There's no other word for it. It
will take us years to get all the details on this. Capman has
gone further in form-change than we dreamed. Every form
in that underground lab explores new ground in form-
change experiment."

He began to leaf through the listings. "Here's an anaerobic form," he said. "It can breathe air, as usual, but if necessary it can also break down a variety of other chemicals for life support. It could operate under the sea, or in a vacuum, or almost anywhere. Here's another one, with a thick and insensitive epidermis—it should be very tolerant of extreme conditions of heat and radiation.

"Then there's this one." Morris waved the listing excitedly. He was unable to remain seated and began to pace up and down in front of the window, where a pale gleam of false dawn was appearing. "Look, he has a complete photosynthetic system, with chlorophyll pouches on his chest, arms, and back. He could survive quite happily in a semidormant state on traces of minerals, water, and carbon dioxide. Or he can live quite well as a normal human form, eating normal food.

"Here we have miniaturized forms, only ten inches high when fully adult. They have a normal life expectancy and a normal chromosome and gene structure. They can breed back to full-sized children in a couple of generations."

Wolf was struck by a sudden memory. "Do these forms have any special project names with them?" he asked.

"They do. They are all shown in Capman's general work notes under the heading of Project Proteus, except for one form—and that one has us baffled at the moment. It's the one we were talking about in the lab last night."

He riffled through the listings and came up with one that seemed much more voluminous than the others. "It's the one with the delay loop that occurs all over the program. We have made several efforts to revive the subject, but we can't do it. He seems to be in some kind of catatonic trance, and when we try and calculate the life ratio on the computer, we get overflow."

Wolf looked at Morris and thought of Capman's note to him in the underground vault. Perhaps Capman was right and Wolf did think in the same way. There was no doubt that he found the intention of the new form obvious, while it had Morris and Larsen baffled.

"Doctor," he said. "Did Capman ever talk to you about the future of the human race—where we will be in a hundred years, for instance?"

"Not to me personally. But his views were well known. He leaned very much toward Laszlo Dolmetsch's views—society is unstable, and without new frontiers we will stagnate and revert to a lower civilization. The United Space Federation can't prevent that; they are too thinly spread and have too fragile a hold on the environment."

Wolf leaned back and looked at the ceiling. "So doesn't it seem clear what Capman's plan was? We need new frontiers. The USF can't provide them unless it has assistance. Capman has been working towards a single, well-defined objective—to provide forms that are adapted to space exploration. The forms you've been describing are ideal for working out in space, or on the Moon or Mars—or for terraforming work on Venus." '

Morris looked blank. "You're right. But what about the small ones, or this catatonic one?"

"He's not catatonic. He's asleep. All his vital processes have been slowed down by some preset amount. I don't know how much, but you should be able to find out if you look at the delay factor in the biofeedback program. Capman set up that delay loop so the software could interact with the form-change experiment in its own 'real time.' "

Morris looked again at the listings in his hand. "Twelve hundred," he said at last. "My God, it's set now for *twelve hundred*. That means that . . ."

His voice trailed off.

"It means that he will sleep for one of his 'nights,' " said Wolf. "That will be equal to twelve hundred of ours. I expect his life expectancy will be in proportion—twelve hundred times as long. That makes it about a hundred and twenty thousand years. Of course, that's not his *subjective* life expectancy—that will probably be about the same as ours."

"But how do we communicate with him?"

"The same way as Capman did in his form-change programs. You'll have to slow all the stimuli down by a factor of twelve hundred. Feed him information at the same rate as he's programmed to receive it."

"But what's the point of it?" asked Morris. "He can't work in space if he's incapable of communicating with the rest of us."

"New frontiers," said Wolf. "We want new frontiers, right? Don't you see you've got an ideal form there for interstellar exploration? A trip of a century would only seem about a month to him. He'll live for more than a hundred thousand Earth years. If you put a form-change machine on the ship with him, he could be brought back to a normal pace when he got there, for the observation work. Combine him with the miniaturized forms you found, and you've got people who can explore the stars with the present ships and technology."

"The delay factor is set in the program," said Morris. "There's no reason to think twelve hundred is a limit. I'll have to check and see how high it could go. Do you think it's possible that the programs would allow him to run *faster* than normal?"

"That's much harder. I don't see how you could speed up nerve signals. But I'm no expert on that, you need to look at it yourself. You can see now why your computer hit an overflow situation when you tried to compute a life ratio. In subjective terms it's still unity, but in terms of an outside observer it's twelve hundred. We need a new definition of life ratio."

Morris was still pacing the room excitedly, listings crumpled in his hands. "There's so much that's new. We'll be years evaluating it without Capman. You have no idea what we lost with his death. I'll have to get back and help the others in the analysis, but none of us has his grasp of fundamentals. It's a gap that can't be filled."

He seemed to have recovered from his earlier shock at discovering that Capman was using human subjects. The potential of the new forms drove all else from his mind. As he turned to leave, Wolf asked him a final question.

"Did the catatonic experiment have any special project name?"

Morris nodded. "Project Timeset—of course, that makes perfect sense now. I must check how big the delay factor can become. I see no reason why it couldn't be ten thousand or more. Can you imagine a man who could live for a million years?"

He hurried out, and his departure took the energy and excitement from the room. After a few seconds, Wolf stood up and went over to the window. It faced out across Old City, toward the coming dawn. He looked at the dark, sprawling bulk of the city beneath him in silence.

"Cheer up, Bey," said Larsen after a couple of minutes. "Capman's death is still eating you up, isn't it? We couldn't have done a thing to help him. And I don't think we should judge him. That's for the future. He did a terrible thing, but now he's paid for it with his life. It's no good you brooding on it, too."

Bey turned slowly from the window, his eyes reflective and introspective. "That's not what's worrying me, John," he replied. "I'm troubled by something a lot less abstract. It's hard for me to believe that a man could be as smart as Capman and yet die so stupidly."

Larsen shrugged. "Everybody has their blind spots, Bey. Nobody's all smart."

"But Capman told us that he knew he might be discovered all along. He didn't know when it might be, but he had to allow for it. He set up elaborate checks to see if anyone was about to discover what he was doing, and when he found we were on to him, he got ready to disappear."

"That's just what he did," agreed Larsen. "He was all set to disappear, but he didn't allow for that monster's trap over in Old City."

Wolf was shaking his head. "John, Robert Capman allowed for *everything*. I don't believe he'd fall into a trap like that. We are the ones who fell into the trap. Don't you see, everything that happened was designed to draw us to pursue him? He knew we would try and follow him—we had to. All that talk about disappearance and a quiet life was nonsense. He *expected* to be followed."

"Maybe he did, Bey. But he didn't expect that illegal form in the tunnel."

"Didn't he, John? He wanted the trail followed while it was hot—just the two of us, without a lot of special equipment and with no preparation. So like a pair of dumb heroes, we rushed in."

Wolf looked down at the streets of Old City, where a phosphorescent green trail of light was slowly spreading; the street scavengers were off on their last predawn search for pickings.

"We should have been suspicious," he continued, "as soon as we ran into that induction field. Who would have set up such a thing—and why? Somebody wanted us to get to Capman without lights or guns. So, sure enough, Larsen and Wolf arrive on the scene without lights and guns."

"But we saw the monster form, Bey, and we saw Capman killed. Are you saying that was all part of the plan?"

Wolf looked at Larsen sceptically. "Did we see it? Did we really? What did we actually *see*? A big, vague form, then Capman dropped the flashlight and the place went dark. We ran. We didn't really see one thing that proved that Capman died down there. When was the last time you ran away from something in a blind panic?"

Larsen nodded. "I'm not proud of that, Bey. I haven't run from anything for a long time. I don't know what got hold of us."

"I think I do. We ran away, but we had a little assistance. I'll bet there was a subsonic projector and a few other items near that pit—all set up to scare the hell out of us as soon as we had the spool of microfilm. Capman even told us, twice, that we had to get the film back to the hospital—so we could justify it to ourselves that we were right to run away. Capman says he 'forgot' to leave it at the hospital, but it would have needed a separate conscious act for him to have taken it from the hospital in the first place —and all the people here say that he never forgot *anything*, no matter how small a detail."

Wolf sighed and peered out through the window. "John, it was a setup. We were moved around down there like a couple of puppets. Capman is no more dead than we are."

Larsen was silent for a couple of minutes, digesting what Wolf had told him. Finally he too came to the window and looked out.

"So you think he is alive somewhere down there. How can we prove it?"

Wolf looked at his own reflection in the smooth glass. He saw a man with a worried frown and a thin, unsmiling mouth. Morris's satisfaction and enthusiasm at Capman's discoveries had not proved infectious.

"That's the hellish part of it, John," he said. "We can't prove it. No one would believe the bits and pieces that I've told you. If we report the facts, and we have to, then Capman will be declared dead. There will be no more pursuit. He will be free in a way that he could never have been if we hadn't followed him."

Larsen too was frowning. "Part of what you say is still

hard to accept, Bey. Capman lived for his work; we've heard that from many people here. Now that's gone from him. What would he do with his life?"

Bey Wolf looked back at him questioningly. "Has it gone from him, John? Remember, there are twenty tanks in that vault, and only fourteen of them were occupied. What happened to the experiments that were in the other six? We know now what the code words in the index file, Proteus and Timeset, were referring to. But I found two others there, too. What about Project Janus and Project Lungfish? We don't know what they were, and we don't know what happened to them.

"I think that Robert Capman has another laboratory somewhere. He has those other six experiments with him, and he's still working on them. You can bet that those are the six most interesting forms, too."

"You mean he has a lab out there in Old City, Bey?"

"Maybe, but I think not. If we wanted to, we could follow him to Old City. He told the Building Committee that he hoped to have twenty more working years. I think that he would look for a place where he can work quietly, without danger of interruption. Would you like to speculate on the forms that he might create in twenty years? I don't think Old City could hold them."

"Even if he's not there, Bey, we ought to check it out and make sure." Larsen turned away from the window. "Let me go and file a report on this—I assume that we won't be going to the Moon today, the way Steuben is expecting us to. I'll request that we send a search party back along the way that we went last night. Maybe we can pick up some clues there."

He left, leaving Wolf alone in the long room. On impulse, Bey went and switched off all the lights, then returned to the window overlooking the eastern side of the city.

Search if you want, John, he thought. *I'm pretty sure you won't find any signs of Robert Capman. What was it his message to me said? "It will be necessary for Robert Capman to vanish from the Earth." I'm inclined to take that literally.*

Wolf began to feel the old sense of letdown and disappointment. After the excitement of discovery and pursuit, there was only another blind alley, another trail that ended in criminality and futility.

Or did it? Something didn't feel quite right. Bey frowned out on the darkened city, allowing his instinct to direct his thinking.

If Capman is what I think he is—and if I am what he thinks I am—then I must also assume that he expected me to see through his 'death.' So what does he expect me to do now? Pursue him. Then he must also know he has a hiding place where I cannot follow him.

It was another dead end. All that was left was Capman's instruction: Learn more form-change theory. There must have been a reason for that. Capman was not a man to provide vague general advice.

And there was still the great inconsistency. On the one hand, Capman was performing monstrous experiments on human children; on the other, he was a great humanitarian who cared about humans more than anyone. Those two statements could not be reconciled. Which left the question, what was Capman *really* doing in his experiments?

Wolf did not know, and Capman did not want to tell—not yet. But if the time for explanations ever did arrive, Bey wanted to be ready to understand it. Could *that* be the point of Capman's message?

Project Janus. Project Lungfish. Something there was just beyond reach. Wolf felt like a man who had been given a glimpse of the promised land, then seen it snatched away. He had to go back to the Office of Form Control now, when what he'd like to be doing was working with Capman, wherever he was. He sensed a new world out there, a whole unknown world of changes.

Wolf's thoughts ran on, drifting, speculating on when he would next meet with Robert Capman. The first rays of the coming dawn were striking through the window, high in the hospital. Below, still hidden in darkness, lay the forbidding mass of Old City. Behrooz Wolf watched in silence until the new day had advanced into the streets below, then he turned and left the room. Capman had disappeared, but the data banks still had some questions to answer. Wolf was ready to ask them.

CHAPTER 9

Sunshine Setting,
Mail Code 127/128/009
Free Colony.
Dear Mr. Wolf,

First off, let me say how sorry I am that I took so long to reply to you. I had your inquiry, then I mislaid it among some of my other things, and I only found it again two days ago. I was going to send you back a spoken answer, but these days they tell me that I tend to ramble on and repeat myself, so I thought that this way would be better. Say what you like about the feedback programs, when you get older they don't let you keep the memory you once had. Just last week, I couldn't find my implant plug for a long time, and then finally one of my friends here reminded me that I had sent it off for service. So I thought it would be better if I sent you a written answer.

Well, one thing is certain. I certainly remember Robert Capman all right, maybe because I met him so long ago. Most of the things that you mentioned in your letter are true, and I was a little surprised that you couldn't rely on what the public records said for the facts on his life. Maybe you are like me, though, and have trouble with the computer call-up sequences.

I'll never forget Capman, and I even remember quite clearly the first time we ever met. We went to study at Hopkins the same year, and we arrived there on the same day—in the fall of '05. It was before they had introduced all that chromosome ID nonsense, and we had to sign in the book together when we arrived. He signed before me, and I looked at his name as he was picking up his case, and I said, joking, "Well, we ought to get on well together, we cover the whole range between us." What I meant was, with his name being Capman and my name being Sole, we had the whole body, from head to toe, between us. Then I said, "Better let me help you with that case," because he was just a little shrimp compared to me. I mean, he was nearly ten years younger than I was. I was twenty-five, and he hadn't quite reached sixteen and was small for his age. I didn't know it at first, but I should have guessed that he was something special—that was the year they put the year for college entrance up to twenty-six, and I was squeaking in myself under the legal limit. He had taken the entrance tests and left his age mark blank, so they didn't find out how old he was until after they had already read his exam papers. By then, they were ready to do something outside the rule book to let him into the college.

You know how it is when you are in a strange place; any friendship seems bigger than usual. After that first introduction, we hung around together for the first week or so, and when it came to the time to assign quarters we agreed that we would share, at least for the first few months. As it turned out, we eventually shared for over two years, until he went off for an advanced study program.

In a way, I suppose that we might have seen even more of each other than we did if we *hadn't* shared quarters. As it was, one of us had to be on the night shift for using the bed (Hopkins was even tighter for accommodation in those days than they are now) and the other had to take a daytime sleep period. Robert took the day sleep period—not that he ever did much sleeping. He never seemed to need it. Many times I've seen him, when I'd be coming home from one of my classes. He'd be still sitting at the desk after working all day on some problem that interested him, and he didn't seem to be in the least bit worried that he'd had no sleep. "I'll just nap for half an hour," he'd say, and he'd do that and then be ready to go off to his classes, perfectly awake again.

You ask what he studied. Well, he was doing biochemistry, same as I was, but he was the very devil for theory. Things that nobody else would worry about—that weren't ever on any examination—he'd tear away at. I used to hear the teachers talking to each other, and they weren't sure whether they were very pleased to have him as a student or just plain nervous about it. You see, with him they could never get away with a glib answer, and they found that out pretty quickly. He'd be back the next day with chapter and verse on the most obscure points if they didn't give him good answers.

I'm not sure how much more description you want. Certainly, the basic facts that you quoted are correct. He was at Hopkins from '05 to '09, to my personal knowledge, and then he went off to one of the European colleges —I think it was Cambridge—for two years, and then he came back again to serve as a research assistant to the Melford Foundation. That's where he became famous, a few years later, when he published the taxonomy of permissible forms. It didn't start then, of course. He was developing the theory long before, in his first years at Hopkins. He would come over to the rest of us with these long lists of symbols on big sheets and try and explain them to me and the other bio students. I don't know about the rest of them, but I didn't have any idea what he was talking about.

As for close relationships, he didn't have many at Hopkins, and I suppose of all the people he knew I must have been the closest to him. He didn't show much sexual interest in men or women, and I don't think he ever formed any sort of bond in the time that I knew him. The nearest he ever got to a contract bond was with Betha Melford, when he was working for the Melford Foundation. She was quite a few years older than he was, but they were very close. The two of them, along with a group of others, who lived in different places around the world, formed a sort of society. They called it the Lunar Society, but I guess that was some sort of joke, because it had nothing at all to do with the Moon. There were some pretty important people in that group, either important then or important later, but I don't think any of them had a close physical relationship that lasted more than a few weeks. We thought they were a bunch of cold characters.

I wouldn't want that last comment to be misunderstood. Robert Capman was a fine man, a man that I would trust with my life. I say that, although we haven't seen each other in the flesh for about forty years. I heard all that talk up from Earth, about his killing people in experiments, but I don't believe it. It's the usual sensation mongering; the news services will say anything for an effect. As I always say, they are not just holo-people, they are hollow people. I don't think that you can believe what they say now, any more than you could believe what they said about Yifter's disappearance, back in '90. I remember that well, too.

Of course, all these things are a long time ago, but I remember them all very clearly, the way you do remember things that happen when you are very young. Nowadays, I don't find things so memorable, but I'll be having my hundred and ninth birthday next week, and I'm enjoying good health, so I mustn't grumble. I'm sorry to have taken so long to get this off to you, but I thought it would probably be better to give you a written answer. You said that you were asking a number of Robert's friends about him, and I wanted to mention that if any of them want to get in touch with me I hope that you will give them my address. It would be nice to see some of them again, and talk about old times with people who lived through them. Of course, I can't go to any place that has a high-gravity environment, but maybe some of them could visit me up here.

I hope this letter will be useful to you, and I hope that the rumors about Robert Capman can be stopped.

Ludwig Plato Sole, D.P.S.

Bey read the letter through to the end, then placed it on top of the stack. It was the last reply to his inquiries, and he'd been lucky to get it. Attached to it was a brief note from the chief physician at Free Colony, pointing out that Ludwig Sole was rapidly losing the ability to use the bio-feedback machines, and thus the information in the letter came from a man of failing faculties. No further information was likely to come from Sunshine Setting. Fortunately, thought Bey, no more was needed. Sole's letter covered much the same ground as some of the others, though he had been closer than anyone during the Hopkins years.

In the eight months since the disappearance, Wolf had painstakingly located forty-seven surviving acquaintances and close contemporaries of Capman. The oldest was one hundred and ten, the youngest almost ninety.

The summary before him, culled from all the replies to his inquiries, was complete but baffling. Nowhere could Bey read any signs of cruelty or megalomania in their descriptions of Capman. Oddness, yes, but oddness that hinted at the solitary mental voyaging of a Newton or an Archimedes, at the lonely life of a genius. Had some chance event, twenty-seven years ago, tipped the balance? "Great wits are sure to madness near allied," no denying it—but Robert Capman wouldn't fit the pattern.

Bey turned to the yellowed sheet that was pinned to the back of Sole's letter. It was faded and almost unreadable, a relic of an earlier age, and it would need special treatment before it could be fully deciphered. It seemed to be an old transcript of Capman's academic records, and it was curious that Sole had made no reference to it in his letter. Bey increased the strength of the illumination on the sheet and varied the frequency composition of the light sources until he had the best conditions for reading the thin blue print.

Robert Samuel Capman. Born: June 26th, 2090.

Date of entry: September 5th, 2105. Category: BIO/ CH/PHY/MAT.

Bey bent closer to the page. Below the general biographical data a long list of numbers was faintly visible. He hadn't seen anything quite like it, but it looked like a psych profile output, one in a different format. He linked through to the Form Control central computer and added an optical character reader as a peripheral. The scanner had trouble with the page that Bey placed beneath it, but after a few iterations, with help and corrections from Bey for doubtful characters, it flashed a confirming message and performed the final scan.

Bey called for character enhancement. He waited impatiently while the computer performed its whirl of silent introspection. The months since Capman's discovery and flight had not lessened the eagerness to trace him; in fact, if anything Bey's determination had strengthened. He was resigned to the fact that it would probably take years. All the evidence suggested that Capman was nowhere on Earth, and it was not practical to pursue him across the Solar System—even if the USF were to cooperate, which they showed little wish to do. Meanwhile, there was form-change theory. It was more evident every day how appropriate Capman's advice had been. New vistas were opening to Bey as he advanced, and there was evidence that he was still in the foothills. At least he had begun to learn how—and how well—Capman's mind worked.

The computer was finally satisfied with its work on character recognition. While Bey looked on impatiently, the screen slowly filled with the final interpretation of the transcript. It was all there, in a slightly different format from the modern displays but quite recognizable. Intelligence, aptitudes, mechanical skills, associative ability, subconscious/conscious ratios, paralogic, nonlinear linkages—they were all listed, with numerical measures for each one.

Bey looked through them quickly at first, puzzled by the low scores in some areas. About halfway through, he began to see a familiar pattern. He stopped, suddenly dizzy with the implications. He knew the overall profile very well. It was different in detail, as any two people were different, but there were points of resemblance to a psych profile that Bey Wolf knew by heart, as well as he knew his own face in the mirror.

Wolf was still sitting motionless in front of the screen when Larsen returned from the central troubleshooting area upstairs. He ignored Bey's pensive attitude and broke out at once into excited speech.

"It's happened, we've had a break on the salamander form. The Victoria office uncovered a group of them, still coupled. If we leave at once we can get the Link entry that Transport is holding for us. Come on, don't just sit there, let's go."

Bey roused himself and stood up. As always, work demanded first priority. He looked unhappily at the display that still filled the screen and then followed John Larsen from the room.

BOOK II

"Beware, beware, his flashing eyes, his floating hair."

CHAPTER 10

The monsters first came to public attention off the coast of Guam. They stood quietly on the seabed, three of them abreast, facing west toward the Guam shore. Behind them, plunging away rapidly to the abyssal depths, lay the Mariana Trench. Faintest sunlight fled about their shadowy sides as they stirred slowly in the cold, steady upwelling.

To the startled eyes of Lin Maro as he cruised along in his new gilled form, they seemed to be moving forward, slowly and purposively breasting the lip of the coastal shelf and gliding steadily from the black deeps to the distant shore. Forgetting his long months of training and feedback control, Lin gasped and pulled a pint of warm seawater into his surprised lungs. Coughing and spluttering, gills working overtime, he surged 150 feet to the surface and struck out wildly for the shore and safety. A quick look back convinced him that they were pursuing him. His glance caught the large, luminous eyes and the ropy tendrils of thick floating hair that framed the broad faces. He was in too much of a hurry to notice the steel weights that held them firmly and remorselessly on the seabed.

The reaction onshore was somewhere between amusement and apathy. It had been Lin's first time out in a real environment with his new gilled form. Everybody knew there was a big difference between the simulations and the real thing. A little temporary hallucination, a minor trompe l'oeil from the central nervous system, that wasn't hard to believe on the first time out with a new BEC form. After all, the guarantees were on physical malfunction, not on sensory oddities. It took long, hard arguing before Maro could get anyone to show even polite interest. The local newsman who finally agreed to go out and take a look did so as much from boredom as from belief. The next day they swam out, Maro in his gills, the reporter in a rented scuba outfit.

The monsters were still there, all right. When the two men swam cautiously down to take a look at them, it became clear that Lin had been fleeing from three corpses. They swam around them in the clear water, marveling at the wrinkled gray skin, massive torsos, and great dark eyes.

When the story went out over the comlink connections, it was still a long way down the news lists. For three hundred years, writers had imagined monsters of the deep emerging from the Mariana Trench and tackling human civilization in a variety of nasty ways. Silly season reports helped to provide some light relief from the social indicators, the famines and the real crises, but they received scant interest from the professionals. Nobody reported panic along the coast or fled to the high ground.

The three monsters got the most interest from the Guam

aquarium and vivarium. A party of marine biologists took a day off from plankton culture and went for a party offshore. They inspected the bodies on the seabed, then lifted them—shackles and all—to the surface, quick-froze them, and whipped them back to shore on the institute's hovercraft for a real inspection. The first lab examination showed immediate anomalies. They were land animals, not marine forms. Lung breathers with tough outer skins and massive bone structure. As a matter of routine, the usual tissue microtome samples were taken and the chromosome ID run for matches with known species.

The ID patterns were transmitted to the central data banks back at Madrid. At that point every attention light on the planet went on, the whistles blew, and the buzzers buzzed. The computer response was prompt and unambiguous. The chromosome patterns were human.

The information that moves ceaselessly over the surface of the Earth, by cable, by ComSat link, by Mattin Link, by laser, and by microwave, is focused and redistributed through a small number of nodes. Bey Wolf, after much effort, had finally arranged that the Office of Form Control should be one of them. His recent appointment as head of Form Control entitled him to a complete interaction terminal in his office, and it was his peculiar pleasure to sit at this, delicately feeling the disturbances and vibrations in the normal pattern that flowed in the strands of the information web. John Larsen had suggested that Bey sat there like a fat spider, waiting for prey, and the analogy rather pleased him. His was, Bey would point out, only one of many webs, all interlocking, and not by any means the most important one. Population, Food, and Energy all had much bigger staffs and bigger budgets. But he would argue that his problems called for the shortest response times and needed a reaction time that some of the other systems could manage without.

Bey was sitting at the terminal, studying a type of omnivorous form that promised to be truly an omnivore—plants, animals, or minerals. He was oblivious to the unscheduled fierce snowstorm that was raging outside the building, and when the priority override interrupted his data link with news of the Mariana Monsters (the press's dubbing of the Guam discovery), his first reaction was one of annoyance. As the details came in, however, his interest grew. It looked very much as though some new group had been using the form-change equipment in unsuccessful experiments, and the results were nothing like any previous line of work.

Although he was fairly sure of the answers, Bey ran the routine checks. Were the experiments authorized as medical research? Were the forms already on the forbidden list? Negative answers, as he expected, came from the data banks. Was quick action needed to stop the appearance of a potentially dangerous form? The answer to that was much harder. The computer pleaded shortage of data—which meant that the decision would have to be made by human judgment, and the human in this case was Bey Wolf.

He sighed a sigh of hidden pleasure and opened the circuits for more data. The physical parameters began to flow in. The cell tests were strange in both chemistry and structure, with a mixture of haploid and diploid forms. The lungs were modified, showing changes in alveolar patterns. A note added to the analysis pointed out the resemblance to animals that were adapted to life at high pressure. Strangest of all, the big eyes were most sensitive in the near infrared —but another added note pointed out that this wavelength region is cut out almost completely underwater.

Bey began to gather printed output. He liked to approach a job by asking very basic questions. What was the objective of a new form? Where was it designed to operate most effectively? Most important of all, what was the probable motive of the developer? With answers to those questions, the next step in the form-change sequence could usually be guessed.

The trouble was, it wasn't working. Bey swore softly and leaned back in his chair. The Mariana Monsters were breaking the rules. After looking at the physical variables of the forms for a couple of hours, it seemed to Bey that they were not adapting to any environment that he could imagine.

It was time to drop that line and try another attack. All right, how had the forms reached their position on the seabed? Certainly they had not placed themselves there. And how had they died? There was information on that in the medical records. They had been asphyxiated. It was a fair guess that they had been weighted with steel after they were dead, then dropped to the seabed. From a surface vessel, by the looks of it—the reports mentioned no sign of skin contusions.

Where had they come from? Bey pulled out the list. He had a complete catalog of the world's form-change centers, especially the ones elaborate enough to include the special life-support systems the new forms would have needed. He was reading steadily through the list of sites, correlating them with the physical changes noted for the Mariana forms, when Larsen returned from a routine meeting on the certification of new BEC releases.

He halted in the doorway.

"How do you do it, Bey? You've only been in this office for a month, and it looks like a rubbish heap."

Bey looked around him in surprise at the masses of new listings and form-change tabulations that cluttered the office.

"They are accumulating a bit. I think they reproduce at

night. Come in, John, and look at this. I assume you didn't get too much excitement out of your review meeting?"

Larsen dropped into a chair, pushing aside a pile of listings. As always, he marveled at Bey's ability to operate clearly and logically in the middle of such a mess of documents and equipment.

"It was better than usual," he replied. "There were a couple of good ones. C-forms, both of them, adapted for long periods in low gravity. They'll revolutionize asteroid work, but there were the usual protests from the Belter representatives."

"Naturally—there'll always be Luddites." Bey still had a weakness for outmoded historical references, even though his audience rarely understood them. "The law will change in a couple of years. The C-forms are so much better than the old ones that there's no real competition. I'm telling you, Capman has changed space exploration methods forever. I know the Belters claim they are losing jobs to the new forms, but they are on the wrong side of the argument. Unmodified forms are an anachronism for free space work."

He switched on a recall display and pulled a set of documents from one of the heaps.

"Get your mind reset and let me tell you about the latest headache. It has the Capman touch. If I weren't convinced that he's not on Earth, I'd be inclined to label it as his work."

Bey ran rapidly over the background to the Mariana discoveries, finishing with the question of where they had come from.

"I suspect that they came into the general area of the Marianas through one of the Mattin Links," he concluded. "The question is, which one? We have twenty to choose from. I don't believe there is any way they could have come in from an off-Earth origin, otherwise I'd have thought they were aliens."

"With human chromosome IDs? That would take some explaining, Bey."

John Larsen went over to the wall display, which Bey had tuned to show the locations of the Mattin Link entry points.

"No, I agree with you, Bey; they've come from a lab here on Earth. If they came through the Links, we can rule out a few of them—they're open ocean, and they only act as transfer points. Have you correlated the big form-change labs with the Mattin Link entry points?"

"I started to do it, but it's a big job. I'm waiting for more output on that to come back from the computer. I'm still waiting for the full identification of the three bodies, too. I don't know why it's all taking so long. I slapped a top priority code on the inquiry."

He joined Larsen over at the wall screen. Working together, they reviewed the locations of the Mattin Links that formed the pivot points for Earth's global transportation system. They were deep in the middle of their work when the communicator beeped for attention. Larsen went over to it, leaving Wolf to record the analysis of the wall outputs. As the first words of the message scrolled onto the communicator display, Larsen whistled softly to himself.

"Come over here and get a look at this, Bey," he called. "There's the reason that Central Records took so long to get you an answer. Are you still as sure that the forms didn't come from off-Earth?"

The message began, ID SEARCH COMPLETED AND IDENTIFICATION MADE. INDIVIDUALS OF INQUIRY ARE AS FOLLOWS: JAMES PEARSON MANAUR, AGE 34, NATIONALITY USF; CAPERTA LAFERTE, AGE 25, NATIONALITY USF; LAO SARNA

PREK, AGE 40, NATIONALITY USF. BIOGRAPHICAL DETAILS
FOLLOW. CONTINUE/HALT?

Wolf pressed CONTINUE, and the detailed ID records appeared: education, work, history, family, credit ratings.
Bey noted with surprise that all three of the men had spectacular credit, up in the mutlimillionaire class, but his mind
was still mainly occupied with the first item of background. The three men were all members of the USF, and
that made for a real mystery. Since the USF had declared
its sovereignty fifty years earlier, in 2142, its citizens had
always been a relative rarity down on Earth. Surely the
disappearance of three of them should have roused a loud
outcry long before their bodies had been found off the
Guam shore.

The two men looked at each other. Larsen nodded in
response to Wolf's raised eyebrows.

"I agree. It makes no sense at all. The USF still have
their ban on form-change experiments. If they won't accept
the C-forms, I doubt if they'd be playing with completely
new forms, even as part of their defense programs. And it's
still harder to believe that they'd bring their failures down
to Earth."

"Even if they could get them here—you know how
tight quarantine is since the Purcell spores." Wolf shook his
head. "Well, we don't have much choice about what to do
next. We have to get a USF man in on this—it's too sensitive for us to handle on our own."

He had a reason to look gloomy. The investigation had
just grown two orders of magnitude in complexity. To go
further without USF concurrence would create an interplanetary incident.

"I'll put a request in," said Larsen. "The less we can get
away with telling them at this point, the better. I'll shove
the bare facts at them and let them decide who they want to

send down from Tycho City. I hope they send somebody who at least knows how to spell 'form change.'"

While they talked, the communicator continued to pump out the information in display and hard copy form. It had reached the point where the requested correlation between Link entry points and form-change labs was being presented—Bey had almost forgotten that he had asked for it. The day promised to be a long and confusing one.

Not surprisingly, BEC was getting into the act as well. An incoming news release set out their official position:

> Biological Equipment Corporation (BEC) today released a formal statement denying all knowledge of the human bodies discovered recently in the Pacific. A BEC representative informed us that the bodies had clearly been subjected to form-change, but that no BEC program developments, past or present, could lead to forms anything like those which have been found. In an unusual procedure, BEC has agreed to release records showing forms now under development in the company. They have also invited government inspection of their facilities.

"That's a new one," said Bey. "They must really be running scared. I've been waiting for them to plead innocent or guilty. I've never known BEC to release their new form secrets before. They must be losing their old commercial instinct."

"Not quite." Larsen pointed at the final words of the message. "I wonder what it cost them to get that tagged on to the end of the news release."

The display continued.

> BEC is the pioneer in and world's largest manufacturer of purposive form-change equipment utilizing biological feedback control methods. The release of BEC

proprietary information to assist in this investigation is voluntary and purely in the public interest.

"There we go," said Bey. "That's more like the old BEC. Old Melford died a long time ago, but I'll bet his skeleton is grinning in the grave."

CHAPTER 11

There generation USF men, like top kanu players, are usually on the small skinny side, built for mobility rather than strength. It was a surprise to greet a giant, more than two meters tall and muscled like a wrestler, and find that he was the USF man assigned to work with the Office of Form Control on the Guam form-change case. Bey Wolf looked up at the tall figure and bit back the question on the tip of his tongue.

It made no difference. Park Green was regarding him knowingly, a sly smile on his big baby face.

"Go on, Mr. Wolf," he said. "Ask me. You'll do it eventually anyway."

Bey smiled back. "All right. Do you use form-change equipment? I thought it was banned for everything but repair work in the USF."

"It is, and I don't. I came this way, and it's all natural.

97

You can guess how hard it is, acting as a USF representative and looking just as though you've been dabbling with the machines."

Wolf nodded appreciatively. "I'm not used to being read so easily."

"On that question, I've had lots of practice. I thought we ought to get rid of that distraction before we get down to work. What's new on the Guam case? I've had orders to send a report back to Tycho City tonight, and at the moment I have no idea what I'm going to say. Did you get a time and cause of death yet from the path lab?"

"Three days ago, and they all died within a few hours of each other. They were asphyxiated, but here's the strange part. Their lungs were full of normal air—no gaseous poisons, no contaminants. They choked to death on the same stuff that you and I are breathing right now."

Park Green sniffed and looked perplexed. "They changed to something that found air poisonous. I don't like that one. How about the way they got to the seabed?"

"They were dropped off twenty-four hours or less after they died. It must have been done at night, or we'd have had reports of sightings. That part of the coast is full of fishing herdsmen during the day. My guess is that they died a long way from there."

"Excuse my ignorance, but I don't follow your logic."

"Well, I'm conjecturing, but I think they were intended for the bottom of the Mariana Trench. Five miles down, they'd never have been found. So they were accidentally dropped a few miles too far west, and that suggests it was done by somebody who didn't know the local geography too well. Whoever did it was in a hurry, too, or they would have been more careful. That suggests it was an accident, with no time for detailed advance planning. Somebody was keen to hide the evidence, as far away and as fast as they could. You don't look very surprised at any of that," added

Wolf as Green slowly nodded agreement. "Do you know something they haven't bothered to tell me?"

The big man had squeezed himself into a chair and was slowly rubbing his chin with an eleven-inch hand.

"It fits with some of the things I know about the dead men," he replied. "What else have you been able to find out about them?"

"Not much," said Wolf. "Just what I got from the data bank biographies. They were Belters, the three of them, all off the same ship—the *Jason*. They arrived here on Earth three weeks ago, rolling in money, and went out of sight. Nobody has any records of them again until they were found dead off Guam. We had no reason to follow them once they had cleared quarantine. They had no trouble there, by the way, which seems to rule out anything like the Purcell spores or any other known disease. They were in the middle of a form-change when they died."

"That's right, as far as it goes," agreed Green, "but you're missing a few facts that make a big difference. First off, you said they were Belters, and technically you're right. They worked the Belt. But in USF terms, they were really Grabbers—prospectors, out combing the Belt for transuranics. They'd been looking for over two years when their monitors finally sniffed Old Loge. Maybe you don't realize it back here on Earth, but the only natural source of transuranics in the Inner System is fragments of Loge that drift back in as long-period comets. The Grabbers sit out there and monitor using deep radar. One good find and they're made for life."

"And the *Jason* hit a good one, I assume," said Wolf. "I couldn't believe their credit when I saw the records."

"A real big one," agreed Green. "They hit about three months ago, and it was packed with Asfanium and Polkium, elements 112 and 114. They crunched the fragment for the transuranics and came in to Tycho City a month ago, all as rich as Karkov and Melford. They started to celebrate, and three weeks ago they came down to Earth to keep up the fun. We lost touch with them then and don't know what they did. We didn't worry. No Belter would live on Earth, and we knew they'd be back when the flesh-pots palled. You can probably guess what they did next."

Wolf nodded. "I think I can, but I'd like to see where you are heading. Keep going."

"They came to Earth," continued Green. "Now, I saw them in Gippo's bar a couple of days before they left the Moon. They looked terrible. You can imagine it, a couple of years of hardship in space, then a celebration you wouldn't believe when they reached Tycho City. If you came to Earth in that condition, wouldn't you find it tempting to hook up for a superfast conditioning session with a biofeedback machine? It's not very illegal, and it would get you back to tip-top physical condition faster than anything else. Costs a bit, but they were rolling in money."

"And easy to arrange," said Wolf. "I know a thousand places where you could do it. They don't have fancy form-change equipment there, but you're talking about some-thing rather trivial. It makes good sense—but it wouldn't explain the forms they were in when they were found off Guam. You couldn't get to those without a fully equipped change center. Now let me tie in our side of it, and see what you think."

He pressed the interoffice communicator and asked Lar-sen to join them.

"I'm going to ask you this cold, John," he said when Larsen entered the room. "Is Robert Capman dead?"

"I thought he was four years ago," replied Larsen. He sighed and shrugged his shoulders. "Now, I'm not so sure." He turned to the USF man. "Bey has always been convinced that it was a setup, and he has me halfway persuaded. I must admit it had the makings of one, but he hasn't been heard of for four years, ever since he disappeared. I agree with Bey on one thing, though; the Guam forms have just the right look to be a Capman product."

"They certainly do," said Bey. He turned to Park Green, who was looking very puzzled. "How much do you know about Capman and what he did?"

Green thought for a moment before he replied, his high forehead wrinkling in thought.

"All I can really tell you is what we hear in Tycho City," he said at last. "Capman was a great man here on Earth, a genius who invented the C-forms, the ones that are adapted for life in space. According to the stories, though, he did it by using human children in his experiments. A bunch of them died, and finally Capman was found out. He tried to escape and died himself as he was trying to get away. Are you telling me there's more to it than that?"

"I think there is," said Bey. "For one thing, it was John and I who handled that case and found out what Capman was doing. Do you have strong personal feelings against him?"

"How could I? I never knew him, and all the things I've heard are not things I know about personally. If he was really using children, of course I have to be against that. Look, what's it got to do with me?"

"That's a fair question." Wolf paced about in front of Park Green's seated figure, his head scarcely higher than Green's despite their different postures. "You have to see how my thoughts have been running. Earth's greatest-ever expert on form-change, maybe still alive, maybe in hiding. Along comes a set of changes that seem to defy all logic, that don't conform to any known models. It could be Capman, up to his old tricks again. But even if it *isn't,* Capman would be the ideal man to work with on this. I should have added one other thing; neither John nor I ever met a man, before or since, who impressed us as much with his sheer brainpower."

Green wriggled uneasily in his seat, still uncomfortable in the higher gravity. "I know you're selling me something, but I haven't figured out what it is. What are you leading up to?"

"Just this." Wolf halted directly in front of Park Green. "I want to find Robert Capman—for several reasons. We think he's not down here on Earth—hasn't been for the past four years. Will you help me reach him? I don't know if he's on the Moon, out in the Belt, or somewhere further out. I do know that I can't get messages broadcast to the rest of the Solar System unless I have USF assistance."

Green nodded understandingly. "I can't give you an instant answer," he replied. "You're asking for a healthy chunk of communication assist, and that costs money."

"Charge it to this office. My budget can stand it."

"And I'll have to check it out on a policy level with Ambassador Brodin. He's down in Paraguay, and you know Brodin, he won't agree to *anything* unless you ask favors in person." He stood up, stretched, and inflated his sixty-inch chest with a deep, yawning breath. "I'd better get to it before I fall asleep—we're on a different clock in Tycho City. What's the best way to travel to Paraguay?"

"Through the Mattin Link. There's an exit point in Argentina, then you'll go the rest of the way by local flier. We can be at the Madrid link in ten minutes, and you'll be to Argentina in two jumps. Come on, John and I will get you to the entry point."

"I'd appreciate that. I've really had trouble getting used to the complexity of your system down here. We only have four entry points for the whole Moon, and you have twenty. Is it true that you'll have more in a few years?"

It was not true, and it never would be. The Mattin Link

system offered direct and instantaneous transmission between any adjacent pair of entry points, but the number and placing of them was very rigid. With perfect symmetry required for any entry point with respect to *all* others, the configuration of the system had to correspond to the vertices of one of the five regular solids. Plato would have loved it.

The dodacahedral arrangement, with its twenty vertices on the surface of the Earth, was the biggest single system that could ever be made. The Lunar system was the simplest, with just four entry points set at the vertices of a regular tetrahedron. The intermediate arrangements, with cubic, octahedral, and icosahedral symmetry, had never been used. Mattin Links away from the planetary surfaces were immensely attractive for transportation, but they were impractical close to a star or planet because of constantly changing orbital distances.

Gerald Mattin, the embittered genius who had dreamed of a system for instantaneous energy-free transfer between any two points anywhere, had died during the first successful tests of the concept. The system that came from his work was far from energy-free—because Earth was not a homogeneous sphere and because space-time was slightly curved near its surface. Mattin had derived an energy-free solution defined for an exact geometry in a flat space-time, and no one had yet succeeded in generalizing his analysis to other useful cases.

Mattin's death came twenty years before the decision to build the first Mattin Link system on the surface of a planet, twenty-five years before the first university was named after him, thirty years before the first statue.

CHAPTER 12

"We have a go-ahead now, but I had to bargain my soul away to squeeze it out of the ambassador. I don't want to waste all that work. Where do we go from here?"

Park Green was back in Wolf's office, shoes off, long legs stretched out. The general confusion of the place had worsened. Computer listings, empty food trays, and maps were scattered on every flat surface. Wolf and Larsen were again standing by the wall display, plotting the Mattin Link access from both the Mariana Trench entry point and the spaceport entry point in Australia. Wolf read off the results before he replied to Green's question.

"North Australia direct to the Marianas—so they could have gone there direct from the spaceport, except that we know they didn't. The Mariana entry point connects direct to North China, Hawaii, and back of course to North Australia. None of those are promising. There's no big form-change lab anywhere near any of them. What do you think, John?"

Larsen scratched his head thoughtfully. "Two possibilities. Either your hunch about the use of the Link system is all wrong, or the people who moved the Mariana Monsters to Guam did more than one jump in the system. Where do we get with two jumps?"

Wolf read out the connections and shook his head.

"That takes us a lot further afield. With two jumps you can get almost anywhere from a Marianas starting point. Up to the North Pole, down to Cap City at the South Pole, into India, up to North America—it's a mess."

Wolf put down the display control and came over to where Park Green was sitting.

"I'm more convinced than ever that we need Robert Capman's help," he said. "We still don't know what was happening when they died. They started on some form-change program, and somewhere along the line it went wrong. I wish I could ask Capman how."

"You never answered my question, you know," said Green. "What do we do next? Where do we go from here? Advertising for Capman won't solve your problem—he'll be regarded as a mass murderer if he ever does show up on Earth."

"I think I can produce a message that he will recognize and be intrigued by, but other people won't understand," answered Wolf. "As for protecting him if he does show up, I'm not worried about that. I feel sure that he'll have found ways to cover himself in the past four years. I've got another worry of my own. I have no way of knowing how urgent this thing is. It could be a once-in-a-lifetime accident that will never happen again, or it could be the beginning of some kind of general plague. We think it isn't contagious, but we have no proof of it. Until we know what we're dealing with, I have to assume the worst. Let me take a crack at that message."

The final announcement was short and simple. It went out on a general broadcast over all media to the fourteen billion on Earth and by boosted transmission to the scattered citizens of the United Space Federation. The signal would be picked up all the way out past Neptune, and a repeater station would even make it accessible to parts of the outer system Halo.

> To R.S.C. I badly need the talents that caused me to pursue you four years ago through the byways of Old City. I promise you a problem worthy of your powers. Behrooz Wolf.

Troubles were mounting. Bey spent many hours with a representative of BEC, who insisted on presenting more confidential records to prove that the company had no connection with the monster forms. The central coordinators' office sent him a terse message, asking if there would be other deaths of the same type, and if so, when, where, and how many. Park Green was getting the same sort of pressure from the USF. Unlike Bey Wolf, he had little experience of that kind of needling. He spent a good part of his time sitting in Bey's office, gloomily biting his nails and trying to construct positively worded replies with no information content.

Two days of vagueness brought a stronger response from Tycho City. Bey arrived in his office early and found a small, neatly dressed man standing by the communicator. His clothes were USF style, and he was calling out personnel records for the three crew members of the *Jason*. He turned around quickly as Bey entered, but there was no sign of embarrassment at being discovered using Bey's office without invitation.

He looked at Bey closely before he spoke.

"Mr. Green?" The voice was like the person, small and precise, and offered more of a statement than a question.

"No, he'll be in later. I'm Behrooz Wolf, and I'm head of the Office of Form Control. What can I do for you?" Bey was suddenly conscious of his own casual appearance and uncombed hair.

The little man drew himself up to his full height.

"I am Karl Ling, special assistant to the USF Cabinet." The tone of voice was peppery and irascible. "I have been sent here to get some real answers about the deaths of three of our citizens here on Earth. I must say at the outset that we regard the explanations offered so far by your office and by Mr. Green as profoundly unsatisfactory."

Arrogant bastard, thought Bey. He looked at his visitor closely while he sought a suitably conciliatory answer, and felt a sudden sense of recognition.

"We have been doing our best to provide you with all the facts, Mr. Ling," he said at last. "We all thought it was unwise to present theories until we have some definite way of verifying them. I'm sure you realize that this case is a complex one and has a number of factors that we haven't encountered before."

"Apparently it does." Ling had taken a seat by the communicator and was tapping his thigh irritably with a well-manicured left hand. "For example, I see that the cause of death is stated as asphyxiation. But the postmortem shows that the dead men had only normal air in their lungs, with no poisonous constituents. Perhaps you would be willing to present your theory on that to me—there is no need to wait for a full verification."

Ling's tone was sceptical and definitely insulting. Bey felt a sudden doubt about his own intuitive reaction to Ling's presence. In the past, dealing with officious government representatives, Bey had found an effective method of removing their fangs. He thought of it as his saturation technique. The trick was to flood the nuisance with so many facts, figures, reports, graphs, tables, and analyses that he was inundated and never seen again. The average bureaucrat was unwilling to admit he had not read what he was given. Bey went over to his desk and took out a black record tablet.

"This is a private interlock for the terminal in this office. It has in it the data entry codes that will allow you to pull all the records on this case. They are rather voluminous, so analysis will take time. I suggest that you use my office here and feel free to use my communicator as the output display device for Central Files. Nothing will be hidden from you. This machine has a full access code."

Bey felt rather self-conscious about his own pompous manner, but it was the right action, whether or not his first intuitive response to Ling had been correct.

The little man stood up, his eyes gleaming. They were a curious brownish yellow in color, with flecks of gold. He rubbed his hands together.

"Excellent. Please arrange it so that I am not disturbed. However, I do wish to see Mr. Green immediately when he arrives."

Far from being subdued, Karl Ling was clearly delighted at the prospect of a flood of information. Bey left him to it and went to give the news to Park Green.

"Karl Ling?" Green looked impressed. "Sure I know him—or know of him. I've never met him myself, but I know his reputation. He's supposed to be one of the inner circle at top levels of the USF. He's also something of an expert on Loge and the Belt. He did a whole series of holovision programs a few years ago, and he used part of one of them in tracing the history of the discovery of Loge. It was a popular program, and he did a good job. He began way back, hundreds of years ago. . . ."

(Cameras move from the illuminated model and back to Ling, standing.)

"School capsules give the 1970s as the first date in Loge's history. Actually, we can find traces of him much further back than that. The best starting point is probably 1766. A few years before the French and American revolutions, a German astronomer came up with a formula that seemed to give the relative distances of the planets from the Sun. His name was Johann Titius. His work didn't become famous until it was picked up a few years later by another German, Johann Bode, and the relation he discovered is usually called the Titius-Bode law, or just Bode's law."

(Cut to framed lithograph of Bode, then to the table of planetary distances. Zoom in on blank spot in the table showing question mark.)

"Bode pointed out that there was a curious gap in the distance formula. Mercury, Venus, Earth, Mars, Jupiter, and Saturn fitted it—and that is all the planets they knew of at the time—but there seemed to be one missing. There ought to be a planet between Mars and Jupiter, to make the formula really fit the Solar System. Then William Herschel, in 1781, discovered another planet, farther from the Sun than Saturn."

(Cut to high-resolution color image of Uranus, rings in close-up, image of Herschel as insert on the upper left. Cut back to Ling.)

"It fitted Bode's law, all right, but it wasn't in the right place to fill the spot between Mars and Jupiter. The search for a missing planet began, and finally in 1800 the asteroid Ceres was discovered at the correct distance from the Sun. Soon after, other asteroids were found at about the same distance as Ceres. The first pieces of Loge had appeared."

(Cut to image of Ceres, zoom in for high-resolution shot of Ceres City and greenhouse system. Cut to diagram

showing planetary distances, with multiple entry between Mars and Jupiter, then back to Ling.)

"There now seemed to be too many planets. As more and more asteroids were found, the theory grew that they were all fragments of a single planet. It was a speculation without hard evidence for a long time, until in 1972 the Canadian astronomer Ovenden provided the first solid proof. Using the rates of change in the orbits of the planets as his starting point, he was able to show they were all consistent with the disappearance from the Solar System of a body of planetary mass roughly sixteen million years ago. He was also able to estimate the mass as about ninety times the mass of the Earth. Loge was beginning to take on a definite shape."

(Cut to image of Ovenden, then to artist's impression of the size and appearance of Loge, next to an image of Earth at the same scale.)

"The next part of the story came just a few years later, in 1975. Van Flandern in the United States of America integrated the orbits of long-period comets backward through time. He found that many of them had periods of about sixteen million years—and they had left from a particular region of the Solar System, between Mars and Jupiter. Parts of Loge were paying their first return visit, after a long absence."

(Cut to animated view of cometary orbits, showing their intersection with a diagram of the system. Run animation backward, to show all orbits coming together at a single point between Mars and Jupiter.)

"This led to the first modern ideas of Loge: a large planet, a gas giant of ninety Earth masses, almost the same size as Saturn. It disintegrated about sixteen million years ago in a cataclysm beyond our imagining. The explosion blew most of Loge out of the system forever. A few parts of the planetary core remain as the asteroids. Other fragments, from the outer crust of Loge, drop back into the Solar System from time to time as long-period comets."

(Move in to close-up of Ling, head and shoulders.)

"That looked like the full story, until we were able to go out and take a close look at the long-period cometary fragments. We found that some of them are packed with transuranic elements. The mystery of Loge had returned, bigger than ever. Why should parts of Loge's outer crust, alone of all the Solar System, contain transuranic elements? Their half-lives are less than twenty million years, in a system that is many billions of years old. They should have decayed long ago. Were they formed somehow in the explosion of Loge? If so, why are they found only in the outer crust, not in the asteroids that came from Loge's core? *How* were they formed? To all these questions, we still have no satisfactory answers."

(Cut to image of Loge again, feed in beginning of fade-out music, at low volume.)

"One final and tantalizing fact. Sixteen million years is nothing; it is like yesterday on the cosmic scale. When Loge disintegrated there were already primates on the Earth. Did our early ancestors look into the sky one night and behold the fearful sight of Loge's explosion? Is it conceivable that another planet might suffer a similar fate?"

(Fade-out as image of Loge begins to swell, changes color, breaks asunder. Final music crescendo for the ending.)

"It still puzzles me why Ling should be appointed to this investigation. He writes his own ticket, of course. Maybe he knew one of the dead Grabbers—he seemed to know everything there was to know about the Belt and the Belters." Green shook his head unhappily. "I suppose I'll have to get in and meet the man and find out what he wants me to do now that he's here. I hope he's not going to try and demote me to being a messenger boy."

Together, Green and Wolf walked back to Bey's office. Karl Ling did not look up as they entered. He was oblivious to his surroundings, deeply engrossed in his review of the autopsy records on the three dead crew members of the *Jason*. Wolf's saturation techniques apparently didn't work on Ling. He became aware of them only when Wolf stepped in front of him and spoke.

"As soon as you want it, Mr. Ling, we are ready to give you a briefing on our findings. This is Park Green, who is representing the USF here at Form Control."

Ling looked up briefly, then returned his attention to the medical records. His glance had taken in the two other men for only a fraction of a second, but Bey had the feeling they had both been scanned and tucked away in memory.

"Very good," said Ling, eyes still fixed on the output screen. "For a start, why don't you answer the most basic question for me. The three dead men had clearly been involved in a form-change process. Where are the biofeedback machines located that were used on them?"

Wolf grimaced at Park Green. "We don't have that answer for you yet, sir," he replied. "Though of course we recognize its importance, and we are working on it."

Ling looked up again. This time, his gaze locked on to Wolf. For some reason, it seemed to have been the answer he was expecting, even hoping for.

"No answer yet, Mr. Wolf? I thought that might be the case. Would you perhaps like me to enlighten you?"

Bey stifled the sudden impulse to go over and choke Ling and managed a cool reply. "If you can, certainly. I must say that it is hard for me to imagine that you could have reached a rational conclusion on such a brief inspection of our records."

"I did not. I knew it before I left the Moon." Ling smiled for the first time and stood up from his seat. "You see, Mr. Wolf, I have no doubt that you and your fellow workers here in Form Control are proficient in your work. In fact, I took pains to verify your excellent reputation before I left the Moon. That is not the issue. The particular situation we have here requires something that by definition you and Mr. Larsen do not have: the ability to think like a USF citizen. For example, if you were suddenly a millionaire because you had struck it rich out in the Belt, where on Earth would you choose to go for your entertainment? Remember, you may choose freely without thought of cost."

"Probably to the Great Barrier Reef, in a gilled form."

"Very good." Karl Ling turned to Park Green. "Now let me ask you the same question. You are a Belter, and suddenly a millionaire. Where on all of Earth would you want to go? What is the Belter's dream of a place for all the most exotic delights?"

Green rubbed thoughtfully at his chin. "Why, I guess it would be Pleasure Dome. I've never been there, and I don't know what it offers, but that's the place we all hear about."

"Right. And of course you haven't been there—neither has anybody else who is not extremely rich. Just the same, it's the USF idea of paradise, especially for people who live out in the Belt. Part of the reason you would *want* to go there would be to prove how rich you are."

He went over to the large map display on the far wall and called out a South Polar projection.

"Now let's take this a little further. Look at the geography. The crew of the *Jason* landed at the North Australian spaceport. That's within easy transport distance of the Australian Mattin Link entry point. One transfer gets them to New Zealand; a second one puts them at Cap City in

Antarctica. Pleasure Dome, as I am sure that you know, Mr. Wolf, though Mr. Green may not, lies directly beneath Cap City in the Antarctic ice cap. Total travel time from the spaceport: an hour or less."

Park Green was nodding slowly in agreement. "I guess so. I'm not used yet to the number of Link entry points that you have here on earth. I don't see where your analysis gets us, though. We need to find a place that has sophisticated form-change equipment. I saw the list of labs that Mr. Wolf has, and I'm sure that Cap City and Pleasure Dome weren't anywhere on it."

Karl Ling smiled ironically. "I feel sure they were not. You saw the legal list." He turned to Bey, who realized what was coming and felt a steadily rising excitement. "Pleasure Dome offers *all* pleasures, does it not, Mr. Wolf? Even the most exotic. Would it not be logical to assume that a number of those recreations involve the use of form-change equipment?"

"It certainly would. That's rather a sore point with me, as a matter of fact. We know that there are illegal form-changes going on there, to cater to some of the more debauched physical tastes. But we have orders to keep out of there. I must say, we usually have no trouble with them. They are very discreet, and since the last trouble, a few years ago, we've had a sort of informal truce with them. I would be surprised to find they have equipment complex enough to handle the Mariana changes, but I wouldn't rule it out. There's plenty of money there, and they could get the equipment if they wanted it. You can probably guess how much power the managers of Pleasure Dome have when it comes to influence in high places. There are rumors about a number of Central Coordinators who go there fairly often."

Ling touched the map controls, and a new image appeared on the display.

"Then this must be our next stop: Cap City, and Pleasure Dome. We still do not have the answer to the basic question: How did those three men become three dead monsters?

"Mr. Green, you should remain here and be available to answer inquiries from Earth and Moon authorities."

Green could not resist a snort of disgust. His view of Ling's order showed clearly on his face.

"Please make travel arrangements for Mr. Wolf and myself," went on Ling calmly. "Take the highest-priority links and the fastest interchanges. Don't worry about finance, Mr. Wolf," he said, seeing Bey's questioning look. "That is not an issue. I can call on the complete financial resources of the USF if necessary to pursue this inquiry."

"That wasn't why I was frowning, Mr. Ling. I was wondering why the Mariana Trench was chosen to dispose of the bodies. Can you explain that also?"

"I have a speculation," said Ling, "and I rather think it is the same one that you have. I even think I know what you are trying to gain by asking it, but that's another matter."

There was a hint of humor deep in his tawny eyes. "Let us indulge our imaginations. The crew of the *Jason* died in Pleasure Dome. The proprietors of that facility looked at their identifications and knew at once that they were all in trouble. They know that the USF looks after its own. They decided that they had to get the bodies off-Earth, and they took them to Australia through the Mattin Link. Unfortunately for their plans, they did not realize how tight the security regulations have become since the Purcell spores found their way in. There was no way to smuggle three bodies into space, so that plan was dropped and they were obliged to improvise another one. Deep water looked attractive. One further transfer through the Link took them to the Marianas. But hasty planning, and inadequate knowledge of the local geography, led to a botching of the disposal job. We know the rest."

Ling looked questioningly at Bey. "Plausible? It is, I admit, no more than a deductive argument, but I think it has a high probability of being right.

"Now, quickly, have preparations made and let us be on our way."

Green hurried out, but Wolf lingered for a moment. During Ling's last exposition, he had been listening intently, studying the manner of the speaker. Ling raised his eyebrows as Wolf showed no sign of leaving.

"You have further business, Mr. Wolf? There is still a great deal of work to be done on the records, and little time to do it."

"I want to make one comment," said Bey. "I've spent my life studying form-change, and I believe that I understand it pretty well. One man is my master in the theory, but when it comes to seeing through exterior changes I will match myself against anyone. I am sure that we have met before, Mr. Ling, and it was under very different circumstances. The problem we have here is an urgent one, and I want to tell you that I do not propose to do anything about my ideas. But I want you to know that I can tell the lion by his paw."

Karl Ling's acid look seemed to soften briefly. There was a hint of a smile again on his lips.

"Mr. Wolf, I really have no idea what you are talking about, and I must get on with this biological work. Perhaps you would like to stay here and help me with it. I have a high regard for your insights. Let's get to work quickly. I want to be in Cap City four hours from now."

After Bey Wolf and Karl Ling had left, Park Green and John Larsen went off together for a stimulant and a sharing of their dissatisfaction. By the third round Larsen had become morose and militant.

"Just our luck," he said. "Those two go off to sample Pleasure Dome, and they leave us here to handle the brainless bureaucrats. It's always the same; we get all the dog work, and those two get all the excitement."

He had never met or even heard of Karl Ling until that day, but fine points of logic were beneath him.

"I'd like to show those two," he went on, sniffing again at the dispenser. "I'd like to show them what we can do without them. Solve the whole thing while they're gone." He slid a little lower in his seat. "That would show them."

Green and Larsen had been matching round for round, but with twice the body mass Green was in much better shape. He watched Larsen sink lower yet, his chin almost down to the level of the table.

"Come on," he said, "if we're going to do it at all, it had better be while you're still capable of it." He lifted Larsen's limp figure easily to a standing position and held him there one-handed while he paid their bill.

"Just let's get a couple of shots of detoxer in you and you'll be as good as new. Once we're all set, let's go over the full records again and see if we can come up with something. We've got Ling's comments to help us. We never had that when we were working before." He walked an unsteady Larsen from the room. "It would do me a lot of good to beat that smarmy supercilious midget to the answer."

Fifteen minutes later they were both cold sober and deep into the case records. There was a long period of sifting before Larsen sat back, snapped his fingers, and said, "Question: What is there about the crew of the *Jason* that made them different from everybody else who was undergoing form-change here on Earth?"

Park Green looked at him and shrugged. "Grabbers? Belters? Super-rich?"

Larsen shook his head. "No. Answer: They had recently been handling large quantities of transuranic elements and probably experiencing high levels of radioactivity. So here's my second question. Did the autopsies look for Asfanium and Polkium in the bodies? Did they even test for a high radioactivity? My bet is that they didn't."

"It shouldn't make any difference, John. We know that the crew didn't die from chemical poisoning, and they didn't die from radioactive dose."

"Of course they didn't—but form-change depends on the condition of the central nervous system. So, final question: What do the transuranics do to that system? I doubt if anyone really knows. It might throw off the fine tuning, and that might make them behave strangely in form-change. What do you think?"

Green shrugged. "It's certainly a long shot, but we should check out the transuranics content of the bodies. Do you know where they went after the postmortem?"

"Sure. They're in the Form Control cold storage center in Manila."

Green stood up. "Come on, then. We'll need authorization for another postmortem, and we'd better find a pathologist to take along with us."

CHAPTER 13

The exit point from the Mattin Link system was in the upper levels of Cap City, almost at the polar surface. Bey Wolf and Karl Ling emerged from the final chamber and looked about them for the elevators that would take them down to Pleasure Dome, four thousand feet below in the polar ice. Above them, the howling winds of an Antarctic July tore at the surface, carrying the groan of protesting surface structures all the way down to the Link exit point. It was not a congenial spot, and they were keen to move downward. As they stood there a soft voice spoke suddenly in their ears.

"Come to Pleasure Dome, satisfy your heart's desires."

Ling looked at Wolf and smiled ruefully. "An omniprojector. What an abuse of a technology. That system would be worth millions to us in Tycho or out in the Halo."

The soft voice continued. "In Pleasure Dome, you can

shed the cares of the world and feel free again, free to fulfill your wildest imaginings. Visit the lustrous Caves of Ice or swim in the Pool of Lethe. Win a world in the great Xanadu Casino or spend an unforgettable day as a shuttle in the Coupling Loom. Be free, be with us in Pleasure Dome."

"Free, at a price," said Bey.

Ling smiled. "These aren't really advertisements, you know. Any message given here is only heard by people who are already on their way to the Dome, so it's preaching to the converted. People just want a reassurance that they are about to spend their money on something really exciting."

The omniadvertising went on, and finally they received a useful comment, "Follow the blue lights to the Temple of Earthly Delights."

Moving along the chain of blue lights as directed, they were soon in an elevator, dropping steadily and swiftly down deep into the polar cap. The entrance to Pleasure Dome was a great sparkling chamber, lined with perfect mirrors, like the inside of a giant multifaceted diamond. The effect was shattering. Walls, floors, ceilings, all were perfectly reflecting. Bey could see images of himself and Ling marching off to infinity in every direction. He struggled to orient himself, to find a view that did not extend indefinitely away from him.

"You'll get used to it in a few minutes," remarked Ling coolly. He seemed quite unaffected by his surroundings. "Pleasure Dome is all like this."

"I didn't realize that you had been here before."

"A couple of times, long ago. These reflecting walls are a necessity, not a luxury, you know—though of course the owners here to do their best to turn the situation to a special feature of the place." He glanced around him with interest. "They've come a long way. When they first cut this city beneath the ice cap, thirty years ago, the big problem was the heat. People produce heat, all the time, from themselves and their equipment. There's nothing you can do about that, but without a special system the ice walls would have melted in no time. You can see the solution. All the walls have been coated with passivine, perfectly reflecting and with a very low coefficient of thermal conductivity."

He reached out his hand and held it close to the wall.

"See, you can feel the reflected heat on your skin. A tiny amount of heat passes through to the ice walls underneath, and a modest refrigeration unit connecting to the polar surface takes care of that very easily."

Bey was looking on ironically. "I must say, Mr. Ling, for a man who is from off-Earth, you have a quite astonishing knowledge of Earth affairs."

"The lunar nights are long. We have plenty of time for reading." Ling's formal reply carried definite hints of humor. Before Bey could comment further, a third person had joined them, moving smoothly and silently across the polished floor.

"Welcome to Pleasure Dome, sirs."

She was tall and slim, dressed in a long white gown. Her skin was pale and flawless, her hair a fine white cloud. Even her lips looked faded and bloodless. She looked at them quietly with cool gray eyes as expressionless as clouded crystal. A Snow Queen. Bey wondered how much of it was natural and how much she owed to the form-change equipment.

"I am your hostess. I will help you to arrange your pleasures. Do not be afraid to ask, whatever your tastes. There are few wishes that we cannot accommodate.

"Before we begin, there are a few formalities."

"You want our identifications?" asked Bey.

"Only if you choose to give them, sirs. They are not necessary. We do need proof of adequate means, but that can be cash or any other method you prefer."

"We are together," said Ling. "My credit will serve for both of us. Do you have a bank connection?"

"Here, sir." The Snow Queen produced a small silver plate from within her gown. Ling placed his right index finger on it, and they waited as the ID was established and the central bank returned a credit rating. As she read the credit, her expression changed. Previously she had been remote and self-possessed, a being without sex or emotion. Now she suddenly lost her composure and for the first time became a young woman. Bey realized that Ling's credit was probably that of the entire USF.

"What is your pleasure, sirs?" A pink tongue licked nervously at the pale lips. Even her voice had changed, become uncertain, tremulous, almost childish. With that much credit available, Bey suspected that there was nothing, literally nothing, that could not be bought at Pleasure Dome. The goods on sale included the body and soul of their hostess, and she knew it. It was dangerous for her to be in contact with such financial power. She could never know when one of Ling's whims might include her as a purchased pleasure.

Ling had read her uneasiness and divined the reason for it.

"We want none of the conventional pleasures," he said. "We want to talk to the men who control the form-change tanks at Pleasure Dome. The men who recently handled three off-Earthers. Don't worry if you do not know what I am referring to—the men we seek will understand fully."

She hesitated. It was odd how her vulnerability had suddenly cracked the glacial shell. There were wrinkles of worry on that perfect brow, and animation in those clouded gray eyes. Ling's request fell far outside the usual list of fancies, and the decision as to how to proceed made her uncomfortable.

"Sirs, I must consult others on this matter. It will take
me a few minutes. If you would wait here"—she led them
to another, octagonal room—"I will return as quickly as
possible. It is a viewing room, as you will see. The scenes
change every two minutes, unless you wish to cancel and
advance to another before that. The control button is on the
seats."

"And this?" said Ling, pointing to the metal cylinder
that stood above each seat.

"Don't worry about it. It is a sensor that will monitor
your responses and move to others that should have increasing appeal to your particular tastes."

As she left them, the room grew dark, then slowly
lightened. They were in the middle of a holo-setting, surrounded by the filtered emerald light of a submarine reef.
Across from them, winnowing the green gloom with giant
questing tentacles, floated a huge octopus. The great eyes
fixed on them, lambent and unblinking.

"An illegal form, I assume?" asked Ling quietly.

"Very much so," said Bey, staring in fascination at the
slowly moving arms. "All the cephalopods are illegal.
There is at least a five percent chance that reversion would
be impossible in that form. I am surprised that anyone
would pay huge sums of money to take such a stupid risk."

"*De gustibus . . .*" said Ling. He shrugged, and the room
again grew dim. When it lightened, Bey at first thought
that they were again in an underwater setting. The light
was again a dappled green. He looked up to the fronded
leaves far above them. The scene was overcanopied by a
continuous growth of vegetation. In front of them, blend-
ing perfectly into the broken patches of light and dark,
crouched the silent form of a tiger. As they watched, the
great muscles bunched beneath the smooth coat, and the
beast sprang. The unsheathed claws ripped at a boar's
throat at the same time that the other forepaw made a

mighty swipe at the exposed backbone. The boar moved its head quickly, intercepting the extended forelimb with a razor-sharp set of long tusks.

"If you don't mind . ..." said Ling quietly, and pressed the button to change the scene. "I hope that is not an accurate reflection of your taste or my own," he said as the light again dimmed.

"I'm not even sure which form we were offered there, the boar or the tiger," replied Bey. "Both of them, I expect."

The light grew brighter, then brighter yet. The man standing in front of them was imperious and commanding. He stood, arms folded, in the blazing light of an Egyptian noon, watching the groaning timber as it moved slowly over the wooden rollers. Heavy ropes held the great block of stone securely on the flat support, and the forms of the long lines of slaves who hauled it slowly across the desert were smeared with sweat and dust. In the distance ahead of them, the long, rising ramp led to the unfinished shape of the looming pyramid.

"A real power kick," said Ling.

Bey nodded. "No man has had that much absolute power for thousands of years. I don't think we really know much about Cheops, but I'll bet that the Pleasure Dome artists have made a creditable shot at the times."

They looked in silence for a few moments at the glaring, empty sky and the tall, white-robed figure standing rock-steady in the paralyzing heat.

"I don't think too much of the power of that monitor to read our tastes," said Bey. "Unless that man is Imhotep rather than Cheops."

The scene was shifting again, the bright white light of an Egyptian morning fading to a flickering red glare. It took time for their eyes to adjust to the smoky firelight. The groan of timber and the sighs of hard-worked slaves had given way to the creak of pulleys and the hiss of a bellows-driven furnace. The men moving around the long table were naked except for their black hoods and leather aprons, and the sweat trickled down their muscular bodies. The man on the table was silent, mouth gaping. His limbs were bound at wrist and ankle with wrappings of cloth and rope, spread-eagled and strained.

A black-cowled figure was approaching the table, brand glowing orange-red in his hand. Bey pressed the button hurriedly.

"Who could want that?" said Ling. Even he seemed moved from his ironic detachment. "I should have guessed it; there is nothing here for people like us."

"How does the machine see us—victims or torturers?" asked Bey.

The scene this time was pastoral and quiet. A young man was sitting alone by a great oak tree, his face calm and thoughtful. The sun was shining, but it was the soft green of a European summer rather than the harsh browns and ochers of Egypt. The birds flew about the garden, and there was the muted sound of distant running water. The man did not move. He was dressed in the shirt and woolen breeches of the seventeenth century. Wolf and Ling looked at each other, both puzzled.

"Do you understand it?" asked Ling.

Bey peered more closely at the man's hands, at the wedge of glass that he was holding. He felt a sudden thrill of recognition.

"Newton," he said softly to Ling. "Look at the hands."

"What?" Ling stared hard. After a moment he made a curious sound, half grunt, half groan. "It is, it's Newton at Woolsthorpe. See, he's holding a prism." His voice was changed from a cynical amused tone to one of fascinated longing. "God, can you imagine what it would be like? To see the world through Newton's eyes, in those years. His *annus mirabilis,* the plague years—he discovered all the basics of modern science, the laws of motion, optics, calculus, gravity. All during those two years when he was at Woolsthorpe to avoid the plague."

Ling leaned forward further, his eyes alight with interest. Wolf, no less intrigued, was wondering how long the scene would remain for their inspection.

"Well, sirs, I am sorry to have taken such a long time."

The soft voice behind them broke the spell. The scene faded. Ling looked at the helmet above his head with respect.

"I would have sworn that there was nothing that Pleasure Dome could offer me with real appeal. Now I know I am wrong," he said ruefully.

He turned to the woman behind him, who had with her an equally striking blond-haired man, also dressed all in white.

"Who programmed this viewing selection?" asked Ling.

The man smiled. "It is not the policy of Pleasure Dome to reveal our working secrets. Just be assured, everything we offer is done as well as history permits. The psychology, if we use the form of a real person, is as accurate as modern methods allow. You are interested in one of the worlds we offer?"

Ling sighed. "All too interested. But we have other business. You have seen the credit I control. We need help. If we don't get it, we can close down the form-change services here completely. I hope that will not prove necessary."

The man nodded. "Sirs, your credit is enough to purchase any pleasure. However, you must appreciate that certain things in Pleasure Dome are not available at any price. The detail of our operations is one. Please state your wishes again so that we can see if we are able to accommodate them."

"We have no wish to cause trouble here," said Ling. "If we wished to, there is no doubt that we could. This is Behrooz Wolf, the head of the Office of Form Control on Earth. I am Karl Ling, special assistant to the USF Cabinet. I tell you this so that you will know we are not trying to trick you. Check our credentials if you wish to."

The man smiled. "That was done as you arrived. Pleasure Dome takes certain precautions, although it does not advertise them. We seek an ID if anyone makes an unusual request—otherwise, the anonymity is total."

Ling nodded. "Good. That saves time. All we are looking for is information. Three men died recently during form-change. We believe that they died here. We want to speak to the men who were in charge of that operation, and we want to see the full records of the monitors that were recording and supervising the form-changes."

The man made no attempt to deny the charge. He was silent for a few moments, then asked, "If we cooperate, you will take our involvement no further, here or elsewhere?"

"You have our word."

"Then come with me." The blond man smiled. "You should be flattered. You are obtaining a service free of charge. To my knowledge, that has never happened before since Pleasure Dome was first created."

The three men walked quickly through a maze of ice caves, fairy grottoes lit by lights of different colors. They came at last to a door that led to an ordinary office, with paneled walls and a functional-looking desk.

The man motioned to Wolf and Ling to sit down on the hard chairs.

"I will return in a moment. This, by the way, is our idea of luxury. Normal walls, furniture, and privacy. We all aspire to it, but our lives here rarely permit us the chance."

He left, to return a few minutes later with his identical

twin. Bey felt that his question about the use of form-change equipment on the staff had been answered. The ultimate bondage: someone else dictated the exact shape of their bodies.

The newcomer was distinctly ill at ease. The idea of talking about his work to an outsider clearly disturbed him. Bey was able to see a new side of Karl Ling in action as he soothed and coaxed the man to become more relaxed and talkative. After a few minutes of introductory chatting, the real interview began.

"All those three wanted was a full-speed reconditioning program," the Pleasure Dome controller said. Once started, it promised to be a torrent of words. "The only thing we did for them that is in any way illegal was the speed. We used the biofeedback machines twenty-four hours a day and provided the nutrients intravenously. It looked like a completely straightforward job, and we didn't give them any special monitoring, the way we would if a customer was to come in and ask for a special change. We can do some pretty fancy things here, though of course we can't compete with the big BEC labs for change experiment. The program that the three of them had asked for takes about a hundred and fifty hours, nearly a week of changing if you run it continuously. I know there are versions that will do the same thing in a third of the time, but believe it or not we take all the precautions we can. I prefer to run the slower version; it's less strain on the people taking it."

"You've run this course many times before, I assume?" asked Ling. The speaker seemed in need of a chance to breathe—all the information had come out as one burst.

"Often, especially for off-worlders. It wasn't my job to ask their origins, of course, but I can make a good guess from their clothes and their speech. If anybody had thought to ask me at the beginning, I'd have told them the three we had weren't Earthers."

He looked at the other blond man, with a hint of a dispute that still rankled.

"Ever since Capman's work on the changes," he went on, "a straightforward program like this one has been completely automatic. The tanks have automatic monitors that control air and nutrient supplies, and the pace of the process is all regulated from the computer. Of course, the subject has to be conscious at some level, because it's purposive form-change that's involved. You understand what I mean, do you, or shall I explain it more?"

He looked at Ling, taking Wolf's understanding for granted.

"Enough," said Ling. He glared at Bey, who was looking smug. "Keep on going."

"Well, the unit is completely self-contained. There's no viewing panel on the tanks, so the only way we know what's happening inside is by looking at the monitors and telltales on the outside."

"How often do you do that?"

"In a simple case like this, once a day. Even that shouldn't be necessary. We never have anything to do, but we check anyway. The three off-worlders had all checked in together and started the program at the same time, so one look a day was enough to monitor all of them. They all had the same reconditioning program. Needed it, too. They looked done in when they arrived—I don't know what they'd been up to."

He paused for a moment. Bey wondered what the staff of Pleasure Dome did for their own entertainment—what would appeal to the men and women who had seen everything, who had provided for every possible taste? Probably something very simple. The chefs of the most expensive restaurants seemed to dine on the most basic fare.

"The evening of the third day," the man finally continued, "I took my usual routine look at the telltales. All three men were dead. I couldn't believe it. At first I thought there had to be something wrong with the telltales, or maybe a programming error for the displays. Then we opened the tanks."

He paused again, reliving the memory.

"It was awful. God, it was like a nightmare. They had changed; they weren't men anymore. They were monsters, with great big glowing eyes and wrinkled skin—just like a horror holo. We checked that they were all dead, then looked at their IDs. I knew, even without that, we had three off-worlders on our hands. Everybody around here really panicked. We thought we might be able to get them off-Earth, but it isn't as easy as it used to be. When we found we couldn't do that, we decided the safest thing would be to put them deep at sea. But apparently that didn't work, either."

There was a long silence. Ling was too engrossed even to give Bey a look of triumph at his reconstruction of events. He was bound in a spell of concentration so intense that he looked blind, his eyes unblinking and focused on infinity.

"Did you do any chemical analysis of the bodies?" he asked at last.

"God, no. We wanted to get them out of here. We weren't about to waste time with tests. There should be records of all the chemistry, though, as it was measured during the biofeedback work. It will all be in the files, still, along with the monitor and telltale records. Blood chemistry and cell chemistry should be recorded continuously."

"Right. I want to examine those now. Bring them here or take us to them."

"I'll get them. But they'll be in raw form. Only a form-change expert would be able to read them."

Ling caught Bey's glance. "Bring them in. We'll manage somehow," he said. "It's a skill you never lose once you've mastered it completely."

John Larsen looked at the spectrograph output, then at Park Green.

"It's far less than I expected," he said. "There are traces of Asfanium in all the bodies, but the amount is very small. There's a tiny trace of radioactivity because of that, but it's not enough to make a big physical effect, even if form-change amplifies it. I wonder if it could be a subtle *chemical* effect? Trace elements, even in microscopic amounts, do funny things to the biochemical balance. We still don't know too much about the chemical properties of the transuranics in the island of stability around 114."

"Well," began Green doubtfully, "we don't know all that much. But we've found no strange properties for Asfanium or Polkium in our work on the Moon. I think it's something different. The crew of the *Jason* never encountered form-change before. They weren't experienced. I wonder if they somehow let things get out of control—they ran into something new, like a trace of Asfanium, and they didn't have the form-change experience to know how to handle it."

Larsen slapped the spectrograph output sheet against his thigh.

"Park, I bet you're on to something. Experience *is* important in form-change work. With inexperienced people, something could go wrong."

"So can we test it?"

"I think so. We already know that Asfanium concentrates in the thymus gland. We can take an extract from one of the bodies and conduct a controlled test to see if funny things happen when you use a form-change program."

Green frowned "It's a nice idea, but where could you get a test animal? I thought the whole point of form-change was that only humans could do it. After all, that's the basis for the humanity tests."

Larsen laughed confidently. "Exactly right. You want to see the test animal? Here it is." He tapped his chest. "Now, don't get the wrong idea," he added as he saw Park Green begin a horrified protest. "One of the things that we get in Form Control is many years of training in form-control methods. If anything starts to happen, I'll have no trouble at all in stopping and reversing it. That's the difference between me and the three Grabbers—experience."

He stood up. "Don't forget, it's a *purposive* process. It only changes you because there is a desire to change. Come on, let's get a thymus extract made here and then go back to the form-change tanks at Form Control headquarters. We'll really have something to show Bey Wolf and your boss when they get back from their jaunt to Pleasure Dome."

CHAPTER 14

The "jaunt" to Pleasure Dome was becoming a grind. The staff employees looked on in amazement as Wolf and Ling worked their way through the monitor records at express speed, reading raw data, swapping comments and shared analyses as they went. They had to deal with a mixture of body physical parameters such as temperature, pulse rate, and skin conductivity, and system variables such as nutrient rates, ambient temperatures, and electrical stimuli. Programs in use as they were swapped in and out of the computer, plus chemical readings and brain activity indices, were all recorded in parallel in the same files. Reading the outputs required many years of experience, plus a full understanding of the processes—mental and physical—of the human body. Ling was tireless, and Bey was determined not to be outdone.

"Who is he?" whispered the Pleasure Dome form-change supervisor to Bey during one of their brief halts to await more data. "I know who you are, you're Head of Form Control; but where did *he* learn all this?"

Bey looked across at Ling, who was deep in thought and oblivious to comments, whispered or otherwise.

"Maybe you should ask him yourself, I've already had that conversation once."

The arrival of more data pushed the question aside.

After thirty-six hours of intense work, the basic analysis was complete. They had an incredible array of facts available to them, but one dominated all others: The crew of the *Jason* had died long, long before their form-change was complete. They had died because the forms they were adopting were unable to live and breathe in normal air. The final forms remained unknown. There were other mysteries. Why were they changing to those forms, under the control of a simple reconditioning program that had been used a thousand times before with never a hint of trouble?

Karl Ling sat motionless, as he had for the past two hours. From time to time he would ask Bey a question or look again at a piece of data. Rather than disturb him with general questions, Bey decided that he would go into another room and try to reach Form Control headquarters. He wanted to check with John Larsen on the general situation. Ling was voyaging on strange seas of thought, alone, and Bey Wolf had developed a profound respect for that man's mind.

It was Park Green who answered the communicator instead of Larsen. He looked very uneasy.

"Where's John?"

"He's in a form-change tank, Mr. Wolf. He went in yesterday morning."

"Well, that's one way to keep the bureaucracy off your back."

To Green's great relief, Bey Wolf didn't seem at all concerned. Even when he explained the whole thing to him, Bey just laughed.

"John's been around form-change equipment almost as much as I have. He knows how to handle it as well as anyone on Earth. But honestly, Park, I'm sceptical about your theory. Those Belters have probably all had use of form-change equipment before. When they use it for injury repairs, it's called regeneration equipment, but it's just the same principle. The only thing the USF is down on is form-change for cosmetics or inessentials."

Park Green looked as though a big weight had been lifted off him.

"Thank heaven for that. I've been worried ever since he gave himself that thymus injection. I thought he might have talked me into letting him do something where he had a big risk. I didn't know enough about all this stuff to argue with him."

Bey smiled at the big man's obvious concern. "Go over to the tank and keep an eye on him if you're at all worried," he said, and signed off the connection. He strolled back to join Karl Ling, who had now come out of his trance and accepted a cup of syncaff, "compliments of Pleasure Dome." Having broken their standard policy by letting them in free of charge, the staff of Pleasure Dome had apparently decided to adopt them. Ling had just politely refused a Snow Queen's offer of an age-old technique to relax him after all his hard work. He looked rather pleased at her suggestion and quite annoyed when she made the same offer to Bey.

"I think I have the answers, Mr. Wolf, and they are fascinating ones. More than I dreamed. If I am right, this is a special day in our history." Ling sat back, relishing the moment.

"Well, Park Green and John Larsen think they have the answers, too," said Bey. "I've just been in video contact with them."

"They do? Without the evidence that we have available to us here?" Ling's eyebrows were raised. "I can't believe it. What do they think we are dealing with?"

Bey sketched out Larsen and Green's theory. It sounded much thinner than it had when he had first heard it. He summarized the situation back in headquarters and finally mentioned that Larsen was now putting the idea to a practical test.

"He injected an extract from one of the dead men and put himself into a form-change tank?" Ling's self-possession failed him. He turned as white as one of the Snow Queens. "He's a dead man. My God, why didn't they consult us before they began?"

He sprang to his feet, hurled the records aside, and grabbed for his loose jacket.

"Come on, Mr. Wolf. We must get back as fast as we possibly can. If there is any chance to save John Larsen's life, it depends on our efforts."

He ran out of the room. Bey, bewildered and alarmed, followed him at top speed. When Karl Ling lost his dignity so completely, it was time to worry.

In the elevator, on the Mattin Link transfers, and through the ground transit system, Ling rapidly explained the basics of his discoveries to Bey Wolf. By the time they reached the Office of Form Control it was hard to say which man was the more frantic. They went at once to the form-change tanks.

Park Green, alerted as they traveled, was waiting for them there. He looked at Ling as though expecting an outburst of insult and accusation. It did not come. Ling went at once to the tank containing John Larsen and began to read the telltales. After a few minutes he relaxed a little and gave a grunt of satisfaction.

"Everything's still stable. That's good. If he follows the same pattern as the other three, we have about twenty-four hours to do something for him. The one thing I daren't do is stop this process in the middle. We'll have to let it run its course, try to keep him alive while it happens, and worry afterward about reversing it. Bring me the tank schematics. I need to know exactly how the circuits work that control the nutrients and the air supply."

Wolf went for them and was back in less than a minute. Park Green was still standing by the tank, looking totally bewildered. When Ling had the schematics, Green took Bey to one side.

"Mr. Wolf, does he know what he's doing? He's an expert on the Belt, I realize that. But he doesn't know about this stuff, does he? Are we risking John's life by letting him do this?"

Wolf put his hand up to Green's massive shoulder. "Believe me, Park, he knows what he's doing. If anyone can help John now, he can do it. We have to give all the help we can and save the questions until later. I'll tell you my views on this when it's all over."

Ling interrupted their conversation. His voice had a reassuring ring of certainty and authority.

"One of you come over here and make a note of the equipment changes that will have to be made. I'll read off the settings as I find them on the charts. The other one of you, call BEC. I want their top specialist on interactive form-change programs. Maria Sun, if she's available, the best they can offer if she isn't. Tell them it's code word circuits, if that will move them faster."

Wolf nodded. "I can get Maria." He hurried out.

The equipment modifications began. At every stage Ling rechecked the telltales. Maria Sun arrived, took one look at the monitors, and settled in by Ling's side. She swore continuously, but it did nothing to lessen her effectiveness as they sweated over the tank. Larsen's condition inside remained stable, but there were big changes occurring. His pulse rate was way down, and there was heavy demand on calcium, nitrogen, and sodium in the nutrient feeds. Skin properties were changing drastically.

"They could have noticed all this in Pleasure Dome if they'd only bothered to look," grunted Ling. "Give them their due, they had no reason to expect anything peculiar. But take a look at that body mass indicator."

Maria Sun swore a string of oaths. "It's up to a hundred and twenty kilos. What's his usual weight?"

"Eighty," said Bey, absorbed in watching the indicators. He longed to see inside the tank, but there was no provision for that in the system.

The work went on. After many hours of equipment change and work on program modification with Maria Sun, Ling finally declared that he had done all that he could. The real test would come in a few hours time. That was when the records from the crew of the *Jason* had begun to go wild. It remained to be seen if the equipment changes could keep Larsen's condition stable as the change proceeded further. The time of watching and waiting began.

As Ling made his final checks on the telltales, Bey realized the mental anguish that Park Green must be going through. He looked at the big man's unhappy face.

"Mr. Ling, have we done all that can be done here?" Bey asked.

"For the moment. The rest is waiting."

"Then, if you will, would you explain all this to us, from the beginning. I got a quick overview on the way here, but Park Green is still in the dark completely, and I'm sure Maria is just as curious."

Ling looked at the three of them as though seeing them

for the first time. Finally, he nodded sympathetically.

"You deserve that, even if I'm wrong. From the beginning, eh? That's a long story. I'll have to tell it to you the way that I imagine it. Whether it's true is another matter."

He sat down, leaned back, and put his hands behind his head.

"I have to begin it sixteen million years ago, and not on Earth. On the planet Loge. Loge was a giant, about ninety Earth masses, and it was going to explode. Now for something speculative, something you may find hard to believe. Loge was inhabited. It had living on it a race of intelligent beings. Maybe they were too intelligent. We know that their planet blew up, and we don't know why. Maybe they were to blame for that. I doubt if we'll ever know. The race had nuclear energy, but not spaceflight."

"Come on now." Maris Sun was looking at Ling sceptically. "You can't possibly know that. I'll buy your Logians, maybe, but you just said we'll never know much about them."

"I know that much, all the same. How do I know it?" Ling was almost pleased by the questioning. "Well, I know that they had nuclear energy because they made transuranic elements. Any *natural* source of transuranics would have decayed by natural processes since the formation of the planet. The only possible way we could find a source of transuranics on Loge—and only on Loge—would be if they were created there, by nuclear synthesis. We don't know how to do that efficiently ourselves, so there's good reason to think that the Logians had a more advanced nuclear technology than we do."

"All right." Maria nodded her dark head. She had changed her appearance since Bey had last seen her and was now wearing the form of an exquisite Oriental. The terrible streams of swearing that came out of that petal mouth when she was hard at work made a strange effect that she was probably quite unaware of. "So, they had nuclear energy. But how could you possibly know they *didn't* have spaceflight?"

"Elementary, my dear Maria." Ling was too engrossed in his explanation to note Bey's quiet reaction to that evidence of prior acquaintance. "They couldn't escape from Loge, not any of them, even when they found that it was going to disintegrate. They must have had some years of warning, some time to plan—but no one got away, not one of them."

Ling rose from his seat. "Wait one moment, I must check the status." He went to the tank, nodded as he inspected the telltales, and returned. "It is still all stable, and the change is accelerating. The next hour or two is crucial."

"We'll stay here," said Bey. "So they could not get off Loge," he prompted.

"That is correct." Ling resumed his relaxed posture, eyes far away. "They had time to plan, so I imagine it was not a nuclear war. Perhaps they had found a way of making large-scale interior adjustments to the planet and lost control. That would be relatively slow.

"What could they do? They looked around them in the Solar System. They knew they were going to die, but was there any way that their race might survive? To a Logian, the natural place for that survival would be Jupiter, or best of all Saturn. They probably never even considered Earth —a tiny planet, by their standards, too hot, oxygen atmosphere, a metal ball crouched close to the Sun. No, it would have been Jupiter or Saturn, that was their hope. That's where they turned those big, luminous eyes— adapted for seeing well in a murky, methane-heavy atmosphere."

Bey suddenly thought of the great, glowing eyes of the Mariana Monsters as they stood guarding the deeps off

Guam. The Grabbers could never have imagined such a fate as they touched down in triumph on the gray surface of Tycho.

"The crew of the *Jason*," he said.

"You are running ahead of me, Mr. Wolf," said Ling, smiling. "Let me keep the story going, true or false—as I said, all this is pure conjecture. Their scientists calculated the force of the explosion for Loge, and they gave a grim report. No life form, even single-celled ones, could survive it. Parts of Loge would be thrown in all directions. Some would leave the Solar System forever. Some would land in the Sun. And some would undoubtedly hit Jupiter, Saturn, and the other planets—including Earth. Was it possible that anything could survive that explosion and long transit?"

Park Green spoke for the first time. "If single-celled creatures couldn't survive, it would have to be something very primitive. How about a virus? That's just a chunk of DNA, without any wrapping."

Ling was looking at Green with an expression of surprise. "That's it exactly. A virus has no 'life-support system' of its own. To grow and multiply, it must have a host cell. The Logians took a chance and packed their genetic material as a viral form."

"And it worked?" asked Maria Sun.

"Not as they expected it to," said Ling. "Or maybe it did. We've never had a ship down to the surface of Jupiter or Saturn, and we don't know what's there. Maybe there are Logians down there, with viral growth of their genetic materials in host bodies.

"Some of their viral material was on fragments of Loge that were blown way out of the Solar System and became part of the long-period comets. That didn't matter. A virus lasts indefinitely. Sixteen million years later, some of the fragments that fell back into the Solar System under the

Sun's gravitational pull were mined by men—not for their Loge DNA, not at all. For their transuranic elements."

"And the Loge DNA began to grow in them?" said Green, his face puzzled. "Wait a minute, that wouldn't work. If that were possible, *every* Grabber would be . . ."

Ling nodded approvingly. "Very good, Mr. Green. You are quite right. Humans are very poor hosts for Logian development. The Loge virus could get into the human body easily enough, and it could even take up residence in the central nervous system. But it couldn't thrive in those unfamiliar surroundings. Wrong atmosphere, wrong chemical balance, wrong shape."

Ling paused and looked at the other three. His manner had changed. He had become the great scientist, lecturing on his own field to an interested audience.

"You know, I knew there was a Logian civilization before I ever came to Earth for this investigation. The transuranics proved it, beyond doubt. Otherwise I would never have been led so quickly to this train of thought.

"I think you can now complete the story yourselves. The crew of the *Jason* picked up Logian DNA in viral form from the fragment that they were crunching for its Asfanium and Polkium. It got into their bodies, and nothing at all happened. They went and had their great celebration in Tycho City, and still nothing happened. But finally they came to Earth—and they got into the form-change machines. At last, the virus could begin to act. It stimulated their central nervous systems, and the purposive form-change process began. It was creating a form that was optimal *for Logians*, not for Earthmen. When that change had proceeded to the point where the changed form could not survive in the atmosphere of Earth, the creatures died. Asphyxiated, in normal air."

Park was looking at the tank containing John Larsen. He had at last realized the full implications of Ling's words.

"You mean that is happening to John, too?"

"It would have happened, and it would have killed him," replied Ling. "He injected himself with Logian DNA along with the Asfanium he took from the bodies. The work we've been doing this past day has been to modify the life-support system of the tank so that it follows the needs of the organism inside it. If you go and look at the telltales now, you'll find that the nutrients and the atmosphere would be lethal to a human being."

Park Green hurried over to the tank. He looked at the monitors and came quickly back.

"Body mass, two hundred kilos. Oxygen down below eight percent, and ammonia way up. Mr. Ling, will John live?"

Ling stood up and went over to the tank. He looked carefully at each of the readouts. "I believe he will," he said at last. "The rates of change are down, and everything is very stable. I don't know if we will be able to return him to his former shape. If we can do it, I think it will not be for some time."

Ling came back to the other three. He looked at Bey Wolf and caught the reflection of his own excitement.

"Look on the positive side," he said. "We've dreamed for centuries about our first meeting with an alien race." He nodded toward the great tank. "The first representative will be in there, ready to meet with us, a day or two from now."

BOOK III

"Let the Great World spin forever, down the ringing grooves of change."

CHAPTER 15

The external lights had dimmed to their late-night glow. Wolf was sitting by the great tank, half-asleep, musing over the social indicators. His weariness showed in the stiff shoulders, the bowed head, and the slack posture. In front of him, the screen display of the global map revealed concentric circles of change spreading out from the Link entry points. He could visualize the frantic activity in the general coordinators' offices as they sought to stabilize Earth's economic system. Even the long-term indicators—fertility, births, deaths, and change rates—would soon be affected unless the new controls produced better results.

"Sorry to be so 'ong, Bey." The sibilant words from the wall speakers broke suddenly into his drifting thoughts. "The BEC peop'e wanted to test more of my visua' responses. Apparent'y I can see everything from near u'travio'et out through the therma' infrared. Rough'y three-tenths of a micron out to fifteen microns. No wonder I've noticed the wor'd is 'ooking strange these days."

Wolf shook his head, took a deep breath, and sat up straighter in his chair. He turned to look into the tank through its transparent side panels. Inside, John Larsen raised a massive, triple-jointed arm and gestured in greeting. His torso was massive, wrinkled and umbonated, with a smooth oval area immediately above the central boss that housed the secondary motor nerve center. The broad skull was dominated by the great jeweled eyes and the wide fringed mouth beneath it. Larsen moved his head forward in the movement that Bey had come to recognize as the Logian smile.

"We had a 'ong session," he said, "but at 'east the doctors seem to think I've kept my sanity through a' this— yesterday they didn't sound too sure of that."

As he spoke, forming the words slowly and carefully, the smooth oval area on his chest modulated in color, from a uniform pale pink, to brown, to soft green, following his words like a sound-sensitive visual display.

Wolf smiled wearily. "That's an improvement, then— you never showed much sign of sanity before the change. Ultraviolet through thermal infrared, eh? More than five octaves on the electromagnetic spectrum, and we see less than one. Can you cover all that range on the chest display?"

"Sure I can. Watch this. Therma' first, then I wi' gradua'y shorten the wave'ength a' the way down. Here we go."

Larsen hooded the nictitating membrane over his prominent eyes and pointed to the smooth area on his chest. Wolf watched in silence. For a while the oval remained gray, then it finally glowed a deep red. Almost imperceptibly, it moved gradually to yellow, then to green, and on to a pale violet-blue before it faded.

Wolf shook his head. "I'll just have to take your word for it, John. I didn't get anything except the usual visual spectrum. You know, you're the ultimate chameleon. When you get through all the tests here, you and I ought to go on a tour. There's been nothing like this in the history of form-change—and we've seen some pretty strange stuff between the two of us."

"I wi' do it, Bey, if you can find a good way of moving me around. You'd have to dup'icate this who'e area." He indicated the inside of the great tank with a wave of a massive forearm. "How much did it cost to set this up so I cou'd 'ive in it? It's comfortab'e, but I'm g'ad it didn't have to come out of my sa'ary."

"I don't know what it cost," said Wolf. "Ling set up the credit and made all the physical arrangements before he disappeared again. I guess it all comes out of some USF budget. He certainly had enough credit to impress the proprietors of Pleasure Dome, and we know that's not easy. I still have no word on him, no idea how he got away from here, where he went—anything."

Larsen nodded his broad, wrinkled head, with its wreath of ropy hair. "You won't hear from him again unti' he wants you to, if you ask me. I found out a'ot about him in those few weeks that he was working with me, making sure I cou'd survive a' right in this form. I'm sure you were right in what you said. 'ing is Capman, no doubt of it. He seems to have found ways to move on and off Earth, and round the So'ar System, that we can't even track."

"I know." Wolf rubbed at his chest, his habitual gesture of frustration. "Losing him once was something that I learned to live with. Losing him the second time is unforgivable—especially when I *knew* he was Capman, knew it in my bones, long before he took off again. He once said he and I would recognize each other anywhere, regardless of disguise, and I believe him. As soon as you're ready for a reverse change, we'll go and have another look for him. I'm more convinced than ever now that we didn't really understand most of what was going on at Central Hospital."

"I don't know what he did there, Bey, but there's no doubt that he saved my skin."

"How long before you can go back to your old form, John? BEC should be getting close to plotting out all the steps. I'm keen to find out the details, but I know they want to find out how to go both ways before they start the reversal."

Larsen laughed, and it came as a harsh, glassy noise over the speakers. "Don't rush me, Bey. First of a', now that I fee' sure I *can* reverse when I want to, I am in 'ess of a hurry. According to BEC, it wi' need a fu' four weeks in a form-change tank, and you know what a bore that wi' be. Anyway, I am not sure that I even want to change back."

Wolf looked at him in surprise.

"I mean it, Bey," Larsen went on. "You know, when I 'ook back on it I know I was not too smart in the human form of John 'arsen. I can remember what a strugg'e I used to have to try and fo'ow your thought processes—and often I cou'd not do it. Now it is easy for me. I used to forget things, now everything I hear or see is waiting to be reca'ed."

He leaned back in the sturdy supporting chair, resting his three hundred kilograms of body mass.

"And there is something e'se. We on'y found out about it during the tests today. I suspected I had it, but I had no idea how we' deve'oped it is. Do you remember the troub'e I had with math? Even with ordinary arithmetic, even with an imp'ant?"

Bey sighed. "It would be hard to forget it, even without total recall. You were practically famous for it. 'Doughhead Larsen,' Smith used to call you in the theory courses."

"You don't know how often I wished he would form-change to a toad—it was his natura' shape. Anyway, ask me something that ought to be hard for me, something beyond John 'arsen's grasp."

Wolf frowned. He scratched his dark head thoughtfully. "John, almost *everything* was. How about special functions? I seem to recall that they were your big hate, whenever they came up in the form-change theories. Do you remember anything at all about the gamma function?"

"How many figures would you 'ike? Suppose I give you six digits and step the argument in interva's of a hundredth? 'ike this. Gamma of 1.01 is 0.994326, gamma of 1.02 is 0.988844, gamma of 1.03 is 0.983550, gamma—"

"Hold it, John." Bey held up his hand in protest. "I don't want the whole table—even if you know it. What happened, did Capman fix you up with a calculator implant when he was working with you in the first couple of weeks?"

"No imp'ant." Larsen laughed again, and Wolf winced at the noise like shattering glass. "It is bui't in, comes free with the form if you are a 'ogian. I don't even know if it is ca'cu'ation or memory—a' I know is, when I want them the numbers and the formu'ae are there waiting. Do you see now why I am in no hurry to change back?"

The glass panel that separated them was thin, but it had to withstand a pressure difference of almost three atmospheres. Wolf was reluctant to lean against it, even though he was sure it would take the extra load with no trouble. He came close to it, and peered through at the alien form.

"Bottom, thou are translated. Much more of this, and I'll feel like a moron. I'm not sure my ego will be able to stand it unless you get started on that reverse-change."

"'et me give it one more b'ow, then." Larsen learned forward, scratching at his side, where the great, gray torso framed the oval central display in his chest. "You have been trying to trace Robert Capman for four years, and you have not succeeded. Now he has disappeared again, and you do not know where you might find him—but do you rea'ize that you have more information now than you ever had before?"

He scratched the other side of his chest. "I think I wi' comp'ain about this skin, it does not fit right."

"More information?" Wolf had lost the last trace of sleepiness. "I don't see how I have more. We know that Ling is Capman, and I've tried to pursue that. I get no cooperation at all from the USF people. Either they don't want Capman extradited to Earth or they don't care either way. I put a call through to Park Green this morning in Tycho City, and he has been told to get back to his other work and not waste time looking for Capman. So where's the new information supposed to come from?"

Larsen had stopped scratching and picked up a green wedge of fibrous sponge. "I have to eat this stuff to keep me a'ive, but I fee' sure it was never the standard 'ogian diet. It tastes 'ike the outf'ow from the chemica' factory." He touched it to the delicate fringes on his mouth, which served as both taste and smell organs. The expression on his face changed. He closed his eyes briefly, then placed the spongy mass down again on the rack by his side. "Now I know how they must fee' in the famine areas when they get their rations of five-cyc'ed pap. Maybe I wi' reverse-change now. It is ages since I had any decent food, I think I am beginning to forget what it tastes 'ike."

"New information, John," prompted Wolf impatiently. "I know you're doing it to annoy, and I know you're sitting there luxuriating in the thought that now you're three times as smart as I am. You ought to realize that anything about Capman puts me on to full alert."

Larsen moved his head forward in a self-satisfied Logian smile but did not speak.

"*How* do we have new information?" went on Wolf. "We haven't had anything useful from the USF, and if you learned something during the weeks you were working with him around the clock, getting adjusted to the Logian form, this is the first time you've mentioned it. So, what's new?"

"'A' right, Bey, no more sta'ing. 'et us app'y simp'e 'ogic, and see what we can deduce. First, think back to your origina' idea that Capman was somehow *responsib'e* for the 'ogian forms that were found in the Mariana Trench. That turned out to be wrong. So, it wou'd be natura' to assume that Capman shou'd have had no interest in 'oge before the arriva' of the unknown forms. On the other hand, Capman—*as Kar' 'ing*— was a 'eading expert on 'oge, and everything to do with it, years ago. 'ong before the forms appeared on the scene. Where does that idea take you?"

Wolf peered into the poisonous atmosphere inside the tank. "*Tokhmir*, John, I hate these conversations in separate rooms. It's worse than a video link."

"Now who is sta'ing? You can come in if you want to, Bey, the air is fine—once you get used to it. Now, answer my question."

Wolf nodded. "It's a good question, and it's an obvious one. I must have been a lot more tired than I realized in the past few weeks. It's been hectic out here since you began to change. All right, let me think."

He sat down and leaned his head forward on his hands. "Capman became Ling. So, either he knew about the Logian forms before we called him in to help or he had some other reason for being interested in Loge. I find I can't believe he knew about the forms before we went to Pleasure Dome—he really was working it all out for the first time there. That leaves only the other alternative: an interest in Loge, but one that was nothing to do with the Logian forms. That sounds improbable to me."

"Improbab'e or not, it is the on'y reasonab'e conc'usion. So now"—Larsen's voice rose in pitch, and the color of his oval breastplate glowed more intensely—"carry the thought to its end point. What is the next step for you to take?"

Bey was nodding, his head still bowed. "All right. You've got something. The added piece is one simple fact: Capman's prior interest in Loge. Now I guess I have to trace the background on that. I think I know the best way to do it. Park Green has access to all the USF data, and he should be able to trace Ling's movements and background." He looked up. "Maybe I should get into one of the tanks myself and switch to a Logian form. I could use the boost in brains."

Larsen nodded seriously, head and trunk moving together. "You may think you are joking, Bey, but it is an idea that you ought to be taking more serious'y. I can't describe how it fee's to be smarter than I was, but I 'ike the sensation. When we get a' the reverse-change p'otted out, there wi' be a 'ot of peop'e who wi' want to try this form."

Larsen opened his mouth wide, revealing the bony processes inside and the rolled, mottled tongue. "Excuse me, Bey. The 'ogian yawn is a 'itt'e disgusting, if I can be'ieve the mirror. If you are going to ca' Park Green, I think I wi' go back to the s'eeping quarters and try and get some rest. We sti' haven't pinned it yet, but the BEC peop'e now think I am on a seventeen-hour cyc'e. A' these tests are wearing me out. Ten hours so far, just on my eyes! At 'east I know what the first reverse-change step wi' be—I want to be ab'e to say my own name." He stood up. "Say hi to Park from me—you know I cannot say he'o to him."

When Wolf had left for the comlink center, Larsen turned and walked heavily through to the inner room that contained the sleep area. His movement was silent but ponderous, gliding along on the round padded feet that ended the bulky lower limbs. In the screened inner area, he went at once to the communications panel that had been built into one of the walls. The thick rubbery pads on his digits were awkward for the comlink's small keys, but he managed to dial a scrambled connection for an off-Earth link. When the circuit was established, Larsen at once began transmission.

Expressions on a Logian face were not easily read by any human, but perhaps some of the BEC specialists who had been working with Larsen for the past few weeks would have seen the satisfaction on his countenance as he began his message. The comlink coded it and hurled it on its way as a tightly focused beam, up to the relay by the Moon, then far on beyond to its remote destination.

CHAPTER 16

The social parameters were tabulated on color displays all around the offices of the general coordinators. Eighteen key indicators in a stylized map format dominated the central office, and summaries in cued form were given by each chart. Next to the ninety-day history was the current ninety-day forecast, showing trends and rate of change of trends.

In the center of the room the six chief planners had gathered, grim-faced, around the circular table. The picture was clear. The perturbations to the usual stable pattern were unmistakable, and they were growing steadily in spite of all attempts to stabilize them. A certain level of statistical variation was tolerable—indeed, was inevitable—but perturbations beyond a certain size, according to Dolmetsch doctrine, would force a major change. The new steady state of the system was difficult to calculate, and there was not a general agreement on it. One school of theorists predicted a partial social collapse, with new homeostasis establishing itself for a reduced Earth population of about four billion. That was the optimist view. Others, including Dolmetsch himself, thought there could be no new steady state solution derived continuously from the old one. Civilization must collapse completely before any new order could arise from the ruins.

None of the planners was a theoretician. For practical people, it was hard to distinguish between theoretical alternatives, where one meant the death of ten billion and the other the death of fourteen billion. Both were unimaginable, but the indicator profile was not encouraging.

The group leader finally picked up his pointer again and shook his head in disgust.

"I can't tell if we're even touching it. There are improvements here"—he gestured at the area centered on the Link entry point in Western North America—"but everything is going to hell again in the China region. Look at that violence index. I haven't looked at the computer output, but I'll bet the death rate from unnatural causes has tripled."

The woman next to him looked at the area indicated. "That's my hometown, right at the trouble center," she said quietly. "Even if we don't know the best course, we have to keep on trying."

"I know that—but remember the rules when you leave today. No public comments unless they're optimistic ones, and no release of anything longer than the sixty-day forecast. God knows, though, that's bad enough all by itself."

They stood up.

"How long do we have, Jed, before we're past a point of no return?" she asked.

"I don't know. Three months? Six months? It could go very fast once it starts; we've all seen the snowball effect

—on paper." He shrugged. "We can't say we haven't worried about something like this before. Half the papers on social stability in the past twenty years have predicted trouble at better than the fifty percent level. Well, there are a few positive things we can do in the next day or two."

He turned to the woman next to him. "Greta, I'll need a summary of the whole situation to send to the USF headquarters. Dolmetsch is up there now, and he can do the briefing. Sammy, I want you to see how the USF reacts to the idea of lending us an energy kernel for a few months and orbiting it above Quito in synchronous station. If we beam the power down, it will help the local energy problem in South America for the next month or two. Ewig, I need the latest data from Europe. I have to brief the council in an hour, and Pastore is sure to ask what's happening in Northern Italy. I'll be back to pick up the material in twenty minutes—I need time to study it before I go in there."

He hurried out. The noise level in the big room rose rapidly as the planners redoubled their efforts to stabilize the world economy. One hope sustained them all: It was not the first crisis of the past half century. They had always managed to find the right combination of restorative measures to arrest the oscillations in the social indicators. But this one looked bad. Like a shore community bracing for the arrival of a hurricane, the planners prepared for a long, hard struggle.

Park Green, seated in the Permanent Records Center six kilometers beneath the surface, completed the listing he wanted. He looked at his watch, whistled, stored the output he had generated into his percomp, and signed off the computer terminal. He sat in silence for a few minutes, reviewing everything he had found, then looked again at his watch. Bey would still be up, even though he was on

Central Time instead of U.T., but if he didn't call him now he would have to wait another ten hours. Park decided to delay his return to the living sections and put in a request for a comlink to Earth.

The connection was almost instantaneous—at this hour, traffic was light. When Wolf's image appeared on the holoscreen, sleepy-looking and irritated, Park decided he must have made a slight error in his time calculation. He concluded that it was no time for the conventional greetings.

"It's a mystery, Bey," he began. "A complete mystery. The records here look as though they are intact, with full data on Ling—personal data—going back for fifty years. I agree with you that Ling is Capman, but how can he be if he has full records like this?"

Bey rubbed his eyes and came more fully awake. "Full records, eh? For most people, that couldn't be faked. But we had evidence a few years ago that proved Capman is a master at manipulating computer software. Stored data isn't safe when he's around. There's a good chance that most of Ling's 'history' is a *constructed* background, made up and inserted into the records by Capman. He must have had some cooperation to do that, though. There must be some leaders in the USF who are helping him—an ordinary Earth citizen would have no way to get started. Somebody up there with you helped Capman get access to your data banks."

"I don't see how they'd do that." Green looked at the computer terminal next to him. "Most of the files here are read-only memory. How could he affect those?"

"Most read-only memory is software protected—it's not special-purpose hardware."

"But how would he know which type he had to deal with? Well, I'll leave that one to you. I've been trying to trace Ling, and all I can really find out is that he isn't on the Moon, right now. According to the records, he's supposed to be down there on Earth. Are you sure he's not there?"

Wolf nodded. "Medium sure—you can't be all that certain with Capman about anything. According to me, though, he's off-Earth. I checked every manifest, coming and going, and every mass record for lift-off. Unless he's found a new wrinkle, we've lost him again from the Earth-Moon system. Did you check the Libration Colonies?"

"Yes. They're easy, because they have no hiding places. He's not there."

"Well, keep looking on the Moon. I won't even guess what form he's wearing now—probably not either Ling or Capman."

Green stood up and leaned against the console. He looked depressed. "Well, Bey, what do you want me to do now? I'm dead-ended here, and you seem to be getting nowhere there. Any ideas?"

Wolf was silent for a minute, recalling his own experiences four years earlier, when he was first hunting for Capman's hidden tracks.

"I can only suggest one thing, Park," he said. "Capman gives this impression that he's infallible, but he's not. Last time I tangled with him I found there are limits to what he can do to change the data banks."

"He seems to have done pretty well here."

"Maybe not. He can change his own records, if he can get access to the protected files, but he couldn't change all the cross-reference files that might mention his name or his actions. That was the way we got a trace on him before, when I went through the medical records from Central Hospital. For some reason, Capman won't destroy other people's records. That's his weakness."

"So what are you suggesting, Bey?"

"We have to try the same method here. We have to track

him from the *indirect* references—other people's records that somehow refer to him."

Green had a very dubious look on his face. "I know what you're telling me, Bey. But honestly, I wouldn't know how to begin a thing like that. I'm no computer hotshot. How would I know *who* would be likely to have a reference to Capman or Ling in his file? There are three million people here in the USF. I can't go through three million personnel records, but that's what you seem to be suggesting."

"There are other ways, if you know how to handle sorts and merges." Wolf hesitated. "Park, is there any way that you could get me a direct hookup to interface with the USF Permanent Data Bank? From here, in my office? It would be enough if you get me a read-only link—I don't propose to try and change any of the files, only to analyze their contents."

"I don't see why not. After all, we have a full cooperative exchange program between the USF and Earth computer banks. Doesn't work too well sometimes, but this shouldn't be hard to do."

"If you can arrange it, I'll take a shot at the analysis myself, from here. If I find anything, I probably won't be able to follow up—but you could help on that, if you're willing."

"I'll be glad to. My trouble has been finding any lead to follow up. Bey, let me check this out and call you back. Tomorrow," he added hastily, noticing again Wolf's rumpled hair and appearance of broken sleep.

"No. Call me tonight if you get approval."

"All right. One other thing I need from you though—a charge code. The comlink hookup will be expensive. Do you have a budget that will cover it?"

Wolf nodded. "No problem." He keyed a fourteen-digit code for transmission to the Tycho City accounting bank.

"One thing about the Office of Form Control, it may run out of toilet paper but they never stint you on comlink costs. One other thing, if you can get access for me but not remote access, take that. I'll make a trip up there if I have to and work from your terminal. It would be better from here, though, so I can keep my eye on John."

Green nodded. "I saw him yesterday, being interviewed on holovision. Do you know, I think he's enjoying himself. He looks strange, but that doesn't seem to bother him. He was there in his tank, and they had a couple of Indian philosophers on the program with him. They started to debate whether John is human. He tied them in logical knots. By the end of the program he used their own arguments and had them deciding that *they* weren't human."

"I didn't see it, but I can imagine it. I wouldn't like to get into an argument with him now—he's smarter than he ever was. If all the Logians had that caliber of mental equipment, it's lucky for us they aren't still around. They'd have us all doing whatever they wanted, and convinced that it was all for our own benefit."

Wolf yawned, and stretched luxuriously. "But you're right, Park. John is enjoying himself—he was a good deal less happy before we were sure that a reverse-change would be possible."

"I'll believe that." Green nodded, and reached out his hand to cut off the connection. "As a matter of fact, I wouldn't mind total recall and increased brain power myself. I never seem to really know what's going on here these days. With Dolmetsch in Tycho City, there are council meetings going on around the clock. The news takes a while to filter down to my level, but there must be trouble somewhere. I'll call you back as soon as I have an answer on your question—that shouldn't take more than an hour or two."

CHAPTER 17

Four years earlier, Bey Wolf had sworn that once was enough; he would never attempt it again. Now he was in much the same situation, but he was faced with something even harder. Instead of sorting through the structure of Central Hospital's medical records, he was working with the data of the whole of the USF. The planetary information file was a maze, and he was in the middle of it, looking for signs of Karl Ling's early work. The path he was following in the records crossed and recrossed itself. First it appeared to be leading to something promising, then it petered out or led him to a restricted record area that only the USF leaders could access. It was a labyrinth without an Ariadne.

Bey plowed doggedly on from his office in Form Control, fourteen and sixteen hours a day. It was almost a week before he had the smell of a lead, another week before he had enough to make it worth discussing with anyone. When he finally dumped his output and cut the connection to Tycho City, he was ready to talk it over with John Larsen. He went again to the viewing panel that connected to the Logian living quarters.

Larsen was not alone. Maria Sun was standing by the viewing panel, along with three other engineers from BEC. Maria, after the help she had given in modifying Larsen's form-change tank when the Logian change had first begun, felt a proprietary interest in the progress of her delivery. Now, however, she was not pleased. She turned to Wolf in exasperation as he approached them.

"Bey, give us your opinion, will you? Who will own the rights to the form-change programs that were involved when John changed? I want to get all the details, but nobody will even tell me who I ought to be talking to. All we get at BEC are hearsay and wild stories about Karl Ling, and the monster here won't tell me a thing."

Bey looked in through the viewing panel to the big living area, where Larsen was sitting comfortably on his specially built chair with its accommodation for the double knee. He gave Bey a nodding of the head that no doubt was the Logian version of an irritating smile.

Wolf could not resist a quick wink at Larsen, which he hoped went unobserved by the BEC group.

"It's only my opinion, Maria," he said, "but I'd say John owns the rights himself, by default. He and Karl Ling are the only ones who know the whole story on the programs that they used, and if you're going to track down Ling, I wish you luck. I've been trying that myself for the past month. It's not easy. I want to talk to John about it."

Maria Sun stepped away from the panel and shook her head in disgust. "I'll come back later, when you've finished." She looked again at Larsen. "According to the outputs I've seen, the life ratio for that form is more than three. I'm really interested in his body."

"—You shou'd have taken me when you had the chance," said Larsen.

She glared at him. "I don't know how much fun it would be to wear a Logian form, but he"—she gestured with her thumb at the inside of the tank—"seems in no hurry to get out of it. If it's comfortable, and if it really lets you live that long, a lot of people will be interested in it even if you have to live in a tank to get the benefit. The fellows back at BEC are talking already of building more big tanks. It could be the hottest thing in next year's re-search budget."

She gave Larsen another scowl. He lifted his great arm and waved at her without speaking. Accompanied by her three companions, Maria swept out.

"She wi' be back," said Larsen as soon as she had gone. "Maria never gives up on a new form."

"I know," replied Bey, pulling a chair close to the ob-servation panel. "Be nice to your girlfriend, John. She did more than anybody else to pull you through when the changes first began—more than I ever could. Well, let's get down to business. This may feel like old times to both of us—tracking Robert Capman through the data banks."

"Except that this time, Bey, I intend to understand what you are doing. 'ast time it was a mystery to me. I've had the opportunity to 'ook at the computer system in the past few weeks, and I suspect that I grasp the concepts proper'y for the first time in my 'ife." Larsen rubbed at the ropy hair on his rounded skull with a bony protuberance that pro-jected from the second joint of his left upper limb. "I hope, though, that this time you do not want to drag me through O'd City—I wou'd have some prob'ems carrying my 'ife-support packages with me."

"If I'm right, we'll have to go a lot further than that," said Wolf calmly. He settled his percomp on his knee and began to call out displays. "Let's start at the very beginning. That means going back more than ten years."

"Wait a minute, 'ing was sti' Capman ten years ago," protested Larsen.

"He was both. I thought that if Ling was an expert on the Solar System, he'd have had to write papers on it—real papers—and that meant that others would have referred in *their* papers to his work. I began by scanning the citation index in the Tycho City reference files. It wasn't easy. I suspect that a lot of references to Ling's work have been deleted, but I managed to trace him. I even obtained a display of an actual paper, published nearly ten years ago. So his interest in Loge—that was discussed in the paper—is real, and it goes back long before Capman was forced to disappear. Any deduction that you'd care to make based on that, John?"

Larsen made a gesture like a shrug, a rippling upward movement of his upper body. "I can make the obvious one. Capman had known for a 'ong time that he might get caught one day. He knew he'd have to prepare his retreat in advance. Somehow, he estab'ished the character of 'ing, and his interest in 'oge was something that he had to deve'op for his own convenience, probab'y because it was important to his continued experiments."

"That's my conclusion exactly." Wolf entered a confirming note to his file. "So then I took a closer look at Ling's publications. That's when I found something a little different from the way that Park Green had described it to us. Ling was an expert on Loge, that's true—but if you look at his publications, the ones that he tried to cover up in the literature, you find that Loge is the minor part of it."

Larsen nodded. "That is no surprise. It is hard to re'ate his interest in form-change to any simp'e interest in 'oge."

"He's interested in the Asteroid Belt. He wrote a series of papers about its formation—and he did a really big series of papers on some specific asteroids. If you catalog all his work, only a few deal with Loge, and most of them concern one group of asteroids. Did you ever hear of the Egyptian Cluster?"

Larsen nodded. "Yes. If you had asked me that a month ago, I'd have to say no, but I can absorb information faster now, and I have had a 'ot of time to spend with the termina' here. Most of the free hours when you were not giving me tests, I have been catching up on my reading."

He leaned back and closed his lustrous eyes. "The Egyptian C'uster. I think I can quote the re'evant texts verbatim for you. 'A group of about one hundred asteroids, with orbits that are different from a' others in the Be't. They 'ie in an orbit p'ane a'most sixty degrees from the ec'iptic.' 'et me see, what e'se?"

Larsen opened his eyes again for a moment. "Excuse me, whi'e I scan my interna' fi'es." He was silent for a few seconds, then nodded. "Here we are. What are you interested in? Members of the C'uster, masses, orbits?"

"How about history."

"No." Larsen grimaced, new wrinkles appearing in the gray skin. "That is an area of the fi'es that I have not read yet."

"That's a relief. I was beginning to think that you knew everything." Wolf consulted his output displays. "Store this away. The cluster was discovered by accident, in 2086, during a deep radar search program. They were surveying the Halo, looking for power kernels. First visited during the Outer System search. According to the Ling paper that I found, all the asteroids in the cluster were formed out of one piece of Loge, after the main explosion of the planet. Most of them are small, five kilometers or less, but there are a few bigger ones."

"That much I know. The data bank 'ists a' the main members. Five of them are bigger than eight ki'ometers in mean diameter—Thoth, Osiris, Bast, Set, and Anubis. No transuranics on any of them. They must have been formed from a piece of 'oge's core. There is a mining sett'ement on Isis, and another on Horus, main'y for the rare earths. No permanent sett'ements on any of them. They seem 'ike a very du' group. Why the big interest in them?"

"I'm getting to that," said Wolf. "You're right, they are a remote lot. It's not the distance, but they're so far out of the ecliptic that it takes a fair amount of fuel to match orbits with them. That's why they aren't a good commercial prospect, even though the lodes of minerals are rich, especially on Horus. The one I'm interested in isn't one you've mentioned. What do you know about Pearl? Anything in your head on that one?"

"Hm. I think I need to go back to my references and dig deeper. I have a 'itt'e information, but there must be more. Pear' used to be ca'ed *Atmu*. That fits in with the idea that it is part of the Egyptian C'uster, but I don't know why it was renamed."

"That's because you've never seen a picture of it. You're quite right; it was named Atmu when it was first discovered. A good name for one of the cluster; oldest of the Egyptian gods. But the first expedition there, forty years ago, changed the name. Other factors seemed more important than the mythology. Pearl is quite small, less than two kilometers across—but it's an odd shape; a perfect sphere of white, fused glass."

"Wait a moment, Bey." Larsen was shaking his great head. "That sounds wrong to me. If it is made of g'ass, it must have been part of the outer crust of 'oge, near enough to the surface to be fu' of si'icates."

Wolf looked up from his records and shook his head admiringly. "It took me a while to come to that conclusion,

John. You're getting too smart for your own good. I finally decided it was part of the outer core, deep enough to be very hot and near enough the surface to have the silicates. It's a very small piece of Loge. The diameter is listed as 1.83 kilometers. Now, do your records include a mass figure for it?"

Larsen's broad skull and upper torso dipped forward in a nod. "I show a mass of about one bi'ion tons. That means —" He paused and looked up at the ceiling of the tank. "That can't possib'y be right. Un'ess . . ."

Wolf was nodding. "Go on, John, let the calculator run free for a moment. You're heading in the right direction."

Larsen shrugged his heavy shoulders, again the upward rippling movement of the body. "With that diameter, it must have a density of 'ess than thirty-fifty ki'os per cubic meter. Fused si'ica g'asses mass at 'east two tons per cubic meter. So . . . *it must be ho'ow.*"

"Quite right." Bey was nodding his agreement. "It's as thin as an eggshell. The references give the inner diameter as about 1.7 kilometers. Pearl is nothing more than a big, delicate glass bubble, blown by trapped gases inside the fragment when Loge exploded. It's classified now as one of the protected asteroids. The USF declared it one of the natural wonders of the system. No one is allowed to land on it—but I think that rule is being broken."

Wolf paused. He felt that there had been an inconsistency in Larsen's replies, but he couldn't put his finger on it. After a few moments, he went on. Larsen continued to sit there motionless, his luminous eyes unblinking.

"Let me give you one more fact, John, then you can tell me what you make of all this. Nine years ago, Karl Ling wrote twelve separate papers on the structure, formation, and stability of Pearl. All references to those papers have been deleted—I had to dig out the information by indirect references. Do you recognize the pattern? It's the one that we saw with Capman's medical records back in Central Hospital."

Larsen nodded calmly. "I see where you are heading. You think that Pear' ho'ds some specia' secret, something that keys you to find Capman. It is p'ausib'e, Bey, but I see one prob'em. You are suggesting that Capman managed to create the person of 'ing, at the same time as he was the director of Centra' Hospita'. How cou'd he do that?"

Wolf stood up and began to pace up and down in front of the viewing panel. His manner was tense and nervous. "I checked that, too. All Ling's early papers show an *Earth* address. His other records show him living on Earth until six years ago, then moving to the Moon. That's the USF files—but the Earth ID files don't show anything for him at all. I suspect that the USF chromosome ID they have is faked. One more thing, then I'm done. Capman's travel records at Central Hospital for the final two years before he was forced to run for it show that he was off-Earth far more than ever before. He always seemed to have a good reason for it—hospital business—but he would have had no trouble making up a reason; he was the boss."

Larsen was nodding his head and trunk slowly, eyes unblinking.

"And so, your conc'usion, Bey? What do you propose to do next?"

Wolf stopped his pacing. His manner was resolute. "First, I'm heading for the Moon. I have to know more about Pearl, and I have to know why Capman was interested in it. I'll be leaving tomorrow. I don't like to leave you out of it, but you're in good hands here. Maria will do all that you need if you want to begin reversion."

"Of course, that is no prob'em. But one thing before you go, Bey." Larsen was looking directly at Wolf, his gaze steady and penetrating. "You ought to ask yourse'f one other question. *Why* do you pursue Robert Capman with such zea'? Even if you think he is a monster, why is he so important to you?"

Wolf, who was turning to leave, was stopped in mid-stride. He swung quickly round to face Larsen through the viewing panel. *"Tokhmir!* You know that, John. There were two other projects in Capman's background at the hospital. We only traced two of them, Proteus and Timeset. What about the others? I want to know what Lungfish and Janus are. They're still complete mysteries. That's what fascinates me about Capman."

His tone was defensive, not quite steady. Larsen looked at him quietly for a few moments.

"Ca'm down, Bey. They are mysteries, I agree. But is that sufficient reason? I don't think so. We've had unso'ved mysteries before in the Office of Form Contro'. You managed to 'eave them a'one after a whi'e, didn't you? Remember when we were ba'ked on the form changes in Antarctica? We were pu'ed off that, and we hated it—but you managed to 'ive with it after a month or two. This has chased you, and you've chased Capman, for more than four years. Think about it, Bey. Do you have to keep up the hunt?"

Wolf's eyes were introspective and thoughtful. He rubbed his fingers absently along the seam of his loose jacket.

"It's hard to explain, John. Do you remember the first time that we met Capman, back in Central Hospital? I had a feeling, even then, that he was an important figure in my life. I still have that feeling." He paused, then shrugged. "I don't know. I'm not a believer in paralogic, and I don't find my own words very convincing. All the same, I have to go. I'm going to tell Park Green that I'll be up there in a couple of days."

He hurried out. It was John Larsen's turn to become

thoughtful. The hulking alien figure sat in silence for a few minutes, then went through to the inner living quarters. He seated himself before the comscreen and opened the high data-rate circuits. When the ready light appeared and the array of sensors was ready, he keyed in the destination. The prompter waited until the link was complete.

Larsen looked at the face that had appeared on the screen.

"Burst mode," he said softly.

The other nodded and activated a switch to his left. Larsen closed his eyes and leaned back in his chair. The smooth gray oval of skin on his broad chest turned to a pale rose-pink, then swiftly became a dazzling kaleidoscope of shifting colors. The area now contained a multitude of separate point elements, each changing color as fast as the eye could follow. Larsen sat rigid in his chair, but after twenty seconds he began to draw in shallow, pained breaths. The brilliant display on his chest flickered on, a bright, changing rainbow shimmering like a winter aurora. The great body was motionless, racked by an unknown tension as the patterns fed into the communicator screen.

Eight thousand miles away, at the global communications center in the South Pacific, the com monitors began to flash red. There was an unexpectedly heavy load on the planetary com circuits. Auxiliary channels automatically cut in. Through a thousand output displays, the worldwide network complained to its controllers at the sudden excess message burden. The load ended as suddenly as it had started. In his tank, Larsen lolled back in his seat, too drained to sign off with his distant receiver.

CHAPTER 18

The journey to Tycho City was supposed to be routine. Wolf had gone by aircar to the nearest Mattin connection, linked twice to get to the Australian exit, and taken a ground car to the North Australian spaceport. After a rigorous USF inspection and certification—no wonder, thought Bey, the staff of Pleasure Dome had given up on the idea of getting the *Jason*'s crew off Earth—a scheduled shuttle took him up to equatorial parking orbit. The lunar connection was due in three hours.

On the journey to the spaceport, and up to orbit, Wolf was preoccupied with Larsen's last question to him and with the simple practical details of his departure. Then, waiting for the lunar transport, he was surprised by an urgent call from Earth. He went along the corridor to the main communications center.

There was a brief delay in establishing the video link.

When the channel was available, Maria Sun's image appeared on the tiny utility screen. Her china-doll face looked grim and suspicious.

"All right, Bey," she began. "You don't have to be nice to us at BEC, I know that. But just let me remind you that if I hadn't helped you, you might not have been able to save John Larsen. So—*what have you done with him*? The USF people at the Australian spaceport swear that he's not with you, and none of the other manifests show any extra people or equipment."

It took Wolf a second or two to grasp her meaning.

"I've not done a thing with him," he said. "You're telling me he's gone, but he ought to still be in the living quarters at Form Control. There's no other place with a life-support system for him. Did you check—"

He stopped. Maria was shaking her head firmly. "We've looked everywhere in Form Control. One thing I'm quite sure of, he's not here. Bey, that system Ling and I fixed up for John is really fancy. If he doesn't have a special environment, he'll die within hours. Are you telling me that you didn't arrange this between the two of you?"

"Maria, I'm as surprised as you are. Damn it, I was with John yesterday, talking about my trip to Tycho City. He didn't give any sign that he wasn't going to stay just where he was. I agree with you; he *had* to stay put, he wouldn't last a minute without that special atmosphere."

Maria bit at her full upper lip. She shook her head in perplexity. "I believe you, Bey, if you swear that's the truth. But then what is going on?"

Bey looked past the viewing screen. He was beginning to feel a prickling sensation at the nape of his neck. A number of small factors from his discussion with Larsen began to sum in his subconscious. The curious arrangement of Larsen's living quarters, the elaborate comlink that Ling had arranged—ostensibly for tuition purposes of the new form—the way that Larsen had steered the conversation, all was coming together. Bey needed to think it out in detail.

"Maria," he said at last. "I told you I didn't know what happened, and I was telling you the truth. But all of a sudden I'm getting suspicions. Let me call you back later. I know John couldn't live without his special equipment, but I don't think we should be too worried about that. Give me a couple of hours to do some thinking and let me call you back."

Without waiting for her reply, Wolf pushed himself away from the console and drifted slowly back through the ship to the transit area. He settled himself in one corner, lay back, and let his thoughts roam freely back over the past few weeks, picking out the anomalies.

They were there. Strange that he hadn't noticed them before. Even so, it was disturbing to realize that he could be led so easily, even by someone he trusted completely. For the future, he would have to remember that he was dealing now with a new Larsen, one whose mind was quicker, clearer, and more subtle than it had ever been in the past. Look at the tuition circuit that Ling had installed. Larsen needed to be able to acquire information from scattered data sources all around Earth. True enough. But why had he needed an off-planet capability, why a complete two-way link, why a circuit rated at many thousands of voice-grade lines?

Wolf's thoughts were suddenly interrupted by a flicker of movement at the port. He looked up in surprise. A crewman was staring in through the panel, held securely against the outer hull by the magnetic subcutaneous layer on wrist and inner ankle. Just above them were the suction cups that provided a grip during the air-breathing elements of shuttle ascent. The crewman was checking part of the antenna. Wolf couldn't resist a closer look. It was the first time he had seen a C-form development in its space environment.

The crewman's skin was thick and toughened, and his eyes were coated with a thick transparent layer of protective mucus. He wore no air tank or protective suit. The modified lungs, structurally modeled after the deep-diving whales, could store enough oxygen, under pressure, to work outside in comfort for several hours. The scaly skin was an effective seal against loss of fluids to the hard vacuum surrounding it. The hard ultraviolet was screened out by abundant melanin surrogates in the epidermis.

Wolf watched as the crewman moved off easily along the hull, quite at home there. He sighed as his thoughts came back to his own stupidity. Larsen had led him, coaxed him easily along, to find out more about Ling, more about Pearl. So Capman wanted him to be aware of that connection, wanted him interested in the Egyptian Cluster—there was no doubt now that Larsen and Capman had been in regular communication ever since Capman/Ling's disappearance a few weeks earlier. Larsen had moved Bey steadily along in his thinking, to the point where Bey had made his decision to set off for the Moon. With that accomplished, Larsen had promptly disappeared. He couldn't have done it without help, but it was quite clear where the help had been coming from. Capman, with resources available to him that Bey could still only guess at, had removed Larsen from the Form Control offices and sent him—where?

Bey was getting ideas on that question, too. Although it was only ten minutes to ship separation, he hurried back to the communications center and placed a quick call to Tycho City. When Park Green appeared on the screen, the first buzzer had already sounded to tell Bey to get back to his seat.

"Park, I'm on my way and don't have time to say

much." It was Wolf's turn to dispense with formal greetings. "Check if there's a ship available with enough fuel capacity to make a trip right out of the ecliptic, up to the Egyptian Cluster. If there is, charter it. Use my name, with Form Control on Earth as surety. Don't say where I want to go with it. I'll see you in twenty-four hours. Tell you everything then."

The purser, his face red-veined with vacuum blossom, was motioning to him urgently. Wolf cut the connection, swung hastily back to his seat, and strapped in.

"Cutting it fine," said the purser gruffly.

Wolf nodded. "Urgent call," he said. "You know, I just saw a C-form working outside the ship. I thought they were still forbidden for USF work."

The purser's expression became more friendly, and he smiled.

"They are. There's a little game being played there. The C-forms aren't USF men at all. They're part of a student exchange program—Earth gets a few specialists in power kernels, the USF gets a few C-forms."

"What do you think of them?"

"The best thing to hit space since the cheap vacuum still. It's only the unions who are holding things up. Job worries." He looked at the readout at his wrist. "Hold on now, we're cutting ties."

As the ship began the slow spiral away from parking orbit, Wolf switched on the small news screen set above the couch. Movement about the cabins would be restricted during the high-impulse phase of the next hour. He turned to the news channel.

The media had picked up from somewhere a surmise that John Larsen was missing. It was a small item, far down on the news priorities. More to the public interest were the latest statements on the social indicators. They were still oscillating, with swings of increasing amplitude.

Even with the power kernel beaming down to Quito, energy was still desperately short in South America. The famine deaths were rising rapidly in Northern Europe. Compared with the mounting crisis that faced the general coordinators, Bey realized that his own preoccupations were a tiny detail. But he could not rid his mind of Larsen's question. Given all this, why was Capman as much on his mind now as he had been four years before?

From where he was lying, Wolf could see ahead into the pilot's station. The computer could handle most things, but the man preferred to operate in manual mode for the beginning of the trip. It was another C-form, added proof that events were moving faster than the union wished. The pilot, hands and prehensile feet delicate masses of divided digits, was manipulating sixty controls simultaneously. Bey watched in fascination while his thoughts continued to revolve around the same old issues.

After the first surprising moonquake, the second construction of Tycho City had placed the living quarters deep underground. Bey, vacuum-suited, rode the high-speed elevator down through the Horstmann Fissure, toward the main city more than three kilometers below. He left it at the optional exit point, halfway down, and walked over to the edge of the ledge. The preserved body of Horstmann, still sealed in his spacesuit, hung from the old pitons fixed in the fissure wall. Wolf looked at the Geiger counter next to the suited figure. The rapid chatter carried clearly to him through the hard rock surface. The half-life of the nuclides was less than ten years, but Horstmann would be too hot to touch for at least another century. The radioactivity could have been lessened more quickly by stimulated nuclear transitions, as was done with the usual reactor wastes, but the lunar authorities were against that idea. Bey read the commemorative metal plaque again, then continued his descent through the fissure.

Park Green had managed to pull strings with Immigration and Customs. The reception formalities were smooth and very brief. Green's grinning face, towering a good foot above the other waiting USF citizens, greeted Wolf as he emerged from the third and final interlock.

"Bey, you don't know the trouble you caused me," he began as he engulfed Wolf's hand in his own. "I didn't know how well known you are. As soon as our people who've been working on regeneration methods found out that you were heading for Tycho City, they started to flood me with calls. They all want to know how long you'll be staying, what you'll be doing, the whole bit. I had a hard time stalling them. They want to meet you and talk about the work that you began a couple of years ago on transitional forms."

Wolf was a little startled. "They know about that work up here? I didn't think it was particularly surprising. All I did was follow up some of the clues that were buried in Capman's work. He had the idea."

"People up here don't seem to agree. If the clues were there, they must have been well hidden. Are you willing to spend some time with them? All they—"

"Look, Park, in other circumstances I'd be glad to," broke in Bey, "but we have no time for that now. Did you get the ship?"

"I think so—it will be a few hours before I know for certain. I've had a problem with that, too. All the forms I've filled out require an actual destination before you can get clearance for any trip longer than a couple of hundred hours. I checked your license, so at least that seemed all right."

"What did you tell them for a destination? Nothing specific, right?"

"I think that should be easy enough. I booked for the Grand Tour, all the way through the Inner, Middle, and

Outer System, right out to the Halo. Once that's approved, there'll be enough fuel and supplies on her to take her anywhere in the Solar System. One thing you ought to know, I charged it all to you—I don't have the credit for it."

"How much?"

Wolf winced at the figure.

"If all this works out," he said, "I'll get everything back. Otherwise, I'll be a slave to the USF for the rest of my life. Well, let's worry about that later."

As they spoke, Green led the way through the long corridor that led to the final clearing section before the main living quarters. He was sliding along in the fast, economical lope that all USF people acquired in early childhood. Wolf, not too successfully, tried to imitate it. The floor of fused rock felt slippery beneath his feet, and he had the curious feeling that the lunar gravity was a little lower than it had been on his last trip to Tycho City, many years before.

"No," said Green in answer to his question. "I think that physics here may be a little ahead of anywhere else in the system, but we still don't have an efficient generator. Gravity's one thing we haven't tamed so far. McAndrew came up with a method a long time ago for using shielded kernels for local gravity adjustments, and that's as far as anyone has been able to go. Nobody's willing to try even that much, down on a planetary surface. What you're feeling is a change in oxygen content. We put it a fraction of a percent higher about three years ago. You'll find that you get used to it in a couple of days."

"A couple of days! Park, I have no intention of *being* here in a couple of days. I want to be well on the way to the cluster. When can the ship leave? I hope it's today."

Green stopped and looked at Wolf quizzically. "Bey, you're dreaming. You just don't know the problems. First, there's no way they can get a ship ready in less than seventy-two hours. Damn it, it has to be equipped to support the two of us on a two-year trip—that's how long the Grand Tour can take. I know we're not really going on that, but they're getting her ready for it. Second—"

"What do you mean, support the two of us? Park, I'm not dragging you on this trip. It's a risky game that far out of the usual system ship routes, and it may all be a complete waste of time. I'm going solo."

Green listened calmly, towering way above Wolf. He shook his head.

"Bey, you're a real expert on form-change, I'll be the first to admit that. But you're a baby when it comes to space operations. Oh, don't say it—I know very well that you have your license. That's just the beginning. It means you're toilet trained in space—not that you're ready to hare off around the system on your own. I'm telling you, no matter how confident you feel about your ability to look after yourself, the owners wouldn't agree. There's no way they'd even let you get *near* that ship unless I go with you—not once around the Moon, never mind the Grand Tour. It's got to be me, or you'll find they push some other USF pilot on to you— somebody you don't even know."

Wolf looked at Green's calm confidence. It was obvious that the big man was telling the truth. He shrugged and resigned himself to the inevitable.

"It wasn't what I had in mind, Park. I wasn't proposing to drag you into all this when I asked you to help in checking Ling's records up here."

Green smiled slightly and shook his head. "Bey, you still don't understand it, do you? I'm not going along because I'm a kind-hearted martyr. I'm going along because I *want* to. Damn it, don't you realize that I've been itching to know what's been going on with John back on Earth since the minute that I set out to come back to Tycho City?

You could almost say that it was my fault that John ever got changed to a Logian form. If I'd been a bit smarter and known what was happening, I might have been able to talk him out of injecting Logian DNA into himself. Get rid of the idea that I'm going along for *your* sake."

Wolf was staring up at the other's earnest face. "Sorry, Park," he said in a subdued voice. "I let my own compulsions blind me to everybody else's. You deserve to come along. I still wish we could beat that figure of seventy-two hours. I didn't plan on spending anything near that long here in Tycho City."

Green was smiling again. "You'll need that much time to prepare. And you still owe me some explanations. Your message from the ship set a new high for being cryptic. We're getting ready to go right out of the System and you still haven't told me why. I heard that John has disappeared, and I know the two things are connected."

"We're not going out of the System, Park, just to the Egyptian Cluster."

"Same thing, to a USF-er. Technically, you're right, of course. The System goes all the way out to the long-period comet aphelia. But so far as anybody in the USF is concerned, when you go to an orbit plane that far off the plane of the ecliptic, you might as well be right out of the System. The delta-v you need is so big, and there are so few things of interest up there. We just don't bother to do it very often. Do you know, I've never even *met* anybody who has been to a member of the Egyptian Cluster. I've been looking up the facts on it ever since you called me from the ship. I still can't imagine why you want to go there."

They were approaching the big hemispherical chamber that marked the city edge. Beyond it, slideways led to the separate centers for manufacturing, maintenance, utilities, and habitation. Agriculture and power were located back up on the surface, 3,500 meters above their heads.

"I'll brief you on all the background as soon as we're settled in here," said Bey. "That won't take me more than a few hours. I don't know what plans you have to spend the rest of the time before we can leave, but I'd like to have another go at the data banks. There may still be things in there that I missed last time on Capman's activities here as Karl Ling."

"You'll have time for that. There will be other things, too." Green pointed ahead of them to where a small group of men and women was standing by a wall terminal. "There's your fan club. I'm sorry, Bey, but I couldn't stop it. Those are the Tycho City experts on regeneration methods. They want to hold a reception later in your honor, and nothing I've said has managed to dissuade them. You see the price of fame? Now, are you too tired, or shall we be nice to them while you're here?"

CHAPTER 19

The *Explanatory Supplement to the Ephemeris, 2190 Edition* lists the mean orbital inclination for the asteroids of the Egyptian Cluster as fifty-eight degrees and forty-seven minutes to the plane of the ecliptic. The cluster's physical data are given at the very end of the reference section, a fair measure of its relative importance in the planetary scheme of things. All cluster members have perihelion distances of about three hundred million kilometers, strongly supporting the idea of a common origin even though any clustering in a purely spatial sense has long since been dissipated. Pearl, with an almost circular orbit, crosses the ecliptic near the first point of Aries. Unfortunately she was riding high, far south of that, when Wolf and Green finally set out.

"Nearly a hundred and thirty million kilometers, Bey," grumbled Green, hunched over the displays. "It will take more fuel to get us there than it would to take us to Neptune. I hope you're right in all those guesses."

Wolf was prowling restlessly through the ship, savoring the half-g acceleration and inspecting everything as he went.

"You say it would take just as much fuel, Park, if Pearl were heading through the ecliptic right now. All we would save is a little time. If I'm wrong on the rest of it, we'll have wasted a few weeks each."

He paused by the radiation-shielded enclosure, eyeing it speculatively.

"It's a pity that doesn't have a form-change tank inside it," he went on. "This ship is plenty big enough to carry the equipment, if there were a suitable tank."

Green looked up briefly. "Remember, Bey, C-forms are still illegal here."

"I know. I was just thinking that we could really use one now to slow down our metabolisms a few times. The Timeset form would do us nicely. How's the fuel supply look? Any problem?"

"No. We could do this twice if we had to. I told the provisioners that we might want to do some unusual out-of-ecliptic maneuvers during the trip. They gave us the biggest reserves the ship can hold."

Green finished his final checking of the trajectory and straightened up. He looked at Wolf, who was still eyeing the closed compartment.

"Eyes off, Bey. You know the USF is ultracautious on the use of C-form experiments. Really, you can't blame us. People are precious out here. We don't have a few billion to spare, the way that you do down on Earth. We'll let you do the wild experiments. It will be a few years before we're ready to play with the form Capman developed in Project Timeset. Meanwhile, we've got our own methods. Did you take a good look yet at the sleeping quarters?"

"A quick look. They're tolerable. I was going there next to look at a few bits of equipment that I didn't recognize. The place looked very cluttered. Why not use one compartment and save on space?"

"That's what I mean, Bey." Green switched off the display and swung the seat around. The legroom at the trajectory monitor had been meant for someone two feet shorter. He stretched his long limbs straight out in front of him.

"You see," he went on, "back on Earth you've been forced to develop methods that let people live on top of each other, millions of you where naturally there should only be thousands. Well, we have a different problem here in the USF. We have a lot of space and not many people, but we've still had to worry about the situation where a small number of people live for a long time in very close contact—in a ship, or a mining colony, or an Outer System settlement. It's even worse than Earth, because there's no chance to vary the company you keep. You have to be able to live for months or years without murdering each other."

Green swiveled his chair around to face Wolf and looked at him with a strange expression. "Bey, answer me honestly. Just what do you think of me?"

Wolf, puzzled by the sudden change in subject, pulled up in midprowl. He looked at Green thoughtfully for a moment before he replied. "I think I know where you're heading, Park, but I'll play the game. An honest answer, eh? All right. You're good-natured. You're a bit of a worrier. You're not stupid—in fact, you're pretty shrewd—but you're also a little bit lazy. You bore easily, and you hate things that are too theoretical and abstract for your taste. We're off to a devil of a beginning here for a long trip together, but you did ask me."

"Right." Green sniffed. "I have trouble with that evaluation—it all rings much too true. Now, let me tell you what you're like. You're as smart as Satan, but you're a bit of a cold fish, and that sometimes throws off your judgment when it comes to people. In fact, you prefer ideas to people. You really love puzzles. You're stubborn, too. Once you get started on something, there's no way of shaking you off it. You're obsessive—but not about the usual human frailties. I'll hazard a guess, but I suspect that you've never formed a permanent link of any kind with either man or woman."

Bey had winced at the accuracy of some of the comments, but he was smiling at the end.

"Park, I didn't realize that you knew me so well—better in some ways than I know myself. So what's the punch line? I presume that you are not proposing that we spend the next few weeks exchanging character assessments. If so, I'm not impressed with your USF ideas on the way to pass the time on a long trip."

Green stood up carefully, looking with annoyance at the low ceiling. "Not at all. Here, Bey, follow me." He started forward, stooped over. "This ship wasn't built for somebody my size. You should have no trouble, but watch your head anyway. I want to show you a few features of this ship that you weren't aware of on your first inspection. We just exchanged character comments, Bey, and we weren't complimentary. But we're still behaving in a civilized way toward each other—even though I'm sure neither one of us greatly enjoys having some of our defects pointed out, even though we know them well enough for ourselves.

"Let me assure you, though, what would happen if you and I were to be cooped up together for six months or a year with no outside contacts and no one else to speak to without a half-hour light-time delay. You may not believe me, but the USF has a couple of hundred years experience on this one. Things would change. Little things about me that you don't like would seem to get bigger and bigger. After three months I'd strike you as impossibly soft and stupid, incredibly big and clumsy, unendurably lazy. And in my eyes you'd be a cold monster, an untrustworthy, calculating madman. Do you find that hard to swallow?"

"Not really." Wolf followed Green through into the separate sleeping quarters, quite large but full of odd pieces of equipment. "I've read about the effects of prolonged small-group contacts, particularly where the people are short of real work to do. Are you telling me that the USF has developed a solution to that?"

"Three solutions. In my personal opinion, none of them is as good as use of the C-forms. Here's the first."

Green reached up above one of the bunks and carefully took down a large padded headgear from its recessed storage area.

"See the contact points, here and here? You attach them to the skin and put the cups over your eyes. It looks similar to the equipment they used in the early form-change work, doesn't it?"

"Close to it." Bey stepped forward and peered at the microelectrodes in the interior of the cap. "It won't permit real biofeedback, though—there's no adaptive control here."

"It's not intended for that. All it does is monitor purpose and wish, just the same as the form-change equipment. But instead of providing form-change feedback, it gives sensation feedback. It's connected to the computer, and that profiles a sensation response for you, maximized for relaxation and peace of mind."

"What!" Wolf was looking at the headgear in disgust. "Park, I don't know if you realize it, but you've just described a Dream Machine. They're illegal on Earth. Once you get hooked on one of these, it takes years of therapy to get you back to a normal life."

"I know. Don't get excited, Bey. This only gets used as a last resort, when somebody realizes that they're going over the edge mentally." Green's voice was grim. "Which would you rather do. Bey? Go under one of these when you start to crack and take a chance that they will get you back to normal—or be like Maniello on the first Iapetus expedition, flaying his partner and using Parker's skin to re-cover the seat of the control chair? I'm telling you, the ship environment does funny things to people. Are you beginning to see why there's more to flying the System than a pilot's license?"

Wolf was looking chastened. "Sorry, Park. One of the problems of living down on Earth—we tend to get the idea that the USF is still a bit backward. For some things it's just the other way around. What else have you worked out here to help you keep sane?"

"These others are the ones that we prefer to use. The first one I showed you is strictly for desperate cases." Green pulled a large blue plastic cover, shaped like a man, from a panel under the bunk. "This one is an inferior version of a Timeset C-form. It's called a hibernator. We inject a combination of drugs to lower body temperature. It kills you, if you want to sound melodramatic about it. The suit holds you in a stable condition at about five degrees above freezing. The effective rate of aging is about a quarter of normal. You can go into it for about a week at a time, then you have to be revived. The suit does that automatically, too. See the monitors on the inside? After four or five days to get the muscle tone back up, you can go under again."

"I don't like the sound of that. You lose a week out of four, completely, while you're in there. Why not use a cryo-womb and make it really cold?"

Green shrugged. "This is safer. The fail rate on cryo-revivals is up near two percent."

"More like one percent, with the latest systems."

"All right, one percent. This thing is just about foolproof. I admit, it's the poor man's version of a Timeset C-form. I expect we'll be using that in a few years. Meanwhile . . ." Green shrugged.

Bey slid open the suit fasteners and looked at the array of sensors running along the whole inside. "Any reason why we shouldn't both use it on this trip? We could cut the subjective time down more if we were both under at once."

Green coughed. "Well, when I said just about foolproof, I only meant that. I would rather that we weren't both under at once. Once in every few thousand times there's a problem with the revivication process. It's nice to have somebody who's awake, waiting around to see if the suit does its job properly and helping out if it doesn't. With both of us under, there's a very small chance that we'd find ourselves on a much longer trajectory than we're planning. Unless we apply the correct thrusts when we get to Pearl, we'll drop back into the Solar System in about seven hundred thousand years. I'd rather not rely on whoever is around at that time to come along and get us out of our suits."

Wolf looked at him closely and decided that Green was only half joking. He looked at the suit, then began to fold it up. "What else do you have? So far I'm not too enthusiastic."

Green shrugged. "I told you, none of these methods is as good as a working C-form." He reached up again into the recess above the bunk and pulled down another helmet, this one smaller and lighter than the first. "This has similar connections to your 'Dream Machine,' but it has a different working principle."

He turned it over. "See these leads? They link to the computer and also to the helmet in the other sleeping area. It still provides a sensation feedback, but in this one it's modulated by what the other person in the system is thinking and dreaming. The computer is programmed to modify those thoughts, before the feedback, to make our impressions of each other more favorable. All the time that we have the helmets on, we are sharing each other's thoughts and emotions. It would be much harder for us—so the theory goes—to develop any hatred for each other. It would almost be like hating yourself."

"I do that anyway, sometimes." Wolf was looking at the helmet with a good deal of distaste. "Speaking personally, Park, I find this device disgusting. It's no reflection on you, but I don't like the idea of somebody else sneaking in on my dreams. Some of the things I think just don't bear to be shared. Whoever thought up this one had a diseased mind—worse than mine."

Green nodded sympathetically. "It's odd that you should say that. Most people don't seem to mind the idea, but I have an instinctive dislike of it. It must feel like a two-way computerized seduction, creeping into each other's hidden territories. Anyway, which one do you want to use on this trip—or would you rather not try any of them?"

Bey looked at the helmet he was holding. "It's not much of a choice, is it? I suppose the hibernator is least bad. I don't mind sleeping for a week, provided we don't feel too bad afterward."

"All right. We'll take it in turns to go under. Really, though, for this trip we don't have to use these things at all. They're not even recommended for trips under a month, and they don't become mandatory until you're going to be six months between stops. Want to skip it completely?"

"Let's see if we get bored at all. You know, Park, I wish the USF was more broad-minded about form-change work. For a start, I feel sure I could set up a system that would work with somebody in the hibernator and use biofeedback to keep good muscle tone. That has to be easy. In fact"—Bey was beginning to sound enthusiastic—"I'll be willing to make a bet with you. I'll wager that I can take a Dream Machine helmet and a hibernator and make a system from them that will do just what I said—and I'll have it finished before we get to Pearl. What's the capacity of the on-board computer?"

"Ten to the tenth directly addressable. About a hundred times that as low-speed backup."

"That's ample. Even if we don't find what I'm looking for, maybe we can take something back with us that will interest the USF."

Green looked at Bey warily and shook his head. "Experiment as much as you like. There's a spare set of helmets and a spare hibernator. But I don't like that mad-scientist look in your eye. I'm telling you now, you don't have a volunteer as a test subject if you think you have it working. When I hear you talk, I sometimes think you're as bad as Capman must be—form-change is the most important thing in the world to both of you." He was silent for a moment, then he sighed. "I only hope I still have a job when I get back. The USF government doesn't take kindly to sudden extended absences without a real explanation. But I'll tell you one thing, Bey, your obsession with Robert Capman seems to be infectious. I just can't wait to get to Pearl."

CHAPTER 20

More than ninety-nine percent of all the mass in the Solar System lies close to the plane of the ecliptic. Of the remainder, the Halo of kernels accounts for all but the tiniest fraction, and that Halo is at the very outer edge of the system, never visible from Earth or Moon with even the most powerful optical devices. For all practical purposes, Pearl and her sisters of the Egyptian Cluster swim in a totally empty void, deserted even by comparison with the sparse population of the Outer System.

The ship climbed steadily and laboriously up, away from the plane of the ecliptic. Finally, the parallax was sufficient to move the planets from their usual apparent positions. Mars, Earth, Venus, and Jupiter all sat in constellations that were no part of the familiar zodiac. Mercury was cowering close to the Sun. Saturn alone, swinging out at the far end of her orbit, seemed right as seen from the ship. Bey Wolf, picking out their positions through a view-port, wondered idly how the astrologers would cope with such a situation. Mars seemed to be in the House of Andromeda, and Venus in the House of Cygnus. It would take an unusually talented practitioner to interpret those relationships and cast a horoscope for the success of this enterprise.

Bey turned the telescope again to scan the sky ahead of them, seeking any point of light that could be separated from the unmoving star field. It was no good. Even though the computer told him exactly where to look and assured him that rendezvous would be in less than an hour, he could see nothing. He was tempted to turn on the electronic magnifiers, but that was cheating as he had been playing the game.

"Any sign of her yet?" said Green, emerging from the sleeping area.

"No. We should be pretty close, but I can't see anything. Did you pick up your newscast?"

"Just finished watching it. It was a terrible picture, though, the signal-to-noise ratio was so bad. I don't understand how they can pick up those broadcasts all the way out to Uranus with a receiving antenna no bigger than the one we have. We're only a tenth of that distance, but the signals seem to be right at the limit of reception."

"We're just picking up one of the power side lobes, Park. Nearly all the real power in the signal is beamed out along the main lobe, in the ecliptic. It's surprising in a way that we can pick up anything at all here. Anyway, what's in the news?"

"What I heard didn't sound good." Green's voice was worried, and he didn't want to meet Bey's eye. "It's Earth again. All the social indicators are still pointing down. I know old Dolmetsch is a prize pessimist, but I've never heard him sound so bleak before. He was being interviewed in Lisbon, and he's projecting everything going to hell before the general coordinators can damp out the swings in the social parameters. He looked as though he was going to say more and tell us the swings couldn't be damped at all, but the interview was cut off short at that point."

Wolf looked out of the viewing port, back to the brilliant blue-white point of light that was Earth. "It's hard to make yourself accept that there are fourteen billion people back there on that little speck. Did you catch any hard facts?"

"Some—but I'm sure they are censoring heavily. Tremendous riots in South America, with the biggest death rate in Argentina. Power blackouts all over. Hints at something really bad in China. It sounded like widespread cannibalism. The general coordinators are even talking of putting a kernel down onto Earth's surface; that gives us a good idea how bad the energy shortage must be."

"It does." Bey looked back at Earth as though expecting to see it wink out of existence like a snuffed candle. "If they lost the shields on a kernel, it would be worse than any bomb in the stockpile. All the Kerr-Newman holes they're using in kernels radiate at better than fifty gigawatts. They'd be mad to take one down to the surface."

"Mad, or desperate. Maybe Dolmetsch has a right to be a pessimist—after all, he invented the whole business. The famine in South Africa is getting worse, too. They are talking now about cutting off all supplies there and using them where people may be salvageable."

Green had joined Bey Wolf at the port, and they were gazing together at the star patterns, each seeing his own personal specter. They stood in silence for several minutes, until Green frowned and looked about him.

"Bey, we're turning. It's not enough to feel yet, but look, part of the star field seems to be rotating. The computer must be tuning us for final rendezvous. Do you remember the setting?"

Bey nodded. "One kilometer surface distance, exact velocity match. I thought we ought to take a look from close in before we get any ideas about a landing on Pearl." He swung the viewer into position and switched on the screen.

"Well, there she is, Park. We've come a long way to see that."

The asteroid appeared on the screen as a small, perfect circle. It glowed softly, but not with the highlights of a reflection from a polished glass surface. Instead, there was a diffuse uniform glow, a pearly gleam with a hint of green in the white. Green frowned and turned the gain up higher. The image seemed to swell on the screen.

"Bey, that's not the way I expected it to look. It's scattering and absorbing a lot more light than it should. It really looks like a pearl, not like a hollow glass ball. Why isn't it just reflecting the sunlight?"

"I don't know, Park. Look at the left-hand side, there. See it? There's something different there, a dark spot."

The image on the screen was still growing steadily larger and clearer as the ship neared rendezvous. It was difficult for Wolf and Green to suppress their impatience as the asteroid's milky surface slowly became more visible. Soon it was obvious that the dark spot was more than a patch of different reflectance, and there were other faint mottlings and markings on the smooth surface, tinged with a cloudy green.

"It's some kind of a pit, Bey." Green hunched closer to the screen. "Maybe a tunnel. See where it angles down into the surface? I don't remember anything like that in any of the descriptions of Pearl."

Bey was nodding his head in satisfaction.

"It's not a natural formation. Somebody's been doing heavy engineering there. See how sharp those edges are?

I'll bet that was cut with a big materials laser. Park, there's no way that Capman—or anybody else—could have done all that without a lot of assistance and equipment. You know what that means? Somebody in the USF has been helping him—and whoever it was has lots of resources to play with."

The computer interrupted his final words with a soft whistle. The orbit match was complete. They stared hard at the nearby asteroid. From a distance of one kilometer, Pearl filled a quarter of the sky. The whole surface shone with a pale, satiny gleam. It was smooth and unbroken, without any irregularity except for the exact, circular hole thirty meters in diameter that showed its black disk near the left side of the image.

They studied it in silence for a few minutes. Finally Bey moved over to the computer console.

"It's no good, Park," he said. "We can't learn much from here. There's nothing to see on the surface. We have to get a look at the inside. I'll bet that tunnel runs right through to the interior. We'll need suits."

"Both of us?"

"Unless you're willing to stay behind here. I know I didn't come all this way to watch. The computer has everything under control on the ship. I think it's safe enough to go in close and jump the gap wearing our suits. Take us in to fifty meters, and let's go."

The two men, fully suited, drifted across from ship to surface. The gravity of Pearl was too small to be noticed. They hovered a few feet from the planetoid and looked at it more closely. It was clear why Pearl shone so softly. Through the many millennia since Loge's explosion, the impact of micrometeorites had pitted the surface, to develop a matte, frosted coating that caught and diffused the light from the distant Sun. Pure white alternated with greenish clouds in a patchwork over the sphere. The two men drifted slowly toward the tunnel. Near the edge, Wolf shone a hand torch downward. Deep channels had been scored in the smooth glass by heavy equipment. The hole narrowed as it descended, ending about fifteen meters down in a smooth plate of black metal.

Wolf whistled to himself, the sound thin and eerie over the suit radios. "That disposes of the idea that nobody's allowed to land on Pearl. Why would anybody put in an air lock down there if it's just an empty shell?" He looked down the steep-sided hole. "Ready to go down, Park? All we need now is the White Rabbit."

They floated together downward to the big portal, untagged the outer door, and went inside. Green took hold of the port, then hesitated for a moment.

"Should I close it, Bey? We don't know what we may be getting into. There could be anything inside."

"I don't see that we have much choice. Either we go in or we go back. I'm expecting to find Capman behind the door and John Larsen with him. If you want to stand guard outside, that's fine—but I'm going in."

Green did not answer, but he pulled the outer door firmly shut and dogged it with the clamps. There was at once a hissing of air.

"Don't assume that it will be breathable," warned Wolf as the inner door swung open. "John should be here, and the atmosphere may be his idea of nice fresh air."

Green snorted. "Bey, give a USF man some credit. Anybody who grew up off-Earth would no more try and breathe untested air than want to live back down on Earth and breathe your soup. Look at the second display panel in the helmet inset. It's registering 6-S. That means it's safe to breathe and a little less than half Earth-normal for pressure. All the same, I'm going to keep my suit closed. I suggest you should do the same."

The inner door was slowly irising open. A pale green light filtered into the lock from the interior of the planetoid. With the port open to its full thirty-meter diameter, the whole of the inside of Pearl became visible. In complete silence the two men drifted forward together, looking about them.

The inner wall of Pearl had a smooth, shiny finish that had been missing on the exterior. No meteorites had marred its perfection. The inner surface was a perfect globe, a little more than a mile in diameter. In the center of the vast, arching chamber, tethered to the wall by long, glittering struts and cables, hung two great metal structures. The nearer was itself another bright sphere of steel or aluminum. Bey, eyeing it thoughtfully, wondered at the source of the materials that had been used in its construction. Certainly they had not come from Pearl itself. Considering the energy needed to transport materials from the main system, it seemed certain that the ball must have been built from metals mined on one of the sister asteroids of the Egyptian Cluster. Bey estimated that the sphere was a hundred meters across. A long tubular cable led from the port where they had entered to another lock on the sphere's smooth face.

The second structure could only be a ship. That made no sense. Bey looked around him again. There appeared to be no way that the vessel, forty meters across at the widest point, could have reached the interior of Pearl—or, once there, could ever leave it. His eyes followed the guide cables that led from the ship to a slightly darker section of the inner wall, directly opposite to the point where they had entered. It had to be a concealed exit. Other cables, running to empty areas in the interior, hinted at the sometime presence of other ships, moored to the inner surface in the same way.

The surface of Pearl, with its wall of translucent glass, provided an efficient conversion of incident solar radiation. The suit thermometers indicated an ambient temperature quite comfortable for human habitation. The inside was lit with the faint sunlight that had been transmitted through the outer walls and suffused about the interior. There were no shadows except those thrown by the torches that Wolf and Green were carrying.

At first Pearl seemed completely silent, a dead world. As their ears adjusted, Wolf and Green became aware of a deep, muffled pulsing, felt more than heard, filling the interior. It came from the metal sphere at the center of the asteroid, regular and slow, like the working of air or nutrient circulators or the beating of a vast heart. Nowhere through the great space of the central bubble was there any other sound or sign of life.

Park Green finally broke the spell. "I'm beginning to think I don't know anything at all about the USF. There's no way this place can exist. That ship up there must be unregistered, and if Capman came here in it I can't even guess where he could have started out from. Not Tycho, that's for sure."

Wolf grunted his agreement. His instincts told him that something was very wrong. He had come to Pearl convinced that he would find Capman and Larsen there. If that were true, surely there should be some sign of their presence. He looked again at the metal sphere ahead of them. Without speaking both men moved to the great hollow cable that led there from the entry port.

As they started along it, the sheer size of Pearl came home to Bey. The far wall looked close at hand, but the vaulted interior of the asteroid could easily have contained tens of millions of Earth dwelling units. They progressed along the cable until their entry lock behind them had shrunk to a small black dot. They both felt more comfortable when they had finally reached the sphere and entered the lock on its shining face.

The first rooms were clearly living quarters. The furnishings were simple, but there was expensive automated equipment to handle all routine chores. Bey, seeing the food delivery system, realized how long it had been since they had eaten. He looked at Green.

"What do you think, Park? Assuming that's in good working order, are you ready to risk the air in here?"

Green was looking hungrily at the dials of the robochef. He nodded. "I think we're safe enough, as long as we don't go through any air locks. This area is a standard USF automat life support, with a few VIP luxuries thrown in. Take a good look at that menu. I'll bet you don't eat like that back on poor old Earth."

Unsuited, they felt a good deal of the tension evaporate. There was still no sign of life, and by the time they were ready to continue their exploration, Bey had become convinced that the whole sphere was uninhabited. After the living quarters came three rooms crammed with monitors and control consoles, exactly like the general control room for a form-change lab—similar, and yet dissimilar. It was bigger than anything Bey had ever seen, bigger even than the research center facility at BEC.

"The tanks should be behind that wall," he said, explaining to Park Green what they had found. "But I don't think we'll find John there. Somewhere, I missed the point. I was sure I was right, then—"

He shrugged and looked about him. Four years earlier he had thought he knew what Capman was doing—only to find that he had been outthought every step of the way. It could happen twice. Capman had *expected* him to unravel the skein that led to Pearl. If necessary, John Larsen could provide a little prompting, since it was clear that he had been in constant communication with Capman ever since the change to a Logian form. Once he knew that Bey was on the way, Larsen had promptly disappeared.

It all sounded so logical—but so unlikely. Bey wasn't sure that he could explain to Park Green just how they had been guided here like a couple of puppets.

While Wolf stood there in silence, Green had been looking closely at the control panel.

"Bey, I know I'm no expert on this stuff, but look at the readouts. They all seem to be from one tank. Could all these be from one form-change station?"

Wolf came forward also. He studied the panels for a few seconds, his face puzzled. "It looks like it, I admit. But there are far too many monitors for one subject. There have to be three hundred of them. I've never seen anything nearly as complicated for one experiment. I wonder if it could be . . ."

He stood, unwilling to state his own belief.

"You and your companion are quite correct, Mr. Wolf," said the speaker grille above the console. "This is indeed all one experiment."

CHAPTER 21

"Capman?" Wolf swung around swiftly to face the grille.

"No, I am not Robert Capman. I am an old friend of his. In fact"—there was a hint of amusement in the light, musical tone—"I could fairly say that I'm a very old friend. Welcome to Pearl. I have heard a great deal about you from both Robert Capman and John Larsen."

Green was looking around him in confusion. "Where are you? The only way out of here looks as though it leads to the tanks."

"Correct. I am in the tank area. It is quite safe for you to proceed through at the moment. I am maintaining the atmosphere at the same level as in the rest of Pearl."

"Should we come through?" asked Wolf.

"Come through by all means, but be ready for a shock.

You perhaps consider that you are past surprise, Mr. Wolf, but I am not sure that the same is true for Mr. Green."

"But where are Capman and Larsen?"

"Far from here. Mr. Wolf, the conversion of John Larsen to an alien form was completely unexpected. It added a new dimension to an activity that was already vastly complex. But it also provided great benefits. Part of the explanation of our activities is not mine to give, and you must hear it from Capman. Part, however, I can tell you. Come through into the tank."

Wolf and Green looked at each other, and finally Bey shrugged. "I'll go first. I don't think there will be any danger. I don't know what we're going to see, but I've had a close look at most things in the years with Form Control."

The chamber that they entered was enormous. It occupied at least half of the whole metal sphere. Bey looked around him in vain for the familiar tank fittings. At first he could see nothing that he recognized. Then, suddenly, what he was looking at made sense. He gasped. It *was* a tank, but the proportions on the service modules were unbelievable. Nutrient feeds and circulators were massive pipes, each two meters in diameter, and the neural connectors were heavy clusters of wave guides and thick fiber-optic bundles. Bey looked around for the origin of the voice, but it was all a complex series of interlocking vats, each one large enough to hold several men. He could see nothing to tell him where to focus his attention.

"Where are you?" he said at last. "Are you in one of the vats?"

"Yes and no." The voice now seemed to come from all sides, and again there was a hint of detached amusement in the tone. "I am in *all* the vats, Mr. Wolf. This experiment has been going on here for a long time. My total body mass must be well above a hundred tons by now, but of course it is distributed over a large volume."

Green, mouth gaping open, was goggling around him like a startled frog. Bey felt that his own expression must be much the same. "Are you human, or some kind of biological computer?" he said at last.

"A good question indeed, and one that has exercised my mind more than a little over the past few years. I am tempted to say simply, yes."

"You're both? But then where is your brain located?" asked Green.

"The organic part is in the large tank straight in front of you, at the rear of the chamber. You can pick it out easily by the number of sensor leads that feed into it. The inorganic part—the computer—is in a distributed network extending through most of the sphere. As you will gather, Robert Capman has shown that the idea of man-machine interaction can go a good deal further than a computational implant."

"But how do you . . ." Wolf paused. His mind was seeing a hundred new possibilities and a hundred new problems to go along with them.

"If there is no one else here," he went on, "how can you get the nutrient supply that you need? And how can you ever change back? I assume that you began as a human form." Another disturbing possibility suddenly suggested itself. "How did you get to be like this? Was it voluntary, or were you forced to take this form?"

"Questions, questions." The voice sighed. "Some of them, I have promised not to answer. Their replies, if you want them, must come from Robert Capman himself. One thing I can guarantee, a reverse form-change would be very difficult. On the other hand, by the time I expect to be interested in such a thing, I feel sure that the capability will be well established—perhaps even forgotten. Enough of that. If you would please turn around. . . ."

The voice, for all its bizarre origin, sounded cheerful and rational, even amused. As Wolf and Green turned to look behind them, a screen flashed into color on the nearer wall of the tank.

"How do I obtain my nutrients, you ask. Very efficiently. My whole life-support system is completely self-contained. Look at the screen and let me take you on a brief tour of Pearl. We are leaving now and heading out to the inner surface."

The screen showed the output of a mobile vidicon that was moving steadily out along one of the connecting cables that led to the inside wall of the asteroid. Seen close up, it was clear that many of the cables were much more than simple supporting members for the sphere. They included tubes, communication guides, and flexible connection points onto which other cables could easily be joined. As the vidicon came closer to the wall, it was again obvious that the image on the screen showed something more complex than the smooth, glassy surface that appeared from a distance. Some patches were lighter than the background and transmitted a light distinctly greener in color.

"Algal tanks!" said Park Green suddenly. "Just like the ones in the Libration Colonies. But these must be cut into the surface of Pearl. See how green the light looks."

"Quite right," said the disembodied voice. "You can see what a great convenience it is to have an asteroid that was almost designed by nature for our purpose. The algae are the source of both my air and my nutrients. We are one closed system, including all the circulation equipment. The thermal gradients do all the work. It is no longer necessary for Capman—or anyone else—to be here to provide services to me. That control console you saw outside is no longer needed here. In fact, I control it myself, through the computer network. The whole of Pearl is a single self-contained environment."

Long experience had inured Bey to just about every conceivable form, but Park Green was much less comfortable with what he was seeing and hearing. He seemed horrified by the implications of the conversation.

"Capman did this to you, did he?" he finally burst out. "Surely he knew what he was creating. You can't move from here, you're tied to Pearl, and you can't do a reverse form-change. You don't even have anyone here to talk to or relate to. You, whatever you once were, don't you see what he's done to you? Didn't you know he's a murderer? How can you stand it?"

"Still more questions." For the first time, the voice sounded irritated. "My name, for what it matters, is Mestel. I need pity from no one. For your other remarks, perhaps I should point out that you are completely captive in your body, at least as much as I am in mine. Who is not? And I possess a degree of control over my own movement, care, and protection that you certainly are lacking. How can *you* stand it?"

"Movement?" Bey picked up on the word. "You mean vicarious movement, through the remote sensors?"

"No—though I have that too. I mean physical movement, as a whole. Wait and see, Mr. Wolf. I admit that I am bound to Pearl for an indefinite period. But why should that be considered a disadvantage? If I can believe the newscasts that I have picked up in the past few weeks, Pearl may soon be the only place left with a decent level of civilization. Or has old Laszlo become even more of a pessimist than usual?

"Perhaps that is enough talk." Mestel's voice became sharper in tone. "I suppose that I do miss the opportunity for conversations without light-time delays. Now I have another duty to perform. Your arrival here was expected, but it was not clear *when* you might come or how many of you there would be. I thought you would arrive alone, Mr. Wolf. Robert Capman believed that Mr. Green would arrive also, and John Larsen insisted on it." A curious amplified noise came from the speaker. Mestel had sniffed. "Whatever it is that makes up the Logian form, there is formidable intellect there. With all the computer assistance that is built into me, I expect to outthink anyone except Capman. Others abide the question, but he is outside normal experience. Now it seems that Larsen can think rings around both of us."

"That's my feeling, too," said Bey. "I knew John very well before the change, and it's not being unkind to say that he was no great intellect. Now he's something special. Robert Capman has always been something special."

"I know you think that. Now let me ask a question that you alone can answer. You have pursued Capman steadily since your first meeting, down the nights and down the days, down the arches of the years. If you wish to pursue him further, there will now be a significant risk to you. You will also be away from Earth for many months. Do you want to proceed on those terms?"

"Wait a minute," said Green. "What about me? I've been in on this from the beginning, at least as far as the Logian forms are concerned. I'm not going to be left out of things now."

"You will not be left out, Mr. Green. You and I, for our sins, will be embarking on a different mission. It is a crucial and a demanding one, but it does not include a meeting with Robert Capman. That encounter is not necessary for us. But there are reasons why Behrooz Wolf needs one more meeting with Larsen and Capman."

Wolf was listening very closely. He was intrigued by the intonation in Mestel's voice and by the slightly old-fashioned and formal manner of phrasing and address. He looked around him again at the tank. Apart from the sheer size, it showed an individual taste in the layout, a little different from the standard arrangement.

"Mestel," he said at last. "Is the layout of this place your work, or did Capman do it for you?"

"Capman and a work crew arranged for the physical labor. That was before I had full control of the remote handling equipment, so I still needed help. Now I could do the whole thing with my waldos. I did all the specifications, though—Robert never did care at all what his surroundings looked like; he lived inside his head."

Wolf was nodding in satisfaction. "Then I'd like to ask you a couple more questions. How old are you, and are you male or female?"

Green looked at Wolf in astonishment. But Mestel was laughing heartily, a musical gale of sound that swept out of a hundred speakers inside the great tank.

"Male or female? Come, Mr. Wolf, is it not apparent that the question is now purely academic? I presume you mean, was my original form male or female? Full marks. My name is Betha Mestel, and I was for many years a female—but never, I'm glad to say, a lady. Robert Capman told me that you have an unmatched talent for reading through an exterior form. I see he did not exaggerate. Can you go further? On the basis of what I have already said, would you like to attempt further deduction?"

Bey was nodding thoughtfully, dark eyes hooded by the half-closed lids. "Betha is not a name much used now. It had a big vogue a hundred and twenty years ago, and you said you are an old friend of Capman." He paused. "I think I am beginning to see a whole lot of things that should have been obvious to me a long time ago. Is it possible that you—"

"Never, as they said in the old days, ask a woman her age." Beneath the flirtatious tone of Betha Mestel's voice there was an undercurrent that was anything but casual. "As you surmise, the answer would take us far afield. I must return to my question and ask again: Mr. Wolf, are you willing to take the risk that a meeting with Robert Capman would entail?"

"Definitely." Wolf's voice was firm, his resolution increased by the implications of Betha Mestel's words. "How do I get to him?"

Wolf paused. The far side of the room was suddenly indistinct, a blur of color in front of his eyes.

"I will get you to him. Mr. Green and I will not go with you; we have our own duties to perform back in the Inner System." The voice was fainter, farther away. "Let me apologize to you for what is about to happen. There are good reasons for this, also. Relax, both of you."

Neither Park Green nor Bey Wolf had heard Mestel's final sentence. Two of the handling waldos came forward and gently carried the two unconscious forms back toward the control room.

One hundred million kilometers above the ecliptic, there is an isolation that is more complete than anything found in the plane of the planets. There were no observers to watch Pearl as the asteroid moved steadily on its three-year circuit around the Sun. The nearest inhabited object was Horus, with its fifty-man mining outpost. That group was far too busy to spend any of their time heavens-watching. In any case, at thirty million kilometers distance, Pearl was at the resolution limit of their best telescopes.

No one saw the great lock in the side of Pearl iris open, and the ship emerge from it like a small, bright minnow darting from the shelter of a hollow rock. The ship fell freely for a while, until it was a safe distance from the asteroid. Then the fusion drive went on. The ship began to move out and down, dipping toward the ecliptic on a trajectory that headed farther from the Sun. The single passenger knew nothing of the motion. He was cocooned deep within the form-change tank at the ship's center.

Soon afterward, the mechanical handlers emerged from Pearl's smaller lock. They went across to the ship that Bey Wolf and Park Green had arrived in. It had remained close to Pearl's surface, with the auxiliary thrusters making the tiny adjustments necessary to hold it at a precise fifty meters from the asteroid. The handlers moved it gently toward the lock, electronically overriding the command sequence that held the ship's position. Once moved inside, the ship was secured firmly by supporting cables that threaded the faintly lit interior.

The currents began to flow through superconducting struts and cables. The interior configuration of Pearl became rigid, constrained by the intense electromagnetic fields within. When the fields had stabilized, the main lock opened again to reveal a power kernel shielded and held in position by the same powerful controls.

The propulsion unit went on. Plasma was injected into the ergosphere of the kernel, picked up energy, and emerged as a highly relativistic particle stream. Little by little, the orbit of Pearl responded to the continuing thrust. It began to change, to shift inclination and semimajor axis.

Betha Mestel was moving house.

CHAPTER 22

It had been added to the air of the room. Asfanil, probably, judging from the lack of general side effects. There
was no headache or uneasiness in the stomach. And yet . . .

Bey Wolf frowned. Something didn't feel quite right.
He ran his tongue cautiously over his upper lip. There was
a faint taste there. No, not a taste, a feeling, like a slight
stickiness. He breathed deeper, and the air felt oddly different, hot in his lungs. At last he ventured to open his
eyes.

—and was suddenly completely awake. He was still sitting in the form-change tank, but he knew from long experience that the process had already run its course. The
change was complete. The monitors were still, the elec-
trodes inactive against his skin.

Full of a sudden alarming notion, Bey reached out a

hand in front of him. He looked at it closely. Normal, except for the color, and that was an effect of the lighting. He breathed again, half relief, half disappointment, and looked up at the odd, blue-tinted lamps above his head.

He was no longer on Pearl. That was obvious as soon as he emerged from the tank. He was on board a ship. It could be the vessel they had seen in Pearl's interior, but the backdrop outside the viewports was of open space, not the gleaming inner surface of the asteroid.

Not on Pearl, and form-changed. But to what?

Bey inventoried his body and could find no change there. He sat down by the viewport to think things through. His body was the same, but his senses felt subtly different. The noise of the ship's engines was wrong, a high-pitched scream of power up at the limit of his hearing. It sounded quite different from the familiar drone of a fusion drive. He looked aft. The equipment was conventional enough, and he could not believe that Capman and Betha Mestel had invented a completely new propulsion system.

Wolf stared out of the port, his face vacant with concentration. Where was he? Where were Pearl, Betha Mestel, Park Green?

He switched on the other viewing screens and tried to gain an idea of the direction in which he was being carried. The Sun was the first reference point. It lay far astern, much reduced in size and brilliance. Its color was changed to a peculiarly intense violent-blue. He peered at it in perplexity. Was it the Sun? It seemed more like a strange star, alien and remote.

Bey looked for other information. Through one of the side screens, a brilliant planet was visible, quite close to the ship. Surely that had to be Jupiter—but it too was the wrong color. The ship was swinging past it, using the planet's gravitational field to pick up free momentum, and the planet itself was only a few million kilometers away.

Bey turned up the magnification of the screen with strangely uncoordinated hands, focusing on the satellites that orbited the brilliant primary.

It was Jupiter all right. There were the four Galilean satellites, all clearly visible, and there was the red spot, itself changed to a peculiar lime-green color. He watched in silence for a few minutes. Io was close to occultation by the great mass of the planet. The satellite's angular separation from the main body was steadily decreasing as he looked on. Just before Io vanished, Bey sat up straight in his seat. He looked again at the Sun and at the lamps inside the ship. Suddenly he understood exactly what had happened. He swore to himself. It should have been obvious to him long before. He looked at the plotter set by the display screen. He had a suspicion what he would find as the end point of the calculated trajectory.

Farside watch tended to be quiet. No parties, no people, not even VIP inspections to provide an irritating relief from tedium. Tem Grad and Alfeo Masti had pulled it three times in four months, and they were beginning to suspect that the random duty selector was loaded against them. Once the big antennae had been recalibrated at the beginning of the residence period, there was nothing to do for the next fourteen days except an occasional personal message from a friend in the Outer System when, as now, Nearside was facing the Sun.

They had run through the usual pastimes left by former duty officers the first couple of times they had been assigned to Farside. Those were few enough, and not too enthralling at that. Now they had retired to opposite ends of the main monitor room, Tem to listen to music and Alfeo to play bridge with the computer. Even that wasn't much fun as far as Alfeo was concerned. He was getting very annoyed with the machine. It was supposed to adjust

its game so that the three hands that it was playing repre-
sented players with roughly Alfeo's level of skill. Instead,
he was being slaughtered, and he couldn't even curse his
partner with any pleasure. After two hours, he was looking
darkly at the screen and wondering if the random hands
that the computer was supposed to be generating were as
open to suspicion as the selection procedure for Farside
watch assignments.

It was a surprise and a positive relief when the communications monitor began its soft call for attention. A ship
was approaching Farside, asking for trajectory confirma-
tion as it neared the Moon. At this time of the month, it
had to be coming from Mars or beyond. Alfeo hit the button that canceled his latest losing hand and activated the
display screen. The computer uttered a low whir of changing peripherals, like a mutter of protest at Alfeo's poor
sportsmanship for quitting when he was behind.

It took a few seconds to get a visual fix on the ship. The
computer took range-rate information from the Doppler
shift in the communications band signals, used that to
compute a relative position, and finally pointed the biggest
telescope to line up on the approaching ship.

When the image of a gleaming white sphere finally appeared on the screen in front of him, Alfeo looked at it
with interest. It didn't seem to be one of the usual
freighters. He glanced automatically at the display beneath
the image giving the ship's distance. Then he frowned,
gasped, and looked again at the image on the screen.

"Tem," he said urgently. "Get over here. We've got a
ship approaching, and according to these readouts she's a
real monster. The screen shows her subtending over six
seconds of arc at the station, and she's still more than sixty
thousand kilometers out. See if you can find her in the
register."

Tem Grad unhurriedly uncoiled his long frame from the

chair and sauntered over to the screen.

"You're star sick, Alf. Six seconds at sixty kay would mean something a couple of thousand meters across. The biggest ship in Lloyd's Register is only three hundred meters. You must be reading the display wrong."

Alfeo did not deign to answer. He merely jerked his thumb at the screen by his side. Grad looked at it, then the numerical displays. He looked again. His expression changed abruptly.

"See if she has a voice channel active, Alf. I think we may have an alien out there."

His voice was excited. Earth, the USF, and the whole Solar System had been pulsing with rumor and talk of aliens ever since the first guarded and cryptic announcements had come from the Office of Form Control on Earth regarding John Larsen's metamorphosis. Speculation had been wild. With so little being said officially, the news media had gone back to the stories of the Mariana Monsters, combing sources in Guam for anything suggestive.

As the voice and video link was completed, Tem hooked in the communicator channel. A chubby, boyish face suddenly appeared on the screen in front of them.

"Hey, I know him," said Alfeo. "I was in school with him, for tertiary vacuum survival. You remember, the courses over in Hipparchus. He's no alien."

Tem gestured him to silence. The voice circuit had corrected for Doppler shift and was now tuned correctly to the sending frequency of the ship.

"This is *Pearl*, requesting approach trajectory approval and parking orbit assignment, Earth equatorial," said Green's holo. "Repeat, this is *Pearl*. Farside, please acknowledge signal and confirm orbit."

Alfeo threw in the second circuit, permitting the computer to provide a message acceptance and a video link of Alfeo and Tem as they worked at the console.

"Acceptance received," said Green after a moment's pause. Then he blinked and leaned forward in his chair, obviously looking at his own screen. "Is that Alf—what was it?—Massey? What are you doing on Farside duty?"

"I'm not sure. Penance, maybe," said Alfeo. "And it's Masti, not Massey. And you're Park, right? Park Green. A better question is, what are you doing in that ship? She's not listed in Lloyd's, and she's very peculiar-looking."

"Watch those comments, sonny," broke in a new voice on the circuit. "Remember, handsome is as handsome does. Look, you and Park can socialize later. We need the highest-priority circuit you can give us to Laszlo Dolmetsch. Is he on Earth or on the Moon?"

Grad held back his questions, responding to the note of authority and urgency in the unknown voice.

"Last thing I heard, he was on Earth," he replied. "That was a week or so ago. I'll try and track him. Meanwhile, I'm giving you a slot that will take you to LEO, eight hundred kilometers perigee, zero inclination. I don't know if you'll be able to get landing permission. With the emergency down there, we've got a ban on everything except top-priority traffic down to the surface."

"We've heard that things are getting bad. The newscasts on the way in were full of it." The four-tenths of a second round-trip delay between *Pearl* and Farside Station was decreasing steadily as the ship flew closer on her lunar flyby. "Anyway, there's no way that Betha could land on Earth. She's not right for it."

"What's the problem?" said Alfeo. "Need a special suit? They can fly one out to you from the Libration Colonies if you're willing to wait a day for it. Where is Betha, anyway?" He stared hard at the screen. "All we're picking up is a picture of you, Park."

"I'd need a special suit, all right," said Mestel. "But I'll guarantee they don't have one that would fit me. How are you doing on that circuit to Dolmetsch? Do you have it yet?"

Alfeo glanced across at the computer output. "We know just where he is now. He's down on Earth meeting with a group from the General Coordinators. I don't have the priority codes that will let me interrupt a session there. I can get a short message to him, that's about all. There's no way that I can give you a two-way unless he wants to initiate it from that end."

"Fine. Send him this message," said the invisible voice. "It's short enough. Tell him that it's Lungfish Project, Phase Two, calling."

"Lungfish Project," said Tem, keying in a second connection. "Right. But what about a message for him?"

"That's all you need. He'll be on the circuit fast, unless the shock knocks him flat."

"But who are you?" persisted Tem. His own curiosity was thoroughly aroused. "Don't you even want to give him your name? You must be a friend of his."

"I was a friend of his long before you two were cutting teeth. But I haven't seen him for a long time, and I've changed a little since then. If you can send a video with the message, give him a shot of *Pearl*. There's no point in sending him the video signal that we're sending you."

"You mean give him a picture of the ship?" Alfeo looked dubious. "You don't look like any ship in the register. I thought I knew every type, but there's nothing that's anything like your size and shape. What sort of drive units do you have? They must be something special."

"They're kernels," said Park Green, "with McAndrew plasma feeds. The same as the Titan freighters, but the bracing is all done internally instead of externally. *Pearl* started out as a natural formation. It was an asteroid in the Egyptian Cluster."

The two men on Farside duty looked again at the image on the screen, then at each other.

"I guess that makes sense," said Tem Grad. "That way, Alf, she'd be in the natural feature listings, not in Lloyd's. Even so, I've never seen an asteroid that looked anything like that." He turned back to the screen. "You know, you should have applied for a reclassification, the way they did when they put drives on Icarus for the solar scoop. You should be classified now as interplanetary passenger."

"Not quite," said Betha Mestel's voice. "For one thing, there's only one passenger—I count as crew. For another thing, as soon as I can get old Laszlo and be sure he'll act on what we're going to tell him, *Pearl*'s status will change again. She'll be *interstellar*, not interplanetary."

"What the devil is all this?" broke in an impatient voice on the incoming circuit. "If this is a hoax, you'd better be ready to answer to the General Coordinators. Who sent that message about Project Lungfish?"

Alfeo turned nervously to the screen, where Dolmetsch's angry face glared out at them. "This is Farside Station, sir. We have a direct video link with *Pearl*, former asteroid of the Egyptian Cluster, now an interplanetary—inter*stellar*—ship." He choked a little at the words and looked at the other screen for moral support. "They requested a priority link to you at GCHQ and asked that that specific message be sent to you."

There was a perceptible pause as the messages went from Farside, through lunar low orbit relay, down to Earth via L-5 relay, then all the way back. Dolmetsch's face was a study as he saw the gleaming sphere appear on his screen. Confusion, alarm, and finally excitement showed there in turn before he finally spoke again.

"Is that Betha? Where are you? The picture that I'm getting can't be from the Cluster; it's much too clear."

"I moved, Laszlo. You know, we were planning to do it anyway in a year or two. We felt we had to advance it. You may be able to guess why—the situation down on Earth, with the economic breakdown, and then the Logian changes to John Larsen. I'm flying *Pearl* around the Moon at this moment, piloting her down to low Earth orbit."

Dolmetsch was nodding his head gloomily. With his great beaked nose, he seemed like some bird of prey ready to dive on its victim. "You're quite right about the situation here," he said. He sighed. "It's getting worse by the hour. We've even stopped trying to keep it secret. We are trying every empirical correction I know, but it's like a sand heap against a tidal wave. Is Robert there with you?"

"No. He has already started on the other mission. Look, Laszlo, you know I can't come down to Earth. All the changes are still going well, and I'm ready to begin Phase Two. We've picked out the target star. There's no way I can approach a planetary surface in this form. But both Robert and I felt that my appearance here might be the only way we could persuade you to act on the information that we want to give you."

"Who's Robert?" said Alfeo to Tem in a low voice. "Weren't you telling me just a few hours ago that nothing interesting ever happens on Farside watch?"

"Come up and match us in orbit," went on Betha Mestel. "Then come over into *Pearl*. Bring the General Coordinators with you, as many as you can. They have to be persuaded even more than you do. The man who is with me, Park Green, will go back to Earth with you. He has all the materials that Robert left here—and he will have the general theory of stabilization with him."

The pause before the answer came back was much longer than usual. When Dolmetsch spoke, his voice sounded guarded and suspicious.

"Betha, we've known each other too long to lie, but I

think you may be very mistaken. You know how long and hard we've looked for a general theory. I've said it before, many times but let me say it again. The work I've done has been useful, no denying it. But at best I've been a Kepler or a Faraday. We're still waiting for our Newton and our Maxwell, to explain all my empirics with a few fundamentals—mathematical laws that underpin everything. Now you're telling me we have it, just when we most need it. I find it hard to accept any coincidence that big. Are you trying to tell me that this fellow, Green, worked out the general theory just like that?"

"No. He's not an economic theorist; he doesn't know even the basics. Laszlo, I've learned something in the past month or two, and you'll have to learn it too. There is now an intellect present in the Solar System that makes you and Robert look like two children. Beginning with what he already knew of your work, he saw how to move to the underlying laws. It took him just a few weeks to do it."

"Weeks!" Dolmetsch sounded even more sceptical. "And we've been working on it for many years. I'd like to meet your superman—and I'll want to see that theory, in detail, before I'll accept or use any of it."

"You've met him already, but you won't be able to meet him now. I'll show you the theory when you get here. It's carried through far enough to define a set of corrective measures that you need to stop the economic oscillations."

"Betha, that's *impossible*, general theory or no general theory. Don't you see, you have to treat the cause, not the symptoms. We have to know what it was that triggered the new oscillations."

"I know. You'll understand too when you see the formal evidence. We can tell you what started it, and you can check it for yourself. The root cause of the problems began the day of the first rumor that we had been contacted by aliens. In other words, the very day that John Larsen completed his change to a Logian form."

Dolmetsch looked thoughtful. "The timing's right," he said grudgingly. "That's when it began, and since then things have become steadily worse. Go on, Betha."

"You can do it for yourself. What's the most likely cause for the instabilities?"

"Psychological perturbation." Dolmetsch frowned in concentration. "We've always suspected that a basic change in attitudes would be the most likely starting point for widespread instability. You're saying that the rumors about Larsen were the beginning? Maybe. People would change their views of many things if they thought aliens were here. Xenophobia is always a powerful force, and there are rumors about immortality and superintelligence already running wild down here on Earth."

He shook his head. "Betha, I'd love to believe you— but doesn't it just sound too unlikely, for the general theory to come along as a solution exactly when we need it?"

"It would be, if the two events were independent. They're not. They are really one and the same. The Logian form produced the instability and also created the intelligence that could understand it and develop a countermeasure. Not coincidence, *consequence*. There was one basic cause for both events—the Logian form-change."

As the conversation proceeded, Pearl was swinging further around the Moon on her approach path to Earth orbit. When the geometry permitted it, the comlink to Earth was automatically rerouted through an alternate path by L-5 relay, and the reception of the signals at Farside began to fade. Tem and Alfeo bent over the screen, straining their ears for the weakening voices.

"I'll be up there by the time you arrive," said Dolmetsch. His voice was firm, and he seemed to have made up his mind. "You don't know how bad it is down here. If I wait longer before we begin new corrections, we may be too late to do any good. Can you begin sending me something here, as you fly in, so that I can get something going even before I get up there to meet you in orbit?"

"No problem. We'll begin sending on a separate data circuit as soon as you can open one for us."

The distortion in the signal received at Farside was growing rapidly. Alfeo had turned the gain to maximum, but the voices were fading in and out as the transmission to the Farside antenna was intercepted by the lunar horizon.

"And where is Robert Capman now?" asked Laszlo Dolmetsch, his voice a faint wisp of sound among the background.

Tem and Alfeo crouched by the console, waiting for Mestel's reply.

"What did she say?" whispered Tem.

Alfeo shook his head. All they could hear was the amplified hiss of interplanetary static, seething and crackling with the noise from suns and planets. Betha Mestel's reply was gone forever, lost in the universal sea of radio emissions.

Farside watch, when it wasn't simply boring, could be most irritating.

CHAPTER 23

Outside the orbit of Jupiter, the Solar System displays a different tempo, a new breadth of time and space. The pulse of Saturn, only fifteen million kilometers ahead of the ship but almost one and a half billion from the Sun, beats thirty times as slowly as Earth's in its majestic revolution about the solar primary. The great planet, even at that distance, looked four times as big as the Moon seen from Earth. From the angle of Bey's approach, the rings made the planet seem almost twice its solid width.

Bey looked at the display that marked the time to rendezvous. Just a few ship-days to go, and he wasn't sure of the speed of the reverse-change process. He suspected that it would be fast—the sophistication of all the form-change equipment on the ship was an order of magnitude better than that of most commercial installations, and many of the programs in the change library were unfamiliar. Even so, it would be better to go into the tank a little early rather than a little late.

Capman would wait for him—that wasn't the issue. Bey didn't want to wait any longer than he had to, to hear Capman's explanations and to confirm the ideas that had been fermenting in his mind ever since his departure from Earth. Longer than that, really. Bey thought back to his own first reaction, years earlier, when John Larsen had told him of the liver without an ID.

The data bank on the ship, primed by Betha Mestel, had informed him of *Pearl*'s mission, bearing back to Earth the precious stabilization equations. It had told him nothing about his own mission. Bey sighed. He would know soon enough.

He took a last look at the ringed planet, growing steadily ahead of him, and at the Sun—still the wrong color—shrunk to a fiery pinpoint, far behind. With a little reluctance, knowing that a boring time was ahead in the tank, Bey set all the ship controls to automatic. He climbed slowly into the form-change tank in the central part of the ship, called out the necessary program, and began the change.

By luck or skill, his timing had been good. When he emerged from the tank, the vast bulk of Saturn was filling the sky ahead like a mottled and striated balloon. The trajectory maintenance system was already operating. The ship was past the outer satellites, moving from Enceladus to Mimas, then beyond, heading for a bound orbit inside the innermost ring of the planet.

Bey looked back at the Sun. It was only a hundredth of its familiar area, but now it was the usual yellow orb, with all traces of blue-violet gone. The tackiness had gone from his lips. When he reached out to touch the control panel, his coordination already felt better. On the panel, the attention light was blinking steadily like an insistent emerald lightning bug.

Bey had no nerves at all—or so he claimed. The tremor in his hand as he reached out to press the connect button had to be, he told himself, a lingering aftereffect of the form-change procedure. He hesitated, swallowed, and finally pressed.

The display gave him an immediate estimate of the direction and range of the signal being beamed to him. The other ship was less than ten thousand kilometers ahead of him, in a decaying orbit that would spiral it slowly and steadily down toward the upper atmosphere of Saturn. When the video signal appeared on the screen, Bey could examine the fittings of the other ship's interior. They were unfamiliar, neither form-change tank nor conventional living quarters. But the figure who crouched over the computer console was very familiar. There could be no mistaking that massive torso and wrinkled gray hide. Bey watched in silence for a few seconds and finally realized that the other was unaware of his surveillance. The monitor must be on a different part of the console.

"Well, John," said Bey at last. "Last time I saw you, I certainly didn't expect we would ever meet here. We've come a long way from the Form Control office, haven't we?"

The Logian figure swung around to face the video camera and looked at Bey quietly through huge, luminous eyes.

"Come on, John," said Bey as the silence lengthened. "At least you might say hello to me." ·

The broad face was inscrutable, but finally the head and upper body nodded and the fringed mouth opened.

"A natural mistake on your part, but my fault. Not John

Larsen, Mr. Wolf. Robert Capman. Welcome to our company."

While Bey was still struggling to grasp the implications of what he had heard, the other spoke again.

"I am pleased to see that you are none the worse for the form-change that you went through on the way here. May I ask, how long did it take you to realize what had been done to you?"

"How long?" Bey thought for a few moments. "Well, I knew I'd been changed as soon as I became conscious in the tank, and I knew it had to be something that affected the senses the moment I saw the Sun. It looked as though it had been Doppler-shifted toward the blue, by a big factor —and I knew that couldn't be real. The ship was heading away from the Sun, not toward it, and in any case it wasn't going that fast. I didn't catch on then, though, and I still didn't catch on when I noticed that the sound of the ship's engines seemed to be at the wrong frequency. Not too smart. But when I saw Jupiter as we swung by, Io was going into occultation. As I was watching it, I realized that it looked to be happening *fast*, much faster than it ought to. Physical laws are pretty inflexible. So, it had to be me. It was a subjective change in speed. I had been slowed down."

The Logian form of Capman was nodding slowly. "So just when did you understand what had happened?"

"Oh, I suppose it was about ten minutes after I came out of the tank. I should have caught it sooner—after all, I already knew all about Project Timeset. Ever since we found your underground lab, I've been expecting to meet forms that have been rate-changed the way that I was. I can't have been thinking too well when I first came through the form-change."

The Logian was nodding his head now in a different

rhythm, one that Bey had learned was the alien smile. "You may be interested to know, Mr. Wolf, that I made a small wager with Betha Mestel before I left Pearl. She asserted that you would take a long time to realize what had been done to you. She thought you would understand it only when you read it out of the data banks that had been loaded on the ship. I disagreed. I said that you would achieve that realization for yourself, and I bet her that it would happen within two hours of your leaving the form-change tank."

Capman rubbed at the swollen boss below his chest with a tri-digit paw. "The only thing we did not resolve, now that I look back on it, is any mechanism by which I might collect the results of the wager. It is three months now since Betha Mestel passed on to Dolmetsch the stabilization equations. She is well on her way out of the system and should not be back for several centuries. She could afford to make her bet with impunity."

The appearance and structural changes were irrelevant. It was still the same Robert Capman. Bey was convinced of it and realized again the insight of Capman's remark soon after their first meeting: the two of them would recognize each other through any external changes.

Before Bey could speak again, a vivid flash of color lit up the screen in front of the console on the other ship.

"One moment," said Capman. He faced the transmission screen and held his body quite still. For a brief second, the panel on his chest became a bewildering pointillism of colored light. It ended as suddenly as it had begun, returning to a uniform gray. Capman turned back to face Bey.

"Sorry to cut off like that. I had to give John Larsen an update on what has been happening here. He wanted to know if you had arrived yet. He's very busy there, getting ready for atmospheric entry, but he wants to set up a standard voice and video link and talk to you."

"What sort of link do you have with him? I saw John change the color of his chest panel, but always one color at a time. You did it with a whole lot of different color elements."

Capman nodded, head and trunk together. "That was for rapid transfer of information. I didn't want to take much time to explain to John what we are doing. Burst mode, we've been calling it. We found out about it soon after John changed, but I wanted to use it as a special method of communicating with him, so we kept quiet about it. It handles information thousands of times faster than conventional methods."

"Are you being literal or exaggerating the rate?" asked Bey, unable to imagine an information transfer rate of hundreds of thousands of words a minute.

"I'm not exaggerating. If anything, I'm understating. I suspect that this is the usual way that Logians communicated—they only used speech when they were in a situation where they could not see each other's chest panels. It's a question of simple efficiency of data transfer. The Logian chest panel can produce an individual, well-defined spot of color about three millimeters on a side, like this."

On Capman's chest panel, an orange point of light suddenly appeared, then next to it a green one.

"I can make that any color, from ultraviolet through infrared. The Logian eye can easily resolve that single spot from a distance of a couple of meters. That was probably the natural distance apart for typical Logian conversation. Each spot can modulate its color independently, so."

The pair of points changed color, then for a moment the whole panel swirled with a shifting, iridescent pattern of colors. It returned quickly to the uniform gray tone.

"I ran the color changes near to top speed there. It's very tiring to do that for more than a few seconds, though John has held it for several minutes when he had a real mass of information to get to me quickly. Now, you can do the arithmetic. The panel on my chest is about forty-five centimeters by thirty-five. That lets me use roughly sixteen thousand spots there as independent message transmitters. If he were here, John could read all those in directly. His eyes and central nervous system can handle that data load. If we were in a *real* hurry, he'd come closer, and I could decrease the spot size to about a millimeter on a side—just about the limit. The number of channels goes up to over a hundred thousand, and each one can handle about the same load as a voice circuit. That would be hard work for both of us, but we've tried it to see what the limits are."

Bey was shaking his head sadly. "I knew there had to be something strange about the com system that you put in the tank back on Earth—there was no reason for it to have such a big capacity. But I never thought of anything like this."

"You would have if we had used it much. It was one of the things that worried me when John was using that mode to send me information when I was on Pearl: Would somebody notice the comlink load and start to investigate it? I don't think anyone did, but as you well know there is really no such thing as a completely secret operation. You always need to send and store data, and sometime that will give you away. John tried to be careful, but it was still a danger."

Bey sat down on the bench next to the communicator screen. "I don't know who could have discovered you. I tried to guess what was happening, and I think I know a part of it—but it's only a part. I assume that John knows the whole story."

"He deduced it for himself within a couple of days after

assuming the Logian form. His powers of logic had increased so much that I couldn't believe it at first. Now, I have observed it in myself also."

There was another flicker of light from the screen in front of Capman.

"John will be in voice communication in a couple of minutes," he said. "He's very busy making the last minute checks on the ship."

"I heard you say he would be making atmospheric entry. Surely he can't survive on Saturn. The form he is in was designed for Loge, and I assume that he's still in that."

"He is—but don't worry. The ship he's in has some special features, as does this one. You can see his ship from here if you look ahead of you. He's already in the upper atmosphere, and the fusion drive is on."

Bey looked at the forward screen. A streak of phosphorescence was moving steadily across the upper atmosphere of the planet. As he watched, it brightened appreciably. The ship was moving deeper into the tenuous gases high above Saturn's surface. In a few minutes more, ionization would begin to interfere with radio communications. Bey felt a sense of relief when the second channel light went on and a second image screen became active.

The two Logian forms were very similar, too similar for Bey to distinguish by a rapid inspection. However, there were other factors that made identification easy. The second figure was festooned with intravenous injectors and electronic condition monitors. It raised one arm in greeting.

"Sorry I couldn't stay up there to greet you, Bey," said John Larsen. "We're working on a very tight entry window. I want to descend as near as possible to one place on the planet. We've calculated the optimum location for low winds and turbulence."

"John. You can't survive down there."

"I think I can. We have no intention of committing suicide. This ship has been modified past anything you've ever seen before. It will monitor the outside conditions and keep the form-change programs going that will let me adapt to them. The rate of descent can be controlled, so that I can go down very slowly if necessary." John Larsen's Logian form sounded confident and cheerful. "Well, Bey, you've had a while to think on the way out here. How much of it have you been able to deduce?"

Bey looked at the two forms, each on their separate screens. "The basic facts about what's been going on for the past forty years. Those are fairly clear to me now. But I don't have any real idea of motives. I assume you know those too, John."

"I do. But if it's any consolation to you, I had to be told them. I don't think they are amenable to pure logic."

"I agree," cut in Capman. "You would have to know some of Earth's hidden history before you can understand why I would rather be thought of as a murderer than have the truth known about the experiments. I am curious to see how far your own logic has taken you. What do you know about my work?"

"I know you're not a murderer—but it took me long enough to realize it. I understand all four of your projects now. Proteus was the basic spacegoing forms, and Timeset was the form that allows a change of rate for the life process. I knew about them four years ago. I assume that Lungfish is Betha Mestel. She's about to go out into a new living environment—interstellar space. How long will she be away?"

Capman shrugged. "We are not sure. Perhaps two or three hundred years. She was always an independent spirit. She will return when she feels that it is useful for her to do so. *Pearl* was arranged to be completely self-contained. Fusion-powered internal lighting takes care of the illumination for the algal tanks when sunlight is too weak for growth—and Betha has a supply of the Logian virus in case she becomes bored with the potential of her present form and wants to try a change."

"I hope I'm around to see her come back," said Bey. "I now think that's a real possibility. You know, John, I didn't follow my first instincts when you told me about that liver in Central Hospital. My first thought was that it must have come from a very old person, one so old that he had not been given the chromosome ID. That would have made him over a hundred, and I decided that no one would use a hundred-year-old liver for a transplant. Then we got an age estimate from Morris in the Transplant Department, and that showed a young liver. That seemed to be the end of the original thought. But it wasn't. Correct?"

"It was not." Capman nodded. "As usual, your instincts were good."

"The only project we haven't accounted for was Project Janus," went on Bey. "I should have realized that you gave your projects names that told something about the work you were doing. And Janus was the two-faced god, the one who could look both ways. You had developed a form-change program that could 'look both ways' in time. It could advance or reverse the aging process. The liver we found was from a very old person who had undergone age reversal as a result of your work. Right?"

Capman's big eyes were hooded by their heavy lids. He was reliving another period of his life, rocking slowly backward and forward in his seat. He nodded. "It was from an old person. Worse than that, it was from an old friend. I could not prevent some of those experiments ending in failure."

Bey was looking on sympathetically. "You can't blame yourself for the failures. Not everything can succeed. I assume that *all* the people who were used in those experiments were your old friends? But they knew the risks, and they had nothing at all to lose."

Capman nodded again. "They had all reached a point where the feedback machines could not maintain a healthy condition. They had a choice. A conventional and rapid death or the chance to risk what remained of their lives in the experiments. As you know, the compulsions we used to achieve form-change were extreme, but even so they did not always work. Let me assure you, the knowledge that their deaths were inevitable did not lessen the loss. When someone died in the experiments, I had killed an old friend. There was no escape from that feeling."

"I can understand that. What I can't follow is your reluctance to share the burden. No one who understood your work would have blamed you for what you were doing. Your friends were volunteers. This is the piece I can't follow. Why did you choose to keep everything a secret— even after your first discovery? Why was it necessary to have a hidden lab, away from the Earth?"

Capman was still nodding slowly and thoughtfully. He sighed. "As you say, Mr. Wolf, that is the key question. In a real sense, I did not make that decision. I am known to the system as a mass murderer, the monster of the century. It is not a role I sought; it was forced upon me. I could even argue that the real villains are Laszlo Dolmetsch and Betha Melford. But I don't believe it."

"Betha Melford? You mean Betha Mestel?"

"The same person. I tend to call her by the name she had before her bond with Mestel."

"What did you think of her, Bey?" broke in Larsen. "You must have met her on Pearl."

"I did. I think she's marvelous, and I can't help wondering what she looked like before the form-changes. Betha Melford. Is she related to *the* Melfords?"

"She is Ergan Melford's only surviving heir. Every

form-change royalty that BEC collects contributes two percent to Betha." Capman paused again, briefly carried into
the past. "The merger with the Mestel fortunes made her
the single most influential person on Earth, but she always
knew the importance of keeping that hidden."

"And now she has given all that up?" asked Bey.

"She did that a number of years ago. Betha is almost a
hundred and thirty years old, and when we embarked on
the age-reversal experiments she had no way of knowing if
she would survive them. Her financial interests are managed by a small group of people on earth and in the USF."

"Including you?"

Capman nodded. "Including me—and also including
Dolmetsch. I told you there are pieces of history that you
need before you can hope to know what has been going on.
None of this has ever been written down.

"My own involvement began when I was still a student,
soon after I came back from studies in Europe. I went to
work at the Melford Foundation and met Betha. Bey Wolf,
if you thought she was marvelous on Pearl, you should
have seen her in her prime. She was tall, and elegantly
dressed, and sophisticated enough to put a cocky young
man who thought he knew everything in his place with one
nod of her coiffured gray head."

"She did that to *you*?" exclaimed Bey.

"Actually, I was thinking more of Laszlo Dolmetsch."
The head nodded in that smiling gesture. "But I suppose it
applied equally well to me. She made a special point of
bringing the two of us together at one of her parties. She
insisted that I take a drink—as a defense mechanism, she
said, until I learned what to do with my hands—and introduced me to half the wealth on the planet. Then, when I
was softened up, she took me outside onto the terrace.
Laszlo Dolmetsch was sitting there, alone.

" 'Laszlo,' Betha said to him. 'This is Robert Capman.

You two will hate each other at first, but you have to get to know each other.'

"Dolmetsch looked no different then than he does now —same big, jutting nose, same sunken eyes. I don't know how I looked at him, but he lifted his head in the air and scowled superciliously at me along his nose.

"Betha Melford shook her head. 'You two deserve each other,' she said. 'Neither of you has the faintest idea of the social graces. Oh well, you'll learn. I'm going back inside now. Come and look for me when you can't stand each other's company any longer. And not before.'

"It took a while before we could talk to teach other. We couldn't get started, but I think we were both scared to go back in and face Betha. She had that effect on you. So Dolmetsch asked me if I knew anything about econometric models. I didn't. And I asked him what he knew about form-change theory. Not a thing, he said. It wasn't until we somehow stumbled on to talking about catastrophe theory that we hit common ground. I had been using it for form-change bifurcations; he had built it into his theory of the effects of technology on social systems. After that we couldn't stop. We went on to representation theory, and stability, and the final limits of technology. It was long after dawn when Betha came back to us. She listened for maybe two minutes—we didn't really take much notice of her—then she said, 'All right, you two, I'm going to bed. Everyone else left hours ago. There's a hot breakfast in the west wing dining room, when you can tear yourselves away. Tomorrow, remind me to tell you about the Lunar Club.'

"That was the beginning." The broad, alien face somehow carried the message that Robert Capman was still staring far back across the years. "We realized after that first night that we *had* to work together. What we were doing was going to change history, one way or another. Betha made sure that we never had any problem with money. And as soon as I had the form-change ideas into a suitable form, we began to feed them into Dolmetsch's programs that modeled the Earth and USF economies. The results were depressing. Most of the changes that I wanted to explore were destabilizing, and some of them were completely catastrophic. The worst one of all was the age-reversal change. A few people might get to live a lot longer, but as soon as the news got out, the economy would blow up."

"But you did the experiments anyway," said Bey.

Capman nodded. "We both believed that there were two conflicting needs. Earth had to be stabilized, if we could do it. But we also had to have a new frontier, off Earth— more than the USF could offer. You know what we did. With Betha's help, we went underground. She financed the operations, and we had help from the rest of the Lunar Club. They were a small group of influential people who shared a common worry about the future. They were modeled on the Lunar Club that flourished in England in the second half of the eighteenth century. Most of them are dead now. Many of them died in the experiments. They were all willing volunteers for the work, as soon as they knew that a natural death was close."

He fell silent for a while. Larsen spoke softly to Bey, switching in a voice circuit that would not include Capman's ship.

"He's lived with this for eighty years, Bey, one way or another, and yet it still gets to him, the death of the people who'd been age-reversed in the form-change tanks. I'll be in atmospheric entry in a few minutes, and out of contact. He needs to get all this off his chest."

"I don't understand how it could be eighty years, John," said Bey. "We only saw evidence that it went back thirty."

"That's when they moved the main base of operations to Pearl. Capman moved what was left into the facility under

Central Hospital. Dolmetsch thought that was an acceptable danger, even if it was discovered. He calculated a limited social effect, one that he thought he could compensate for."

"John, how much of all this do you understand now? Will the general theory of stabilization really work?"

"Within limits. We still can't let people know that age reversal is possible. I understand most of this—I helped Capman when he was working out the theory, in the past few months. Make no mistake, Bey. You know how I've changed mentally since I became a Logian form—but Capman has changed just as much, and you know where he started from. I still can't follow his thinking. I can't describe the way this form feels. You should take the change yourself and know it firsthand."

Larsen stopped speaking and looked across at the display screen in his control cabin. "I'm close to entry. We'll lose radio contact very soon. I should be able to reestablish it in a few hours." He switched back to a circuit that connected him also with Capman's ship. "Sixty seconds to signal blackout."

"John," said Bey rapidly. "I still don't know why you're going down there. There must be a big risk."

"Some. Less than you think, as we have calculated it. Why are we going down there? Come on, Bey, use your imagination. We think there's life down there, and we think humans in Logian form can live there. It's our second beachhead, an area ninety times as big as Earth. If the collapse comes—and we hope it won't—we need some other options, off-Earth."

The quality of the voice transmission was rapidly deteriorating as Larsen's ship dug deeper into Saturn's atmosphere. Larsen obviously knew it too. He raised one heavy arm and spoke his last words rapidly. "See you soon, Bey. Come on in, the water's fine."

Bey looked through the forward screen, watching the trail of ionized gases that glowed from Saturn's face behind Larsen's plunging ship. The entry was a daunting prospect. Saturn's surface gravity was almost the same as Earth's, but with an escape velocity more than three times as high, movement to and from low orbit was a difficult feat for any vessel.

"Don't worry, Mr. Wolf." Capman had come out of his reverie and read the expression on Bey's face. "This has all been calculated very closely. Unless there are unknown forces at work in Saturn's lower atmosphere, the danger to John Larsen is very small."

"And you are intending to follow him down?" asked Bey.

"Perhaps. Let me answer the question behind the question. Obviously, we could have exchanged all the information between us by radio link. Why did I think it necessary to bring you all the way to Saturn in order to talk to each other? After all, in my present form it is obvious that we cannot meet in person, even if there were reason to do so."

"That will do," said Bey. "I might have chosen different words, but the meaning is the same."

"Then since I asked your question, would you care to attempt to give my answer?"

Bey smiled. "There is one obvious answer. You want me to join you in this experiment. To change to the Logian form and descend to the surface of Saturn."

"And then?"

"As I said, that is the obvious answer. Unless I am losing my ability to read a little deeper, it is not the whole answer. I can't provide the rest of it."

Capman was sitting perfectly still in his chair, big eyes unblinking. "It is not simple," he said. "Like many things, it involves a choice. Tell me, in your investigation of my background, did you ever see a psychological profile?"

Bey nodded. "An old one. When you were still in your teens."

"That would do. Did you notice anything peculiar about it?"

"You're joking, of course. As you know very well, it was similar to mine—more similar than I would have thought possible. I must say, I found it very encouraging in some ways. You showed low scores on some of the same things as I did—intelligence, for instance. Until I saw your profile, mine had always worried me a little."

"We don't fit well on the standard charts, either of us," said Capman with the nodding smile of the Logians. "I doubt if I would fit them at all in this form. But we are a little different—not a lot, but enough to worry me that some people like us are failing the humanity tests. You may be interested to know that *you* just squeaked through. Well, that is irrelevant at the moment. Shortage of people, even of people like oneself, is not Earth's current problem. Let me get to the point. I brought you here to offer you a choice. It is one that I would not make to anyone else. I can do it in your case only because we have that curious affinity of mind. Both branches call for self-sacrifice of a sort."

Bey began to feel again a rise of tension, a suspicion coming from the base of his brain. "To change to the Logian form and explore Saturn . . ."

Capman nodded. "Or else?"

"To return to Earth and continue the work on the control of form-changes? Laszlo Dolmetsch and the others need advice from somebody who really knows form-change theory. If I choose Saturn, you will return to Earth yourself."

"That is correct. If that is your choice, to remain here, I will borrow your outward appearance and go back to Earth. One of us must be there. No one would question Behrooz

Wolf's return, or knowledge of form-change."

"It must be quite obvious to you that I would prefer to stay here. The mental advantages alone of the Logian form are enough to make me want to choose that alternative."

"I know." Capman sighed. "That cannot be denied. All I can say is that the return to Earth, and all its problems, would not be permanent. When Earth's troubles lessen, or become hopeless, or you find and train your own successor, the Saturn experiment will still be here. There will be other work to do—Betha was the first of the Lungfish series, not the last. But it is your decision as to the next step. I am prepared for either role."

"How much further can form-change be carried? Betha Mestel suggests that we are only at the beginning."

"We are." Capman bowed his head. "I am beginning to suspect that the boundary that we impose between the animate and the inanimate is an artificial one. If that is true, form-change has no real limits. We can conceive of a conscious, reasoning being as big as a planet, or as big as a star. It would have to be a mixture of organic and inorganic components, just as Betha is; but that presents no logical problems. I have a more fundamental question: At what point would the result cease to be human? If our tests for humanity are valid, any human—or alien—and machine combination that can achieve purposive form-change should be considered human. I can think of worse definitions. Tell me, have you made your decision?"

Bey was silent for several minutes, watching the clouded face of Saturn speeding by below the ship. "Tell *me*," he said at last. "Do you remember the time that we were in Pleasure Dome, waiting for the decision as to whether they would let us talk to the people who were in charge of the form-change operations?"

"Very well. Why do you ask?"

"Just before they showed us Newton, in the garden at

Woolsthorpe, there was a scene of a torture chamber. If the Snow Queen was telling the truth, that scene showed something that one of us wanted. Would you agree that we were the victim, not the tormentor?"

"I believe so."

"Then *who* was the victim, Behrooz Wolf or Robert Capman?"

Capman sighed. "I have wondered that, too. I do not think the machine would tune to an interest that was not common to both of us. We were both the victim."

Bey nodded, his face intense. There was a lengthening silence as the two forms, man and Logian, watched the brown and crimson thunderclouds of the planet rear and clash beneath their ships.

EPILOG

"The music stopped and I stood still, and found myself outside the hill."

CHAPTER 24

It couldn't happen again, but of course it had. Tem Grad and Alfeo Masti had been picked out for Farside watch. The two men landed the runabout that they had flown over from Nearside next to the group of domes and went slowly over to the main entrance lock. They went inside and looked miserably about them.

"You know the problem, Tem?" said Alfeo, walking through from the main room into the sleeping quarters. "This horrible place is beginning to feel like home. Another two tours of duty here and I'll be afraid to go back to Nearside."

"I know." Tem dropped his case on the bunk and patted it. "Well, this time I'm ready for anything. I brought a natural features listing to supplement the Lloyd's Register. If somebody puts a drive on Jupiter and brings it past here, I'll be able to slap the correct ID right on it."

"This might be your chance," said Alfeo. "Isn't that the com monitor over in the main area? Somebody's trying to call us. Want to grab it?"

Grad ran quickly back to the main communications room and was gone for a few minutes. When he returned he looked puzzled.

"Jupiter?" asked Alfeo.

"No such luck. It was a standard one. Long trip, though. She'd flown in all the way from Saturn orbit. It was one of the ships in the Melford fleet, requesting Earth approach orbit."

"That sounds routine enough. Why the frowns?"

"There was one thing about it I didn't understand—not the ship, the pilot. After he'd given me the ship's ID, I asked him to identify himself for our records."

"Was he somebody special?"

"Not really; I'd never heard of him. It was the way he put it, as though it was somehow supposed to be a joke."

"You never did have much of a sense of humor, Tem. Did he sound amused?"

"Not at all. Sort of sad, if anything."

"So what did he actually say?"

"He said, 'This is the *real* Behrooz Wolf, returning to Earth duty.' "

ABOUT THE AUTHOR

Charles Sheffield is Chief Scientist of Earth Satellite Corporation. He is a past-president of the Science Fiction Writers of America and of the American Astronautical Society, a Distinguished Lecturer of the American Institute of Aeronautics and Astronautics, and a Board Member of the National Space Society. Born and educated in England, he holds bachelor's and master's degrees in mathematics and a doctorate in theoretical physics (general relativity and gravitation). He now lives in Bethesda, Maryland.